How Insensitive

RUSSELL SMITH

HOW INSENSITIVE

The Porcupine's Quill, Inc.

CANADIAN CATALOGUING IN PUBLICATION DATA

Smith, Russell, 1963-
How Insensitive

ISBN 0-88984-143-8

I. Title

PS8587.M58H6 1994   C813'.54   C94-932319-5
PR9199.3.S55H6 1994

Published by The Porcupine's Quill, Inc.,
68 Main Street, Erin, Ontario NOB 1TO
with financial assistance from
The Canada Council and the Ontario Arts Council.
The support of the Government of Ontario
through the Ministry of Culture, Tourism and Recreation
is also gratefully acknowledged.

Represented in Canada by the Literary Press Group.
Trade orders are available from General Distribution Services.

Readied for the press by John Metcalf.
Copy edited by Doris Cowan.

Cover is after a photograph by Jeremy McCormack.

For Katherine Bruce

ONE

'BUT TORONTO, MAN, I don't know,' said the Vancouverite. They were parallel with a highway now; outside the glass
long trucks inched ahead of the train. 'I don't know how anyone could live there. I couldn't live there. I need to be able to
get to the beach, or at least *out of the city*, you know? In Vancouver you can just drive, and before you know it you're right
there. You got the mountains, the water, the most, I bet the
most beautiful scenery anywhere in the world.'

Ted couldn't remember the man's name. He had known he
was from Vancouver as soon as he had seen the red hair, the
Gore-Tex pack with a Super Natural sticker on it. The trucks
glinted in the afternoon light; the highway was full and slow-
moving. Ted pushed his glasses back up on his nose, picked a
thread off his tweed jacket. Now the Vancouverite was talking
about white water rafting.

'It's just the most incredible rush. It's almost like ecstasy,
although I would never do something like that on ecstasy. I've
thought about it, but I'd never do it. Colin did it, my friend,
when we were in New Zealand. You ever done bungee cord
jumping? He did it on ecstasy. Colin would. This guy's done
just about everything. But those New Zealand guys will do anything on those bungee cords. Big time. We saw one guy go
over on a skateboard, not too dangerous, no. One guy goes
over all the time on a motorcycle. They love it.'

A thin strip of deciduous trees now separated them from the
highway, which veered away gradually. Ted felt a little sick. 'Is
it safe?' he asked the Vancouverite, who grinned.

'Safe?' he said. 'There's nothing safe about it.' He spread his heavy hiking boots out towards the seat before him and clasped his hands behind his head.

'So why are you going to Toronto?' said Ted.

'Oh I'm just flying from there. I'm going to Japan. Colin's meeting me there, we're going to spend a year in Japan.'

'You're going to teach?'

'Yeah. Teach English. Melanie's already there, she can get us a contract with the same company. We're just going to stay in Kyoto for six months though, and then travel. I've been to Thailand but I'd like to spend some more time in Burma, Bali. And this time I'm going to get to Goa, see the hippies. You know, I believe that it's really good for you to see other cultures. See as many cultures as you can. You realize when you're out there like, whoa, mine isn't the only way of doing things, you know? And then there's the financial side of it. Melanie's already hauled some major coin. Of course you spend a lot living, but I guess if you're smart you can come away with major cash. I guess it's better than tree-planting. And I've done that three summers anyway. But Toronto, man.'

The Vancouverite eyed Ted. 'Look at this.' He gestured out the window. 'Look what they've done to the land here. It's all highways and overpasses and industrial parks. You spend two hours commuting every day ... '

'Well, actually, I – '

'And you live there for more than ten years you're poisoned anyway. I mean the pollution, the toxins in the water. *Fuck*, man. They've done studies. The rate of birth defects is like unbelievable. And you go crazy, living like that. It's fucked up, man. You're running around trying to make more money than everyone else and going to the right clubs to see and be seen, you know? and talking on your cellular phone. I can't believe these guys you see driving around in their Porsches making sure everyone sees them talking on the phone so they know how *busy* they are. You see these guys talking in *restaurants*, like give me a break. Are you really that busy that you can't wait

8

till after you eat? Or do you just want everyone to *know* that you're busy? You know? Too, too fucked up.'

'Well,' said Ted, 'for what I want to do, I guess you, I think you really have to be there.'

'Which is what?'

'Well, I'm going to try to get into film, I think.'

'Oh yeah.'

'Or some kind of writing. I have a couple of degrees that are not really useful, but I ... '

'Hey,' said the Vancouverite. He leaned forward, holding one finger in the air. 'Education is never useless. As soon as you start looking at it in economic terms, you're fucked. I think it's really really important to do what interests you. And it's all profitable in the end. You know, in my Dad's firm, he says they're looking *especially* for ... '

'Right. I know. That's why I studied psychoanalytic feminism.'

'Oh yeah.' The Vancouverite sat back. 'Where? McGill?'

'I was at Concordia. In the cultural studies program. Have you heard of it?'

The Vancouverite shook his head. He looked out the window.

'We did literature, film, television, politics, all as one discipline. It's pretty well a post-structuralist program.'

'Oh yeah,' said the Vancouverite faintly. 'So what did you get, a ph.d.?'

'No. A master's. I just finished it last spring. I'm supposed to start my ph.d. in a week. But I'm not going to.'

'Oh yeah. Why not?'

'Well ... ' said Ted. His stomach tightened with the cramp he knew to be nervous. 'Excuse me.' He rose.

Ted walked through two sleepy cars until he found the little galley where the bar trolley had stopped. A sullen woman in a grey VIA uniform was tearing open bags of foam cups. Ted convinced her to sell him a beer, and she said he had to drink it in the same car where he bought it, so he went through the sliding door.

The next car was so smoky Ted stopped on the threshold. It was obviously being used as a bar car, since bar cars didn't exist any more. In the first few rows, with their backs to him, loud students were drinking beer. The only spaces to sit were in the central seats, the ones that faced each other in groups of four. A big man with a beard sat in one, next to the aisle, with two beer cans on his folding table. He had a plaid shirt and a cigarette. He looked up at Ted dubiously.

Across the aisle, in a seat by the window, sat a young man with sleek black hair. He stared out the window, motionless. Ted saw that his hair was tied back in a tiny ponytail, but the sides and back of his head were shaved. He wore a navy blue wool suit of expensive cut, a mustard shirt and a bright floral tie. His shiny shoes had heavy leather soles. A plastic glass of amber liquid sat before him. Ted waited for him to feel the stare and turn, but he was lost in his gaze. Or perhaps he was so composed he was simply unperturbed by starers. So Ted stared.

The man must have been about Ted's age. But it took Ted a moment to realize that he was beautiful. His jaw was chiselled, his nose fine. Bright blue eyes. Perhaps he was gay. Ted looked at the bearded man, who looked ferociously back. He had a tattoo on his forearm. Ted hesitated, then made his first Toronto decision. He approached the young man.

'Someone sitting here?'

The man turned tranquilly, smiled up at him with easy warmth. 'No, no. Please.' He gestured to the chair.

'Thanks.' Ted sat opposite him, pulled out his folding table and poured his beer. Warm, it foamed and spilled on the plastic. He said 'Shit,' and got up to trouble the sullen woman for a napkin.

When he returned to his seat the young man was still

smiling, but looking out the window. His legs remained crossed; his body had not moved an inch since Ted had seen him first.

Ted drank in silence for a few minutes. He looked at the stranger's untouched whisky. 'Do they serve any good Scotches?' he asked.

'It's not Scotch. It's rye. When I travel by train I like to feel at one with the common man.' He turned his smile back onto Ted. 'But then I find I can't stomach it.'

Ted smiled back but felt his face heating up and looked down at his beer. He began to pick at the label. 'Is Export what the common ... the working class drinks in Toronto?'

'It's what they will drink until some brilliant post-literate television ad campaign filled with negative images of fire escapes filmed by epileptic cameramen turns it into the beer for people with education. For people like you and me. Then it will become the fashionable underground beer. It will be a beer for the black-baseball-caps-on-backwards set. It will be the beer to be universally despised by actors and environmentalists and all the serious people who can't stand to think they are influenced by advertising or fashion, which are essentially the same thing, the rape of the third world, as I'm sure you're aware. You know, the ugly people. Max,' he said, holding out his hand.

'Ted. You work in advertising?'

Max didn't reply, turning back to the window. He reached out for his whisky and took a sip.

'I guess you live in Toronto,' said Ted.

'I have worked in advertising, yes. I did some advertising. I don't now. You're from Montreal?'

'Well, not any more. I'm moving. Everything I own is with me on this train.'

Max raised his perfect eyebrows. 'A Montrealer moving to Toronto? That's unusual. You know you'll hate it, don't you? Or do you already? Hate it?'

'Well I'm not originally from there, Montreal. I'm from the East Coast. So I don't really ... '

'So you don't have the Montrealer's desperate inferiority. Good. Montrealers say they hate Toronto because they can't smoke anywhere, but they never ask themselves, why must I smoke so much? Because they know the answer is "Because I'm such a desperate failure". Everyone smoking in those artistic cafés they're so proud of on the Main is "about to get a band together" or "about to get some recording time, for a demo." And of course they can't really speak French. They love the idea, and they've signed up for some lessons, but it's easier just to smoke. And get inarticulate French boyfriends who play a little jazz keyboard – not piano, keyboard, it's a little electric Casio like the ones you see in the Holiday Inn piano bar. We have them here, in the centre of evil too. There's fashion hip and then there's dirty hip. Dirty hip is the Idiot Cats crowd. Krishna Wilson's people. They hang around in the Hive. You know them?'

Ted shook his head.

'You're a student?'

'Yes. Was.'

'Concordia?'

'Yes.'

'Cultural studies?'

'Yes. Do I really give that away?'

'Foucault in your jacket pocket.'

Ted laughed shortly. He drank from his beer.

'Lozere is head of that department. Is he still stripping bare Western ideology?'

'That's right.'

Max sighed. 'I do worry about Lozere's health.'

'You were at Concordia?'

'No. So you've had enough? Not going on to do your ph.D.?'

Ted looked at his lap. 'It seems pretty pointless now. I

don't see the point of going on publishing articles on "Re slash Productive Gender Politics and the Post-Modern Baby" in all those tiny little journals with slashes in the titles. It just suddenly died in me. I have this friend who just finished an article on female ejaculation, which some American feminists are, well, claiming to be possible.'

Almost imperceptibly, Max raised one eyebrow; a faintly encouraging smile flickered over his lips.

'His article's called "The Muse of Masturbation, Re slash Writing and Feminist Intertextuality as Resistance", and he's going to publish it in the *Journal of the Missouri Semiotics Circle*. It's coming out in three years. Three years. I heard that and it all just went to hell in my head.'

Max shook his head in a show of dismay. 'Indeed. It's all so depressingly *eighties*.' He sighed. 'But we're not rid of it yet. Even here. There's a fellow, a bum really, who writes books and publishes them himself and sells them on the street. Have you heard of him? Zack Rudnicki? I don't know if that's his real name. He's never been published by a real publisher. He sits out in the street in the coldest weather with a sign around his neck saying "Buy my book". He's an amusing fixture. Well, there's a magazine you may know – the *Referent*? Used to be *Intratext*, Brad Cransome ed?'

'Oh yeah, yes.'

'Right. Well, the erudite Cransome bought one of Rudnicki's books. Gave it to his top marxian critic. Forget the fellow's name. The critic loved the book. You understand that Rudnicki's essentially a dweeb; his books are sort of anti-establishment science fiction, just like the stories you might have written in high school. At your high school he would have been a wargamer. Bag of twenty-sided dice in his pocket.'

'Right.'

'The critic saw all the stories as – these stories involve piles of excrement building up all over a futuristic city, or language police in the subway, you understand, and all the sensitive

artistic protagonists die horrible ketchupy deaths at Big
Brother's hands. So the critic saw all the stories as post-marxian
deconstructions of suburban consumer society and the frag-
mented late-capitalist world. Brilliant work. There was a
phrase he used, something like ''deconstructs not only the context but the very discourse of Western canonical literature''.
Something like that. Poor old Rudnicki, out on Yonge Street,
he's never even heard the word canonical, although he may
have seen ''deconstructs'' in *Flare* this month. They called a
bright orange windbreaker ''deconstructed''. Anyway. The
Referent is defunct now.'

'Really?' said Ted. 'Really? I thought they – '

'Well,' interrupted Max, 'it's technically still in existence.
They will probably put one more issue out. But after that
they're finished. I wouldn't give them longer than four
months.'

Ted nodded, afraid to ask Max how he knew. Max turned
to the window, looking serene. The more Ted studied him the
younger he looked. He couldn't be more than twenty-five. He
could have passed for twenty-three. He didn't seem gay. Not a
trace of effeminacy, no affectation of manner. He spoke easily,
with a smooth voice.

'So you're going to look for some writing work?' Max said
suddenly.

'Ah, yeah,' said Ted. 'I hear there's a lot of technical writing work, corporate newsletters and – '

'No,' said Max, shaking a finger. 'You don't want to get
into the tech-writing rut. It sucks the life out of you and kills
you. And every time you tell them you're leaving they offer
you an enormous raise and seduce you back. You end up worrying about which stall has the best lamb's lettuce in St
Lawrence Market.'

Ted laughed. 'I don't know if I have a problem with that.'

'There are only so many CD players you can buy.'

Ted looked out the window.

'Have you,' said Max, 'ever written a screenplay?'

Ted smiled. 'Hey, you know the program I was in. Of course I have.'

'And that's what you really want to be doing?'

'I've thought about it, yes.'

'And you'd like to try some freelance magazine work?'

Ted laughed. 'Yes. I suppose you hear this a lot, on this train? Is that what everyone's trying to do? Christ, there's no hope for me.'

'I've never ridden this train before in my life,' said Max. 'Do you have a place to stay once you get there?'

'Yeah, a friend has a spare room.'

'Who's your friend?'

'Oh, you probably wouldn't know him. He's a very square guy. I knew him at Southern Ontario. He's a bond-trader now.'

'You did your B.A. at Southern Ontario? I know quite a few people from there.'

'Were you there?'

'No. But perhaps I know your friend.'

'John Reynolds?'

'Too funny. John Reynolds. Yes. I know him. You may find he's not so square now.'

'You know John? That's very funny. John's an old friend of mine ... he's never mentioned your name.'

'Oh, I've met him here. So he's a bond trader now? I suppose that's what he was when I met him. John Reynolds. That's where you're staying?'

'Yes. He shares a big house in the Annex.'

'You should be all right then,' said Max. 'Listen, are you serious about this film script? Because I could put you in touch with some useful people.'

'Shit yes,' said Ted. 'Anybody at all.'

'All right. And magazines. Could you do lifestyle?'

'Sorry?'

'Profiles of designers, restaurant reviews, pop-psych relationship columns.'

'Christ,' said Ted.

'Much more fun than covering city hall for the *Star*. And better paid. And higher profile. I'll put you in touch with Derek, at *Cities*. He's useful to know. He's a bit of a tough nut, but he'd love you.'

'Sure,' said Ted.

And so they talked. Max gave him a list of names; he told Ted always to say he was a friend of Max. The landscape changed from fields to industrial parks; subdivisions of identical town houses, apparently unconnected to any metropolitan development, swelled up to touch the tracks and receded. The highways and overpasses grew more numerous. Ted got up to get them two Export. Max drank his quickly, because he was getting off at Oshawa. It seemed incongruous to Ted, who asked whether he was visiting a boring relative, but Max just smiled. They exchanged phone numbers as Max pulled on an off-white raincoat that appeared to be made of linen. He had a worn leather bag with him. Ted promised he would be in touch.

He watched for Max walking away on the crowded platform in Oshawa but didn't see him. As the train pulled out under a suddenly overcast sky, Ted watched the empty streets of the town's outskirts pass. No building was higher than two stories tall. He saw a store front marked 'Ted's Fish And Chips'. Ted sat back and sipped his Export. He felt fine. Oshawa was all right, really. He couldn't see Toronto from where he sat, facing the back of the train, but he knew it rose before them, glittering.

TWO

JOHN'S HOUSE was on a leafy Victorian street. It was brick, narrow and crooked. The whole terraced row, gabled and pointy, slouched on itself at crazy angles. There was a string of plastic Chinese lanterns hanging on John's little veranda; three bicycles were locked to the banister. The brightly painted house next door belonged to Portuguese: its little garden was an image of the Virgin, a pattern made of coloured stones. The other neighbour had recently renovated: the brick was sandblasted, wooden shutters inside were tightly closed. A blue plastic box, for recycling, was before each house. The front door of John's house was open, so Ted walked in, struggling to get his duffle bag through. In the front hall was a stack of photographic equipment: metal poles, lights, sheets of coloured plastic. He walked past it, calling out, into a bare living room painted dark green. There was a girl sitting on a sofa, doing nothing. She looked up at Ted. 'Hi,' she said shortly.

'Hi,' said Ted, dropping his bag. 'I'm Ted. I'm John's friend.'

'Hi,' said the girl blankly. 'I think John's asleep.'

'Oh. He's back from work early. Did he tell you I would be staying here?'

'John's not working,' she said. She was wearing very little actually: a pair of black footless tights, a painted T-shirt, bare feet. Straight black hair cut at a fashionable angle hung across half her face. If she hadn't been slightly plump she would have been what Ted found sexy. She was short.

'Okay,' said Ted. 'Do you live here too?'

'Yes. I'm Go-Go.'

17

Ted shook her hand, which seemed to embarrass her. She giggled. 'I'm waiting for someone to show up. You should wake John up. He's been asleep all day.'

'Sure.' But he hesitated, looking around him. There was nowhere to sit but the one sofa. He looked at the framed Schiele reproduction, the nineteenth-century print of some English college. Two pairs of skates lay in the middle of the floor, next to a kerosene heater. Bright plastic handbags were pinned to one wall.

'That's my collection,' said Go-Go. 'They're all genuine sixties.'

'I suppose the old print is John's.'

Go-Go shrugged. 'His dad's college or something.' She was staring at Ted. 'You must be one of his Southern Ontario friends. Would your parents be interested in buying some South American native art? Because I just got back from travelling and I have some really special pieces.'

'I don't think so.' He smiled. 'My parents live in New Brunswick.'

'Oh. Aren't you hot? That's a nice jacket.' She got up quickly and fingered the green tweed.

'It's my professorial look,' said Ted.

'I think that's really cool. With the jeans. Like a professor or something. And the glasses. Are those Roots shoes?'

'Yes.'

'Cool. I haven't seen those for a long time. Did you get them here?'

'No. In Montreal.'

'Cool. You can't get them here any more. I remember they used to have the best boots. Roots boots. Everyone wanted to have them because they were so expensive and like so earthy, which I think is really funny now. Did you used to wear the negative heels ones?'

'Yes,' said Ted a little wearily, for he was well used to gleeful reminiscences about seventies clothing. 'Yes, I did.'

'It would be so great to find a pair now. I think that would be the coolest.'

'I guess so,' said Ted, looking around. 'I'm not sure. I don't really get the irony thing.'

'The what?'

'I mean the whole they're-so-tacky-they're-great thing I don't get. Of course if you really *like* them ... '

'Oh, I love them. Don't you? Are you a writer like John?'

'I ... John's a writer?'

'Well he's trying to be.'

'Hey dude.' John was on the stairs, in a terrycloth bathrobe. He was still tall and blond, but his face was grey. He stepped down shakily. 'Hey dude,' he said, holding out his hand.

Ted shook his hand happily, remembering how with John he was always aware of his own thick brown hair, cut undemonstratively short, his brown eyes, his glasses and his height. John looked a little older, but he was still handsome, the plane of straight blond hair still cowlicked out of his blue eyes in a clean sweep to the back of the head. He flicked it back now, and coughed, and Ted smiled.

They went into the bad-smelling kitchen, where John drank juice. 'Jesus Christ,' he said hoarsely, gulping. 'Jesus Christ. I was at the most incredible place last night. It was about the fourth party we'd gone to, and you had to go up this fire escape outside a warehouse and climb through this loading window. And inside they had gauze sheets hanging all over, and slide projectors beaming random images on them and the walls. You know, like a Renaissance statue, then a Coke can, then the word "family", and so on. You can make yourself tea or coffee or anything if you can find it. I don't drink coffee. There's no food right now.'

'Sure. You should throw this garbage out. So what's this, not working?'

'Working? Oh yeah. You didn't know. I haven't worked for CIBC for months now. I got laid off. There were naked fags dancing, almost naked, fags in garter belts and stockings and G-strings dancing – oh yes, and a teledildonics program you could play with. The fags were dancing with dykes with shaved heads, on risers, with spotlights on them. Everyone just stood around watching. It was kind of boring after a while. Miranda was there. She wanted to leave as soon as we got there.'

Go-Go had come in to listen. 'Who did it? Submarine?'

John nodded. 'Submarine's parties are the best,' he said to Ted.

'So what are you living on?' asked Ted. 'Have you got any work lined up?'

'Yeah, I'm going to be working with my uncle. He's got a project setting up with Mexico. International finance. The Mexican stock market is an incredible place to make money.'

'I'm sure,' said Ted. 'There's forty percent unemployed in Mexico. It's about the only way to make money. Putting a few companies under. So when does this start?'

'In a couple of months.' John pulled a pack of Camels from his bathrobe pocket, lit one with shaky hands.

'Good Christ,' said Ted. 'You smoke. You're smoking.'

'You want one?'

Ted shook his head. Go-Go took one, saying 'I have shrink at seven,' and left the room.

'So I guess you don't row much any more,' said Ted.

John laughed, then began to cough. The cough grew until he was racked and wheezing.

'You okay?' said Ted. 'Choking? Water?'

This began John laughing again. 'Jesus Christ,' he hacked happily. 'Jesus Christ.'

'So you're not working. No more bond trading, no more suits, no more champagne in bars with stock tickers? Was it that you burned out, do you think, the way they say you do?'

'Actually,' said John, panting, 'the part with the champagne I learned to like. The rest you can't do for too long. You meet a lot of people though.'

'Oh,' said Ted, 'I met the most incredible guy on the train; he said he knew you. Incredibly well-dressed guy called Max.'

'Max? You met Max? Jesus. It's been months since I saw Max. What's he doing now?'

'I was hoping you would tell me.'

'Shit, I don't know Max, really. I used to go to his club, that's all.'

'His club?'

'Spleen. All his clubs went under all at once and he disappeared for a while.'

'He *owned* clubs? How old is he?'

John shrugged, narrowing his eyes as he exhaled. 'I met him once at the opening party for Dionysus. He had this thing where – he owned a lot of buildings in town, or rented them, I don't know, and he would open up a new club every few months and close down the old one, so everyone always had a new club to go to. He was smart, because as soon as everyone knew about one they didn't want to go any more. You know how it happens.'

'Right,' said Ted.

'And he always kept them cool. No signs, no advertising, except sometimes just a full page of black in *Next* and everyone knew what it was for; only open one night a week, you had to know when. Anyway, he would throw these giant parties to open them, and you could just walk in and there would be free food, free booze for hundreds of people, and then he just wouldn't show up. I met him at one of these parties, Dionysus I think – that's where they used to have DDA nights on Saturday –'

'DDA?'

'Diesel dykes on acid; supposed to be the best dyke night in town. I never went, of course, but I heard about them. So I went to this Dionysus party and of course I got completely hammered and I was looking for Max because I knew what he looked like and I'd talked to him on the phone at *Haze* –'

'*Haze* magazine? He worked for them?'

'Yeah, before it went under; it was his baby. He was the publisher. I wanted to pitch this story to the editor about this sex game all the bond traders were playing on their computers, I wanted to write about it, and I thought it would be a *Haze* sort of thing, you know; they'd have a big photo over two pages of something close up and you wouldn't know what it was, and a half page of text superimposed and six different typefaces so you could hardly read it, and it would be on computer sex for stockbrokers, is it perfect or what? They'd have some title like "Orifice Boy" printed backwards.' John paused for a drag on the cigarette. 'So I called the office and I just got Max. He was charming. And *Haze* went under just after. So I was hoping I could talk to him at this Dionysus party but he wasn't there, so I just drank like a roadworker on payday, looking at this incredibly tall woman in bondage gear. Max used to send invitations to all the modelling agencies so there was quite a crowd. I kept eating all this black food, I remember, all the food on the buffet was black, and the only beer they were serving was Black Label, of course.' John rolled his eyes. 'It's usually just a big black warehouse space. There was dancing upstairs, so I'm up there sweating at three in the morning, I'm dancing with some guy I think, who is voguing, and Max just walks through, completely calm and sober, beautiful suit, a girl on each arm, and he walks through the crowd shaking everyone's hand and asking them if they're having a good time, and then he leaves. I stopped him just before the stairwell and I, God, I must have been a mess, completely wasted and sweating, and I just bumbled through something about thanks for helping me at *Haze*, and he was incredibly polite, considering the state I was in, and then he left. That was the only appearance he made at the biggest party of the year, which was his own.' John got up. 'You're staying in Georgina's room.'

Ted followed him upstairs. 'How many people live here?'

'Five, I think, at the moment, more or less, not counting you. Georgina's leaving for Japan tomorrow for two months, I think. Which is fine with me, which you'll understand if you've ever lived with a model.'

'Oh. Is that her stuff in the hallway?'

'What stuff?'

'The photographic equipment.'

'Oh that. Shit, I don't even see that any more. That's been there for months. No, it belongs to her prick boyfriend Lucas, who's a photographer, but he lives in LA now. That stuff is probably rented. It's worth all kinds of coin.'

John opened the door to a dark room. He walked across a futon strewn with clothes to pull up the bamboo blind. The air was close but perfumed; the futon covered most of the floor. The walls were bare except for two postcards pinned above a dresser: a Klimt painting and a photograph of Marilyn Monroe. An oriental marionette made of wood lay crumpled in one corner. Lacquer bangles, wooden earrings, underwear, sweatshirts and running shoes covered every surface; they overflowed from the dresser drawers and the wicker basket in the corner. Behind the door hung several wide-brimmed hats with ribbons. There was no mirror. On the dresser was a stack of oblong cards. Ted picked one up: it bore three photographs of a woman with perfect features and straight blond hair, posing on a beach, in a café, on a car. 'Georgina de Kerk,' it said, with her height, measurements, glove and hat size.

'Christ,' said Ted.

'She doesn't really look that good,' said John. 'I guess she'll clean some of this up before she goes,' said John. 'I'm not sure when she's leaving though.'

'You mean I could be sleeping here tonight, me and her underwear here, and she could walk in? This is crazy. Where is she now?'

John looked at him, narrowing his eyes as if confused. He smiled. 'Relax, man. This all your stuff?'

'I've stored some trunks at the station until I find a place. So who else lives here?'

'Well you've met me and Go-Go, and then George, and then Malcolm, he's an actor, very much an actor, and then the Mole. He lives upstairs.'

'The Mole?'

'I forget his real name. He does some computer stuff at U of T. You'll never have to see him; he works all the time.' John's face froze. 'Oh my Christ. What's the time?'

'Seven or so.'

'Shit. Shit. I said I'd call Miranda. She's got something ... ' He ran out of the room, up the stairs to the attic. Ted followed him into his room. John sat on the futon, dialling. 'Miranda's got this opening, but I don't know where I ... Ellen? Jennie. Jennie, it's John, how are you?' John listened, then laughed. 'No, no. Listen, is Miranda there? Oh. Do you have the number there? Would Lisa have the number? Do you have Lisa's number? No, no, it's okay, I'll call Jack. Do you know about this thing of hers at Q-Space? That's moved, right? Yeah, Richmond and something. Hang on, hang on, I've got another call. Hello? Hey dude, hey. Right on. No, I was at the Submarine thing. You weren't there. Wild. How was – oh yeah? They're open now? Listen, where are you going to be tonight? Yeah, we'll probably end up there. What about this thing for Suckmeat at the Aquarium? Yeah, yeah, I know. No, Miranda's at her mother's and I don't have the number. Hang on, I've got Jennie on the other ... '

Ted inspected the room, wading through clothes. He peered at a photograph of a rowing team and stepped on a CD, cracking the box. A silk shirt was draped over a chair before a desk piled with unopened letters and photo magazines. Ted picked up a magazine called Vortex. Under it was a Playboy.

'Okay,' John was saying. 'Two four five Sorauren. Wait, I don't have a pen.' He gestured to Ted, mouthing 'pen.' Ted produced one; John dictated. 'Two four five s-o-r-a-u-r-e-n. And who do we have to know at the door? Donna who? Spell it. M-i-h-a-i-c-h-u-k. For Christ's sake. Okay, we know her, right.

Okay. Maybe we'll run into you at Penumbra.' He hung up. 'Okay, we'd better go. Do you want a shower or anything?'

'Listen,' said Ted, 'I'm pretty tired; I had to get up really early this morning to – '

'No, no, listen man, this is a good one. Really. And you'll meet Miranda and the gang. I'm going to take a shower.'

John pulled a towel from under some clothes and left the room. Ted heard the shower from downstairs. He sat for a moment on John's futon, then went back to Georgina's room and sat on her futon. It was getting dark. He knew he would go out with John.

After his shower, Ted put on a clean shirt. He went back upstairs, where John was standing in front of his full-length mirror, doing up the buttons on a white silk shirt. He wore baggy jeans and cowboy boots.

'I don't know about the boots, dude,' said Ted.

John looked at him with a grimace. 'Well I don't know about striped shirts, dude. Or Levi's straight legs. Or brown shoes. So let's not talk. Those aren't Roots, are they?'

'What's wrong with the shirt? This is my favourite shirt.'

'Very comfortable, I'm sure.' John was putting on a soft navy sportsjacket.

'Wow,' said Ted. 'Beautiful jacket. Beautiful. How much do you pay here for something like that?'

'Normally, about five hundred. It's cashmere. I paid fifty at a sample sale. I'll get you onto the sample sale circuit. You have to know where they are; there's no advertising for them. Usually in a warehouse or something, and you pay cash. A lot of the stuff is what the models have worn in shows. I can put you on Jordie's mailing list if you want. And Miranda always knows about them.' John buttoned the shirt's top button, then pulled the cuffs out from under the jacket's cuffs so they dangled.

Ted took off his glasses and polished them. He fingered his own open collar. 'Maybe I can borrow a shirt,' he said.

'Sure. Closet.'

Ted fingered the row of shirts: soft cotton, linen, silk, and a pile of T-shirts with faded rowing team logos. 'People dress up more here, I guess.'

'This isn't dressed up. No one dresses up.'

'Oh.' Ted pulled out a white linen shirt.

'The idea of dressing up is rather suburban, I think,' said John. 'The idea is to look good, not to dress up.'

'But you look good by dressing up.' Ted suddenly felt exhausted. He hadn't eaten since a plastic VIA sandwich at noon, and his beers with Max had left him dry.

'You look good by being stylish. And actually, for your information, it's politically cooler if only the guys are stylish.'

'What?'

'Chicks are traditionally supposed to worry about style, so now if they're cool they don't. It's that whole correct-cool thing. It's bad to dress up if you're a chick.'

Ted laughed, doing up the buttons on the scratchy shirt. 'Chicks. I haven't heard that word for a while. Sounds a little room two-twenty-two now, doesn't it?'

John looked around. 'No.'

Ted put his jacket over the shirt. 'I've never worn linen before. It scratches.'

'Chicks love it.'

Ted mouthed the word 'chicks', trying it on. 'Are you seeing any ... chicks?'

'Me? No. No.' John was slicking his hair back with gel. 'By the way, for your reference at this party, you can't say chick. Only chicks can say it. If a chick says it, it's extremely cool, but if you say it it's bad. Same with fag and dyke.'

'Only chicks can say fag and dyke?'

'Only fags and dykes.'

'I see.' Ted opened the Playboy, flipped through it quickly. 'I can't say chick, fag or dyke. What about to you, here?'

'To me, when we're alone?'

26

'Yes. What am I allowed to say?'

John smiled at himself in the mirror. 'To me, you can say splitarse, fudgepacker and carpetmuncher. You ready to go?'

THREE

AFTER THE Q-SPACE reception Ted felt all right. There was free champagne and caviar and somebody had trained a bright light and a video camera on him for a few minutes as he stood next to the artist, a gay Californian in a linen suit who kept smiling at him. Ted had never been on television before. And he had had a few crackers so he didn't feel quite so sick. Now he was in John's car with the cracked windshield, with Jean-Luc and Jean-Paul from Quebec, whose breath smelled of garlic, and a big prep called Doug whom no one seemed to know. Jean-Luc and Jean-Paul were painters, and they seemed amusing together. They sat together in the front seat, one on the other's lap, giggling. 'He ain't heavy,' Jean-Luc kept saying. Then he sighed. 'Mon dieu, mon dieu. Je suis un vieux boudoir plein de roses fanées.'

Ted laughed. Miranda and Julia and Isabel hadn't shown up, so they were going to look for them at Penumbra. They were moving fast on big downtown streets between office buildings. 'It's just like de bobsled on TV,' said Jean-Paul. 'We're all so lucky to sit so close together.' He was caressing Jean-Luc's forehead. Finally they parked on a sidestreet and tumbled out of the car.

'Where is this?' said Doug.

'This is Illyria, lady,' said Ted.

'Never been here,' said Doug.

Penumbra was just a door framed with twisted scrap metal. Just above it were metal letters embedded in concrete that spelled LASCIATE OGNI SPERANZA VOI CH'ENTRATE. Inside it was very dark and crowded. All the men seemed to

28

have long, curly black hair. There was a roar of frenetic music, the jackhammers and screaming Ted knew to be Belgian industrial hardcore, for he had volunteered for his college radio station. He squeezed past a group of three women with peroxided crewcuts to the bar. He leaned next to a black man wearing dark glasses and a headset with a little microphone attached. There didn't seem to be any wires leading from the headset to anything else. The two women behind the bar were dressed as vampire daughters, with teased black hair and blood-red lips. Ted found them beautiful. Above the bar were six video screens on which were silent images of Jimi Hendrix smashing flaming guitars and an edited tape of spectacular motor-racing crashes.

Ted found he couldn't concentrate on anything and so when one vampire daughter jerked back her head at him, signalling that it was his turn to order, he hesitated and provoked a sneer, missing his turn. She turned to the two long-haired men beside him, who made a gesture which she understood: she jerked open two bottles and slammed them on the counter before them. Over the roar, Ted heard bits of what one was shouting in the other's ear.

'We just weren't growing as people ... Oh, no, no, we're best friends, maybe we should always have been.'

Ted looked at the one part of the bar that was illuminated: a low lamp hung over a pool table. A crowd was gathered to watch a large black man with dreadlocks playing. He wore cowboy boots and a T-shirt that read 'Fuck dancing; let's fuck'; he was very quiet and serious, with a cigarette stuck to his lip. His opponent was a tiny Chinese girl with enormous horn-rimmed glasses. She wore the same blood-red lipstick and spandex catsuit as the bartenders. The spectators swayed slightly with the thundering music.

In his ear Ted heard, 'So they can't get in to the movie so he decides why don't we go see *Phantom*? He spends a hundred and sixty bucks on two tickets, just like that, I mean I can't compete with that, and why should I?' Above the bar, race cars spun and burned. Figures ran onto the track with extinguishers. 'You know? Why should I?'

'Are you okay?' John was beside him. 'Miranda's here.'

'Johnny!' screamed a woman approaching them through clusters of black jackets. She wore a man's motorcycle jacket over what were clearly expensive clothes: wide silk trousers, a linen blouse. Her black hair was held back by a hairband, and this pulled strings in Ted which had been mute since his University of Southern Ontario days. Her porcelain skin and faint freckles confirmed the memory: all of her spoke of privilege. She rushed at John and embraced him, talking rapidly. The two women who followed her fitted the mould even more closely, in jeans and hairbands, looking displeased. Ted knew they had worn pearls with their sweaters at school. He smiled at them and they smiled weakly back, looking over his shoulder.

'And you're Ted,' said Miranda, turning to him and grasping his hand. 'Johnny's told me all about you.' She smiled brilliantly and Ted felt a dull and familiar trouble in his belly because he realized that he found her quite beautiful, more beautiful than the bartenders or any of the models in black tights. He decided to hate her. She introduced him to Isabel and Julia, and then to two tall men who stood back a little: Arthur the blond prep who smiled and shook Ted's hand firmly, and sullen Roger, who didn't look like the others. He smoked a filterless cigarette, he hadn't shaved, he wore a suede jacket and cowboy boots.

'No, no, the thing for Suckmeat was last night,' said Miranda. 'I wouldn't have gone anyway, I'm so sick of the Aquarium. Do you know,' she turned to Ted, 'I have this thing about I can't remember where I was the night before. Sometimes I try to remember where I was last night and it's completely blocked out. Cindy asked me on Wednesday if I wanted to go down to the Aquarium and I said well I guess, I haven't been down there for so long, I never go there, and then when I got there I realized I'd been there just the night before. Johnny tells me you're a writer, have you talked to Roger?' Roger was looking around and scowling. 'He's a writer. Rodge, have you talked to Teddy?' Roger looked at her, shook his head and shook Ted's hand. Miranda left them. Roger fixed his eye on something over Ted's shoulder.

'What kind of writing do you do?' said Ted.

'Novel,' said Roger, shrugging. He sucked on his cigarette and turned around. Arthur was leaning to his ear to tell him something with animation. He was pointing at a young woman. Ted looked around for John. He saw Miranda greet a very young ugly little man with sideburns and heavy horn-rimmed glasses. She kissed him just below the ear. John was pushing through a crowd towards Ted.

'Hey dude,' he said, 'Miranda knows your friend Max.'

'Really? How?'

'Don't know. But she says he might be here later.'

'Max? Really? Love to see him. Always love to see Max.'

Miranda approached them. She put her arm around Ted and massaged the back of his neck with her fingertips. 'Are you lovely boys going to the Aquarium?'

'What, now? Are you going?' said John.

'It's too hot and smoky in here. Don't you want a place where we can talk?' She smiled at Ted.

John said, 'The Aquarium's getting a bit tired, don't you think?'

'Teddy, don't you feel like just *relaxing*?'

'Sure,' said Ted. 'I've never seen any of these places.'

In Arthur's car Miranda was talking about someone whose name Ted had not heard mentioned. 'Get out of me! That woman, I swear, is such a Trojan, gunning people off like that. I mean what a *tea-roll*. She treats me as if I'm Medea. Seriously, am I Medea?'

John murmured in Ted's ear, 'The Aquarium needs a good dissing, really. No one disses anything around here.'

'*Yes*, he's a lawyer,' Miranda was saying. 'Didn't you see the brown shit smeared all over his mouth? And she's like Miss DES Daughter ... '

Ted asked her, 'I hear you're a friend of Max's.'

'Max? You know Max? He might be at the Aquarium later on.'

'Really? You spoke to him today?'

'Oh no,' said Miranda.

The car stopped with a jerk outside a bar with a glass façade. There was red light and music inside.

'Just look how easy it is to get a parking space here,' said Arthur. 'That shows just how sucky this neighbourhood is.'

'It's a land of bad mistakes,' said John.

Inside, the crowd was smaller than in the last bar, and the people seemed cleaner, but less animated. Few were talking. Most just leaned against walls or the bar. They seemed younger than Ted, and very thin. He stared at a beautiful girl.

'Don't bother, dude,' said John in his ear. 'She's a model.'

Then John was gone. Ted tried to talk to Miranda's friend Isabel, one of the prep girls, but she answered his questions in monosyllables and soon turned her back. He looked around for Miranda and saw Julia, the other one, talking to a tall man with thick blond hair in a long ponytail. He wore a leather jacket and dark glasses. Ted stood beside them, listening.

'No, seriously,' the man was saying. 'Spadina station, the moving sidewalk, in that long tunnel? I could ride it all day. I walk as fast as I can and the air rushes by and the fluorescent lights and I feel like I'm in a movie. It's totally Ridley Scott. I've spent hours on it.'

'Oh,' said Julia, without looking at Ted. 'Ted this is Andreas, he's just got five million dollars to do a movie.'

'Really? You're producing it?'

'Writing, directing, producing,' said the man.

Ted looked down at Andreas's feet and saw that he wore silver-tipped cowboy boots. 'What kind of movie?'

'It's about my family here, my heritage. My roots are Icelandic.'

'Oh I see. Who ... where did you get five million?'

'You can get grants. There are a lot of grants. You should look into it.'

Ted laughed. 'What makes you think I make movies?'

Andreas shrugged. 'Everyone needs grants. There are ways of getting them. Don't you need one?'

'Sure, but, ah, for writing. I'm a writer.'

The director raised his eyebrows. 'Oh boy, you need a grant. Do you write screenplays?'

'Yes. Yes.'

The big man rolled his eyes. 'Then you should get a grant.'

'Yes, I suppose I should.'

Julia squealed. 'Oh my *God* I hate this song. I *hate* this song. It's so *tired*.'

Ted nodded. 'Beef Syringe again. It's the second time we've heard it this evening. I didn't realize how big the Newcastle sound was here.'

'Oh,' said Julia. 'Is this the Newcastle sound? I heard about that but never knew what it was. It's this?'

'These guys started the whole Newcastle thing. That's how we know all the rest of them, Bad Hats, Bile Ducts, Doggymeisters ... '

'My God I've never heard of any of them,' she said. 'I've probably heard them all but there's no way I'd know any of the names. You write screenplays?'

'Well, no, I write, ah, fiction, but I'm trying to get into magazine writing here, you know, book reviews, movie reviews, that sort of thing.'

'Oh.' She looked at the video monitors. A long-haired group was playing silently on one screen, next to another which showed endless scenes of horror-film violence. They seemed to be all taken from Cronenberg films: a head exploded, then a hand emerged from a chest, insects crawled

33

from eye-sockets. Andreas noticed someone and called to him, 'Ho! Thomas!'

Another tall man in cowboy boots and a ponytail approached them, and shook Andreas's hand warmly. 'Thomas can help you get a grant,' Andreas said to Ted.

'Oh? You've received a lot of grants?'

'No, no. It's my job. I help people get grants.'

Andreas put his arm around Thomas. 'Thomas is a professional grant adviser. He will come up with a project for you, fill in the right forms ... '

'You can make a living from that?'

'Sure,' said Thomas. 'There's a huge demand right now. If I didn't do it artists would have to work at it full-time. They'd have no time for anything else.'

'If,' said Ted, having difficulty concentrating, 'I have the money to pay you to do that then why would I need a grant?'

'Oh, you can find ways of paying for my services.'

'Don't tell me.'

'Yup. Grant Research Grant. CACA has one, plus the OCAA, their deadline's next week.'

'Right.' Ted nodded. 'Beer?'

'Sure. Thanks.' Thomas and Andreas handed him their empty bottles. Again, the bar proved daunting. Ted slammed down the empty bottles to get attention, then imitated another man, scowling and holding two fingers up in an x. The waitress looked at him. Gaining in confidence, he frowned harder, made the x sign again, then held up three fingers on one hand. She smiled and slid him three Export.

Julia was standing alone when he returned to their spot. 'I guess we'll drink these,' he said.

She looked at him as if confused by the sentence, but took a beer. 'Did you go to university?' she asked suddenly.

'Doesn't it seem so?'

'Well, I don't know.'

'Yes.'

'Where?'

Ted hesitated. 'Concordia. I did cultural studies.' The way she was looking at him made him ask aggressively, 'Where did you go?'

'I did art history at McGill,' she said quickly, as if nothing could be less interesting. 'What's cultural studies?'

Ted told her.

'I guess that's how you know about the English music.'

'Well, I suppose. It never occurred to me that I knew about that. Everybody ... everyone in my program listened to music. And talked about it all the time. Don't you?'

'Oh sure, sure.' She paused. 'Do you know Derek at *Cities*?'

'I don't know anyone,' said Ted with sudden fatigue.

'Because if you're interested in writing for magazines I could put you in touch with him. He's kind of uptight, but that's the kind of thing he might be interested in, you know, English music. That's the kind of thing you could really sell. Or just write about the stuff you did in school, you know, anything intellectual like that, as long as you don't come across as a snob.'

'Wait, Derek, Max mentioned him. At *Cities*. What is *Cities*?'

'Oh, you know, *Cities* magazine, it's like what's going on in home renovations, that sort of thing. I guess it's mostly for people like, you know, people who live north of Bloor. What we used to call yuppies. They have a good restaurant column, that's what most people read it for.'

Ted shrugged. 'Sure, I'd love to talk to him. You could set it up for me?'

They exchanged phone numbers. Julia promised to talk to Derek. Ted remembered Max and asked her if she had see him, but she didn't even know who he was. Julia drifted away and Ted studied the crowd, looking for Max. He saw Roger the writer approaching him and stiffened. Roger carried two beers. He handed one to Ted.

'Thanks,' said Ted guardedly.

'Too funny,' said Roger. 'You know Johnny.'

'Yeah.'

'You row?'

'No.'

Roger nodded sagely, swaying. He was very drunk. 'Well,' he said, holding out his hand, 'Good to meet you man. I hope I'll see you at Miranda's party.'

Ted shook his hand, then Miranda had her arms around his neck. 'Teddy! Please please please come to my little pahr-tee. Just a few friends for drinks and I'd love you to come. Chrissy!'

And then she was gone, embracing someone else. Ted glimpsed someone, the back of someone's head, under the video screens behind her, that made him jump. He almost shouted out. A tall man whose head was shaved at the sides, with a small, shiny ponytail. He was wearing a dark jacket with big shoulders and talking rapidly to another man.

'Max!' Ted called out, and began to move towards him, but the bar was suddenly crowded; he had to shoulder his way through two tight groups.

As he approached, the man turned and stared: it was not Max, but an ugly Italian boy with a wide face and a brutal smile.

Ted looked up, pretending to stare at the video screens. The two men turned back to the bar, and Ted noticed that they both had the same haircut.

He looked around for John. Immediately, against the far wall, he saw Max, definitely Max, the same navy suit and noble savage haircut. He smiled with relief and waved.

But when the man turned to him and frowned, the face dissolved into someone else's: not Max either. And both his friends wore dark suits and slicked-back hair; Ted hadn't noticed that. He gulped his beer. John was approaching. 'Johnny. I keep seeing, or thinking I see ...' Ted shook his head.

John smiled, looking around. 'Whatever, dude.'

'Forget it.'

'You ready to go?'

Laboriously, they made their way to the door. Ted saw Isabel waving to him and waited for her as she pushed her way through to them.

'Bye!' she said brightly, and kissed him on the cheek. He felt her breasts touch his arm quickly through her thin blouse. Then Julia kissed him too, and hugged him.

The wide street was surprisingly cold. John began to walk into the wind, along the row of closed dry cleaners and fabric stores.

'How far are we from home?' said Ted.

'Far.'

'Couldn't we take a taxi or something?'

'Have any money?'

'Sure. I'll pay for a taxi.'

'Right on, mon.'

'Doan FUG wid me, mon,' said a voice close to them. A man with dreadlocks glared from a doorway.

In the taxi John said, 'So what's the story with Janet? She's staying there?'

'Yes. It's all over.'

'Really?' John turned to look at him. 'Wow, eh?'

'Yeah. Finally. It's a good thing.'

'Oh. And how's she taking it?'

'Very well. Very well. She's being very strong.'

'So she's doing a lot better, eh?'

'Oh yes. She's completely off the medication now. She's going out more, doing things for herself. Signed up for some courses.'

'Well, that's good. That's great.'

They watched the storefronts pass; some drunks fought in a brightly lit intersection, then were obscured by a bright empty streetcar. It rumbled past them at high speed. Suddenly, Ted knew he was about to cry. He looked out his window.

'So,' said John, 'This is a good thing, right, this end of the Janet thing, this Toronto thing? Is this a good thing?'

'Oh yeah. Definitely.' Ted stared doggedly out his window.

'Well that's good. Do you think you made the right decision?'

'No.'

FOUR

THE DOOR OPENED and Ted jerked his head and opened his eyes. The room glowed with a subterranean pink light. He could see the pink paper blind, lines of daylight around it. He was lying on a sea of clothes. Someone came in quietly, stepped over him and fumbled in the closet. He turned his head and saw her, the blond girl in the picture, whose room it was. 'Oh hi,' he said, sitting up. A wave of pain sloshed across his head.

She turned and said softly, 'Hi, it's okay, don't wake up. I'm just getting some stuff.'

'I'm Ted,' he croaked. He gathered the sleeping bag around his waist; he was only wearing briefs. He looked at his crumpled socks on top of the pile at the foot of the futon. Georgina was bending with her back to him, wearing a sundress. Her exposed shoulderblades jutted and glided as she struggled with something in the closet. He watched her thin neck, the straight blond hair. 'I didn't realize you'd still be here,' he said.

'It's all right. I'm leaving and it's all yours.' She had an extraordinarily soft voice. She straightened and turned to look at him, smiling.

Ted ran his hand through his hair. 'I was out late with John last night,' he said, and coughed.

'That's where it is,' she said, and pulled at something Ted was sitting on. He shifted and she pulled out something silk.

'Sorry.'

'It's all right, I'm finished.' She left the room, leaving a strangely sharp scent in the air; it must have been one of those natural oils. Ted felt dirty and sprawling; he wanted to leave the room quickly, to clean it up. He pulled up the blind and dressed quickly, afraid that Georgina would suddenly reappear.

The kitchen was bright and still bad smelling; John was nowhere. Sliding glass doors led onto a patio of broken stones. Through them Ted saw Georgina's back in sunlight. He poured himself a glass of water and stepped into the sun, squinting.

'Oh, hi,' she said. She wasn't reading, just sitting with a glass of water barefoot in the sun. It was as hot as summer, but dry and clear. It reminded Ted of registration, standing in queues with forms.

'Indian summer,' he said.

'I love it.' She smiled into the sun, closing her eyes.

'So you're off to Japan.'

'Tomorrow.'

'Wow.' Ted sat on a shredded lawn chair, shading his eyes and looking at her. He wished he had unpacked some shorts.

'Do you want any breakfast?' she asked. 'There's juice, I think.'

'Thanks. I checked. There isn't any. I might make some coffee though. Want some?'

'Mmm. Sure. No, I don't drink coffee. I love the smell though. I'll try it if you make some.'

Ted didn't move, feeling the sun on his arms and forehead. 'So you're going to be modelling over there?'

'Mmm.'

'Have you been there before?'

'Oh yes. I've spent a lot of time there. It's where I go when there's no work here.'

Ted tried to imagine her on the boulevards at night, under the flashing Sanyo signs, towering over chattering black-haired men.

'You in school?' she asked.

He told her the story. She was excited by psychoanalysis and feminism; she had taken a feminist course at Simon Fraser. And a friend of hers had just gone into analysis. 'Do you believe in it?' she said.

'Well, as an intellectual theory, sure, it's very interesting. As a series of paradigms, I mean like a series of archetypes which we can see as models ... or more as analogies, metaphors for human behaviour, patterns of human behaviour which recur, it's very interesting if you compare it to stories, in books and films. It can be a useful way of seeing things, because all interpretations are a part of the fiction anyway. But it's basically just fiction, a fictional set of models.'

'But as therapy, I mean.'

'Therapy? Oh no. No no. That would be like going to see a Marxist therapist or Catholic therapist or a ... some kind of New Ager or something. Reiki or something. It's just fiction, like any religious system. There's no basis in science. Freud was basically a philosopher.'

She laughed, confusing Ted.

He asked, 'You like it over there?'

She didn't answer for a moment, staring straight ahead. Then she shook her head.

'So you're not looking forward to going?'

'No.' She turned her head away and Ted realized she was crying. He looked up at the sun. He was not surprised or frightened, for he was used to people crying easily, but it always made him tired. He wanted to close his eyes and go back to sleep. The best thing to do was always ignore it, not say anodyne words of comfort which were embarrassing, nor to use it as an opportunity for sex, which came easily with it. There was something terribly sad about this, though, her silent crying in the bright garden, looking away from him. He broke his rule and looped a finger around one of hers, lying flat on the seat of her chair.

'Why are you sad?' he asked in a conversational tone, holding on to her finger.

She didn't answer, but tried to giggle, wiping at her face.

She shrugged and shook her head, sniffling.

Ted remembered the pile of lights and poles in the hallway. 'Do you have someone here you're leaving?'

She laughed, then shook her head again. 'No.'

'You just don't want to go?'

She paused, and seemed to have regained composure. 'You're being so sweet,' she said in a normal voice. She was still staring out at the garden, hardly squinting in the glare. Ted looked at a mole under her ear, and felt a sudden surge of intimacy. He was embarrassed to have seen the little blemish, as if he had accidentally brushed against her in a train. To his vague disappointment, she had stopped crying.

'I guess I am just upset about leaving, I guess,' she said, smiling at him. Her tears had left no trace on her pale skin. 'I haven't had a lot of sleep lately. Listen, I really want to do something really nostalgic for me. I used to have breakfast every day in the Bakery, you know Bepo's Bakery on Bloor? I know it's kind of sickening.'

'Sickening? Why?'

'Oh, well it was kind of the trendy place for a while. It's still full of actors and models. Looking at each other.' A frown crossed her face. 'And I used to have a croissant and a hot chocolate there every morning, when the sun was on the other side of the street. It was a real ritual for me, and it was good, because it was so.'

Ted waited, squinting.

'Quiet there, I guess. It was so beautiful. It was really beautiful.' Her voice broke on the last phrase but her face held together. She smiled up at the sun. 'So listen, I was wondering if you'd want to come there, today, with me, for a last croissant sort of thing.'

Ted spoke enthusiastically. 'Sure. Sure. There's nothing here to eat anyway. I'd love to see the place.'

As the two of them left the front door a fit black man in a tank top rode his mountain bicycle across the sidewalk, up to the veranda. 'Hi,' he said in a deep voice as he lifted the bicycle onto the porch. His muscles bulged and shone. 'Malcolm,' he said, holding his hand out to Ted.

'Oh, I'm sorry, Ted, this is Malcolm,' said Georgina.

Ted shook his firm hand and marvelled at his perfect face, his cabled legs.

'How are you babe,' Malcolm said to Georgina, kissing her below the ear. 'Beautiful day.' His voice was so velvety Ted found it vaguely embarrassing. Malcolm smiled brilliantly at him from under his Indonesian pill-box cap, his hands on his hips. 'Good to have you here.'

'I'll see you around,' said Ted as he and Georgina walked away. Malcolm waved enthusiastically after them.

'Wow,' said Ted. 'He's in good shape.'

'Oh Malcolm's a lovely man. Such a lovely man.'

'He's the actor, right.'

'Yeah, dancer, actor.' She looked at him quickly. 'He's gay you know.'

'That guy? That guy is gay? You couldn't hear it in his voice at all.'

'Well he's an actor, right. Oh he's such a sweetie.'

They had to walk through leafy blocks of narrow Victorian houses to Bloor Street. Ted talked animatedly of university politics and rival factions in British pop music. He found that Georgina had met Max but wouldn't talk about him. She didn't know where to find him. 'Oh don't worry,' said Ted proudly, 'I have a number for him.'

He was also pleased to see the Bakery: it was crowded with people their age wearing the little hats that Malcolm had. The glass walls had been rolled back so that there was no demarcation between the canopied terrace and the interior. On the sidewalk next to the terrace, pimply young skinheads were playing with devil sticks, juggling one stick in the air with two others. They played very badly, and kept dropping the sticks.

Ted and Georgina walked through the skinheads, refusing

43

their requests for change, bought croissants at the counter and weaved through the canvas bags between the tables to find their own. When they sat, Georgina jumped up again. 'I'll be right back.'

Ted watched her rush out past the patio tables. He felt a strange nervousness. She looked fragile and frightening as she ran through the cars across the street, with her sundress flying and her bare feet. She had walked all the way there in bare feet, easily, and this was a bad sign; it reminded him of the heavy-metal girls from Saint John suburbs he had kissed at bonfires in junior high. He looked around at the crowd. Two short-haired women with heavy necklaces came in and stood at the door.

'By the window,' said one, pointing, 'if we can. I so crave the light at this time of year.'

'Well of course,' said the other, 'it's a spiritual need. It's a spiritual need at this time of year.' As they passed Ted he saw the dull glass pieces hanging from their necklaces: crystals. 'The vegetable soup isn't vegetarian,' said one as they sat down.

Next to him sat two businessmen in suits. They were both balding, with wire-rimmed glasses, and file folders and coffees. 'Now Bob I think that's unfair,' one said. 'I think that's unfair. You can ask anyone, *anyone* in my section about the project and they'll tell you they think it's going, it's proceeding they way we, you and I first saw, ah, envisaged it and they're, they're happy with it.'

'Well Jim, in my perception that's not a, that's not a true.' The other mopped at his face with a handkerchief. 'Perception. That's not a true perception.'

Ted thought of Max and looked out to the street for Georgina. There was no sign of her, so he stood up to find the telephone. He found it downstairs, near the bad-smelling washroom, but there was a girl in combat boots speaking into it. He waited behind her. 'Look, don't tell me,' she was saying. 'Don't even tell me. Because I'm holding a cigarette and I'd probably burn myself or something.'

Ted went to the toilets; when he came out she was still talking. 'Uh-huh. What did you drink with it? Did you drink milk? Do you drink milk? You don't like milk. I don't like milk. I like chocolate milk though.'

He gave up and walked up the stairs, to see Georgina standing forlornly at door of the cafe, holding a bunch of flowers. 'I was just in the washroom,' he said as he approached her.

'Oh,' she said sadly. 'Are we staying?'

'Sure, of course. I was just in the washroom. See, my stuff is still on our table. Let's sit down again.' They sat, and Ted looked nervously at the flowers.

'Here,' she said, proffering them and then pulling them back. 'Maybe they have a glass or something.' She stood up and went to the counter for a glass of water. 'They're for you,' she said as she sat down again. 'For being so nice and coming out with me.' She was bright pink.

Ted felt his own face heating up. He thanked her awkwardly.

'Have you just broken up with somebody?' she asked after they finished the croissants.

'What makes you think that?'

'John told me.'

'Oh. Well I guess you know then.'

'Yes.'

There was a clatter from the sidewalk as a skinhead dropped all three of his sticks, and Ted felt the tide of confession rising in him. After this, he knew, there would be no turning back from Georgina. His stomach heaved. He pushed away his chocolate-stained plate and told her about Janet.

FIVE

THERE WERE LONG dappled shadows on the Victorian street as Ted leaped up the stairs to John's veranda. There were new bicycles locked there; he paused to squeeze the brakes and examine the gear systems, humming. The door opened and a tall, bony man, his age, came out and stared at him. 'Hi,' said Ted. 'Ted.'

'Hi.' The man looked down at the bike Ted was touching, frowning. He looked angry. He wore square wire-rimmed glasses and a T-shirt that was too small for him with a faded logo; the words were 'System 9 AmeriCon'.

Ted let the bike go. 'I'm John's friend, staying here. You're ...' He almost said 'the Mole'.

'Oh.' The man nodded, looking out at the street and pursing his lips. He kept nodding for several seconds. Ted looked at his ribcage, his narrow shoulders, visible through the cheap T-shirt. The Mole was awfully thin, utterly white. His short black hair looked dirty. He had corduroy jeans of a kind Ted hadn't seen since high school, running shoes and an enormous technical watch with revolving dials and buttons. He nodded, looked at it and turned to Ted with an expression of fury. Ted reflexively stepped backwards. 'Well,' said the Mole. 'Time I jacked in. Cyberspace awaits. Wheeeep,' he whistled as he bent to pick up his plastic Loblaws bag full of binders. 'Nerk nerk,' he said, walking purposefully down the stairs and jerking his elbow up and down like someone doing a chicken imitation. 'See ya,' he called as he walked away, waving. 'Look out for black ice.'

Ted was still laughing when he reached the top of the stairs,

46

the door to John's attic domain. John was lying in bed reading a magazine. He looked up with a knowing expression as Ted entered. 'Had a funny day?'

'Look out for black ice, dude,' said Ted, pulling the Playboy from under its cover. 'The Mole is excellent. I couldn't have invented him.'

John grinned. 'Mister technofanboy. First time I met him he told me he was doing this impersonation of Tonto, you know the Lone Ranger's guy, as a Chinese surfer, with this Chinese-Californian accent. He'd draw his lips back over his teeth and squint his eyes and say, "Su'fs up, bohss". And you'd have to say, "Tonto, where's Trigger?" and he'd say, "Pretty rad, bohss."'

'Too good. What does he do, exactly?'

'He's a funny guy,' said John. 'For a while he told me about this program he was working on which was supposed to make a dictionary and a concordance of all the elvish words in *Lord of the Rings* – you remember *Lord of the Rings*? Took me a while to realize he was joking. But you know what he does work on? Fucking virtual reality programs. You know, three-dimensional models on a screen that move when you move your hand in this sensor-glove or something?'

'Yes, friend. I published a paper on it,' said Ted, stretched on the floor and flipping the pages of the Playboy. 'And you don't say virtual reality any more, you say immersive interface, or you talk about something specific, like multiple-user role-playing, and besides, you don't, because it's been done to death.'

'Well, anyway, that's what I thought the Mole was working on.'

'*Lord of the Rings*,' said Ted. 'God help us. Funny about the *Lord of the Rings* though, I mean what is it about computers and wargames, D and D and that fantasy stuff – remember the air-brush posters of guys with armour and swords we used to have in high school? What is it about the dweeb factor that links those two things? A desire for violence in a non-physical world. There's an essay in that. *Je me demande.*' He began to whistle.

'So, had a funny day?'

'What do you mean?'

'High spirits? You've been out all day and you're in very high spirits.'

'I was with Georgina,' Ted said nonchalantly. 'She's going away tomorrow so she wanted to have fun.' He sat up, pulled out the centre-fold and rapidly folded it again.

'Where did you go?'

Ted shrugged. 'Breakfast in the Bakery. She seemed nice enough to me.'

'Uh huh.'

'Then we, ah, walked a bit, went to Yorkville, got some ice creams. Oh yeah, and then she showed me this big new record store, three floors, banks of video monitors, dj booths, and I couldn't believe it, they have a whole *floor* of rock videos to *sell.* I mean, who would want to *buy* a rock video? To *own* one? They're by definition temporary things. You own it, it's use-less. They have nothing beyond the surface of the moment.'

'Uh-huh,' said John, raising his eyebrows.

'But I did like the CD listening posts. You just pick up the head phones and –'

'Ted, I live here. I've been there.'

'Right. But I mean what's cool is that they let you know what's hot, you just plug into it. It's like the stock market, turning on the ticker to see what's happening. It's like there's this big global mechanism that decides what CD's get chosen for that listening post next, it's like some enormous, uncontrolled, inhuman machine that's constantly changing shape. And there's this machine that will show you twenty-five seconds of the video of your choice. Which is of course all you need, from my point of view. What impresses me is that they understand so well, I mean the kids who run the place – and they are *kids,* these guys in gothic hair and surfpunk bandannas are the *bosses*

– they understand the brief, no the transient nature of the technological culture these repeated images spring from. It's all so totally postmodern, you know, fragmentation – '

'Ted. Kids are stupid. They don't read. They have no attention span. Rock videos are stupid. The kids love it. It's easier than TV. That's all there is to it. I don't think there's – '

'No, no, there's much more to it than that. These kids have an interesting intuition. There's something that links the fragmentation and transience to the simulacrum, you know Baudrillard's – '

'Ted. You tell all this to George?'

Ted looked at him blankly. 'I guess I did. Sure.'

'Uh-huh.' John lay down again on the bed, linking his hands behind his head. 'And she loved it.'

'Well, I don't know. She listened, sure. What do you mean?'

'Go on.'

'Oh, I guess that was it. And then we went to a gallery in a warehouse on Spadina, there was a group show with one of her friends in it. A sculptor called Anthony, bit of an asshole, tall guy, tight black jeans and five o'clock shadow, you know. Ego. Touched her a lot. But she was touching everyone a lot too, you know how they all hug and kiss. All these girls in second-hand dresses and army boots. Reminded me of Concordia.' Ted gave a short laugh. 'The show was interesting, for student work, although there was a bit too much painting, you know, old-fashioned oil painting, for my taste. I can't believe people aren't sick of that.'

'Why would they be?'

'Well, it's all so heroic. You know, it's the whole macho artist-as-master thing. The only interesting thing was some Polaroids. Polaroids with ball-point-pen text on them. That was okay.'

'Uh-huh. Well. Seems like you can take the boy out of Concordia, but you can't ... '

Ted laughed. 'Yeah.' He paused. 'Actually, I don't know. I don't know anything about painting, about art any more. Some of those paintings were pretty, but ... It's too confusing.'

'Uh huh. Well. Seems like you and old George hit it off just fine. She's going away, dude.'

'Hey, I know it.' Ted rose, began fiddling with the CD player.

'Where is she now?'

'Ah. That I wasn't clear on. She had to go somewhere and I take it she's spending the night there. She doesn't leave till tomorrow and she said I could have her room.'

John sighed, looking at him wearily. 'Right. Dude –'

'Let's not talk about it,' said Ted.

'Right.' John swung his legs off the bed. The stereo popped into life with a long swish of computer-generated white noise, then the sound of breaking glass superimposed over John F. Kennedy repeating that he was a Berliner.

'Didn't expect you to be this hip,' John shouted over the noise.

'I'm not. George gave it to me, she didn't like it. Anthony, your friend the sculptor, gave it to her.'

'Christ, this is an import. Wasted on you people.'

Ted suddenly felt sick, as if he'd had too much chocolate. He couldn't remember why he had spent the day with Georgina instead of looking for work. He turned the music down and fumbled in his pocket for Max's phone number. 'Gotta call Max,' he said, picking up the phone.

'Miranda's party tonight,' said John, getting undressed.

'Oh yeah.' Ted dialled, waited for the ringing. 'Do you really think she wanted me to – Hello? Hello?' The woman had answered in some foreign language. 'Yuh, is Max there? Max. I don't know his last name.'

He repeated the number. 'Oh. Sorry.' He hung up. 'Chick didn't even speak English. Never been a Max there. That's definitely the same number.' He peered at the crumpled slip of paper, then threw it into the waste basket. 'Shit.' He sat down heavily. 'Okay.' He looked around the room, its piles of laundry and magazines, the matte-black stereo components. The music had changed to a the sound of a television evangelist shouting over some Gregorian chant. They had altered the chant somehow so it was similar to the James Bond theme. 'HEY POOR,' shouted the voice. 'YOU DON'T HAVE TO BE JESUS.'

'Okay,' said Ted. 'Let's go to a fucking party.'

Showered and dressed, he went downstairs to wait for John. In the middle of the kitchen, Malcolm the actor and Go-Go were embracing. Malcolm still wore his pillbox hat, and his arms were shining knots around her shoulders. He released her and said hello to Ted as he entered. 'Okay?' Malcolm said to Go-Go, smiling widely.

She nodded.

Malcolm turned to Ted, holding out his hand. 'So, how're you doing?' he boomed. 'John tells me you've come to settle.'

Ted shook his firm hand once again, although he wasn't sure they needed to. He explained once more about writing work in Toronto. Then he asked Malcolm about acting, and Malcolm recited a long list of projects at major theatres, CBC pilots and workshops. 'I've just come back from Banff, was there this summer. Beautiful. Incredibly beautiful. Well, I have a rehearsal.' He stuck out his hand again. As he shook Ted's, he moved his face very close. 'Good luck, man. Great to meet you.'

Once he had gone, Ted turned back to Go-Go. She was bending over the garbage in her black tights, sorting it into two bags. 'Fuck, fuck, fuck,' she sang. She stood up and looked at Ted, blowing hair out of her face. 'Look. This.' She held up an empty tin can. 'Does not go in here. Nor does this. And this.' She pulled up a banana peel. 'Goes in the compost. Honestly, it's not difficult. Do you know how much fucking landfill space is left in this city? And do you know where we have to fill after there's none left here?'

She seemed genuinely angry. John sat down at the kitchen table.

'You look nice,' she said. 'You going out?'

'Miranda's party, I guess.'

She rolled her eyes, turned back to the garbage.

'You know her?'

'Rosedale,' she said to the far wall. 'They all know each other there. Everyone at that party has known one another for years, since elementary school. They're all sick of each other and Toronto, they're dying to go to New York and they talk about it all the time. They're all terribly, terribly bored.'

'Why don't they go then?'

Go-Go was washing her hands in the sink. 'A *very* smart question, Mister Ted. Nobody knows. They're just stuck, that's all. They can't get out.'

Ted looked at his watch. 'You coming?'

'Well.' She looked at her watch. 'I have shrink at eight. And my friend Mike is coming into town tonight, I think. I should be around for him.'

'Where's he live?'

'Montreal, right now.' She fiddled with a dishcloth. 'Well, I don't really know if he's coming or not. I don't really have to be around for him. Maybe I'll meet you guys later on.'

In the car, somebody else's car, some friend called Jeff who was in L.A., Ted asked John who Mike was.

'Go-Go's waste product boyfriend. Bike courier, skull and crossbones kind of guy. Crazy, drinks, does a lot of chemicals. Into body adornment. Religious self-mutilation shit. Bad news.'

Then they were in the wide street of enormous houses, stone and neo-Tudor half-timbered, where Miranda lived. There were lawns and flowerbeds and stone fountains. 'Her parents' place?' asked Ted as they walked towards a heavy wooden door.

'No, she and Diana rent the top floor here. Her parents live next door, I think.' He rang the bell. 'They all grew up here too.'

And then the door was wide open and Miranda was kissing them and introducing them to big blond boys in button-downs who crushed Ted's fingers when they seized them, in the bright entrance hall with black and white tiles on the floor. 'Get you a beer, Ted?' they roared.

In the living room he saw Julia and Isabel; they kissed him on the cheek, looking pained and drawn. Diana was tall and beautiful, and she had a fat friend called Caroline who had just come back from England. He saw Arthur the prep and Andreas the filmmaker and the grant-getter; they all shook hands. John shouldered his way ahead of him, through to the sparkling kitchen, where he tried to open the fridge to get beer out. As Ted watched the struggle, he saw Roger the sullen writer, who pretended not to see him. He was leaning on the counter on the range, set into an island in the middle of the room, talking earnestly to a small girl in black. His mouth was close to her ear; he spoke very softly, with several smiles. She giggled often, as if shocked.

John handed him a beer and shouted 'David! Dave!'

A tall man with a crooked nose, in a rumpled suit and a loose tie pushed his way to them. 'How you doing man?' said John, pumping his hand. 'How's the law?'

'The law. It's great.' Dave's voice was loud and cutting. Ted could picture him talking on the phone, his feet on the desk, berating a police officer. 'It's fun. I'm quitting. I guess it's not wall-to-wall fun, not three-sixty degrees fun, I guess. There's not a high fun-to-bullshit ratio.'

Ted found himself squeezed out of the conversation by the angle of their backs. He looked at the the small man standing next to the fridge, alone, and instinctively held out his hand.

'Brian,' said the man nervously. He had longer hair than the rest of them, and a plaid shirt. 'You from around here too?'

'Ah, no, no, I just arrived. I was in Montreal.'

Brian brightened. 'I'm from Prince Edward Island.'

'No shit. I grew up in New Brunswick.'

Brian's face broke into a wide grin. He clinked his beer bottle against Ted's. 'So how long you been up here? You like it up here or wha? You know these people or wha? Oh, yeah, I know. They seem really friendly but it's hard to get to know them. It's like they're all pissed off at one another all the time, you know? Like they'll tell you this club is really boring and stupid and awful, and they go there every night. It's like they're too cool to like anything. I'm sick of it. I can't stand it.'

'You're going back?'

'Well, there's not much for me to do back there.' Brian looked down at his beer.

'How long you been here?'

'Five years,' said Brian.

'Five *years*?' As he said it he saw Go-Go's black triangle of hair, her head at an angle to keep it out of her eyes. She squeezed into the kitchen with her jacket still on, looking unhappy. He met her at the island, next to Roger and his friend.

She tried to smile. 'Don't know anyone. John here?'

Ted pointed him out. 'Take your wine?'

'Sure. Open it.'

'No need. Lots open. Keep this. Take from the rich when they offer.'

'Smart.' She sighed, ramming her hands into her jacket pockets.

'You don't look very happy.'

'I don't know why I came,' she said with venom.

'Hey, listen, this is all right, free beer, big friendly preps, Miranda's —'

54

'Oh listen, tell me about Miranda. Tell me all a fucking bout her.' She played with the zip on her jacket.

'What's wrong with Miranda? She rude to you?'

'Oh it's ... nothing. Nothing. Listen, I'm not comfortable here, I'm going to go.'

'Did Mike show up?'

She shook her head. 'I'll see you later.'

Later, Ted found John laughing in the living room with more girls called Henrietta or something. John turned to him, bleary-eyed. 'Fine for *you* to say,' he blurted. 'Fine for *you* to fucking say.'

'You know it. Hey, dude, what's the – '

John had accosted a passing prep. 'Hey, you've got some nerve,' he shouted. He turned to the girl at his side, who laughed nervously. 'Is he bothering you? Is he bothering you, ma'am?'

Ted pulled him away. 'Hey, have another beer, man.'

'Some nerve,' John muttered. 'Road to hell paved with unbought stuffed dogs, remember that?'

'You know it.' They both sat down on a sofa. 'Christ,' said Ted. 'Everything's a fucking mystery here. Why do you people all hang out together if everybody hates each other.'

John looked at him, unfocused. 'Easy, dude. What are you talking about?'

'Go-Go, Go-Go just comes in and says – '

'Oh listen, Go-Go, *Go-Go*'s just a fucking little – '

'Right,' said Ted, standing up, 'I don't need to hear it.' He went to the kitchen to get another beer; when he returned John had moved. There was an awkward man in a beard and a tweed jacket sitting on the edge of the sofa, staring into space. Ted sat beside him. 'Hi.'

The man turned very slowly, and paused before repeating the greeting in a soft voice.

'Ted.'

Gingerly, the man put out his hand. 'I suppose you went to a private school too.'

Ted noticed, on his tweed lapel, a tiny red pin: an Ontario flag. He laughed nervously. 'No, I wouldn't say that I did. I went to a public high school in a small town in the Maritimes.'

The man raised his bushy eyebrows. 'Oh,' he said in a voice like an owl. He peered at Ted with wide eyes. He's some kind of loony grad student, thought Ted. Metallurgy or paleontology or something. 'Most of these people are from private schools,' said the man. He was rubbing his hands slowly up and down his thighs, staring fixedly down at them.

'You went to a public school,' said Ted.

Almost inaudibly, the man said, 'No.'

'Excuse me,' said Ted.

He found Miranda in the kitchen. 'Someone told me I have a nice posture,' she was saying. 'I said nice posture? Thanks a lot, Queen Vic fucking toria. Teddy!' She squealed, and put her hands behind his neck. 'You know, I'm so, so glad Johnny brought you.'

'Yeah. Listen, who's that guy on the sofa, in the beard?'

'Oh.' Her face suddenly closed, became blank. 'Did you talk to him? Was he okay?' Her voice was much quieter.

'Yeah, sure, he was okay, maybe a little strange. He just seems really out of place here.'

'Well, he's been sick. He's Diana's brother.'

Ted looked across the room at Diana, her bright smile and the way she moved her cigarette to her mouth, her sleek black dress, and couldn't believe it. 'He's *Diana's* brother?'

'He's just come out of hospital, actually.' She was speaking very softly. 'He's been very sick. He's probably pretty heavily medicated right now, just so he could be here without being difficult. Maybe that's why he seemed strange. It's been very sad and hard on the family. He's the eldest.' She was speaking distractedly, watching Roger making his small friend laugh.

Ted craned his neck to see through the door to the living room. The man was still sitting, staring into space and rocking slightly. 'Christ, I can't believe he's from the same family. Mad woman in the attic, eh?'

But Miranda had turned away and put her arms around a newcomer. Before he left the room Ted saw Roger kiss the small woman just below the ear.

Half an hour later Ted was sitting alone on a couch, watching John flirt drunkenly and with astounding success. He rose to go to the washroom. The stairs were full of men in sweaters talking about purchasable items and their worth.

'Two fifty horse,' said one with wide eyes.

'Shaft?' said another.

'Oh yes, strictly inboard. Not inboard outboard. Shaft, of course.'

They both turned to look nervously at Ted as he ascended the stairs, but seeing it was another man they relaxed.

'Excuse me,' said Ted.

'No problem, man,' they all said warmly. 'No problem at all.'

Ted walked down a carpeted corridor, looking for a washroom. He passed an open door and glanced inside. For a second he glimpsed Miranda and Roger the writer standing next to a brass bed in the middle of a bedroom, a woman's bedroom. Their faces were strained and very close together; they were talking intensely, in low tones. Ted looked away.

When he emerged from the washroom the bedroom was empty.

Ted persuaded John to leave Jeff's car behind. 'You've got some nerve, buddy,' John repeated to himself all the way to the subway.

Ted could see the glow of buildings downtown. 'Drinking, right. It's good, right?'

'Drinking. Good,' said John. 'Sure. Good for you.'

In the yellow light of the train, Ted said to him, 'Everybody seems to know Max but nobody knows where to find him. I bet if I could find him he could open a lot of doors from me.'

John grunted from behind closed eyes, his head swaying loosely in the motion of the train.

'Met a great Maritimer. Sounded as if he'd just got off the train, then he said he'd been here five years. You like it up here or wha? Like I'd just met him in the Legion. Hey.' He poked John. 'Do you know Diana's brother? The crazy one?'

'Yeah,' John breathed, opening his eyes. 'Poor guy. Big embarrassment for the family.'

'Embarrassment! That's it, isn't it? I mean it fits perfectly. He's the one who goes crazy, and nobody talks about him. He's the one who manifests whatever tensions all these people – I mean they're so *polite*, aren't they? They're so well-trained, they must be hiding tension all the time, and he – '

'Would you rather they cried and had to make up all the time, like Janet's friends at Concordia, or the BFA's at Southern?' John spoke wearily. 'Would you rather have every coffee with a friend a kind of therapy session where you say, How *are* you, *really*, it's *me*?'

'No. No I wouldn't. It just strikes me as clichéd that one of them should crack up so completely. It's like an argument against wealth. It's sheer Bunuel.'

'Right. I don't know who the hell Bunuel is, and I'm pretty sure poor people crack up just as regularly as Isabel's family does, but I can tell you that you're right about the skeletons in every closet over there. You dig deep enough. Did you meet Miranda's sister?'

'Caroline? Fat one? Just came back from England? It took me a while to figure out she was her sister. But she's nice. Nice girl.'

'Yeah.' John talked with his eyes half-closed, as if through immense fatigue. 'Those girls, Julia, Diana, Caroline, they've been together so long they know each other better than they know themselves, you know? But Miranda's done okay. The only casualty of that scene was her sister.'

'What scene was this?' Ted watched another bright station slip away through the windows.

John glanced at him. 'You know Miranda was moving with a real crowd in high school. The really serious crowd.'

'Serious?'

'Money, cocaine. Older people. This was the early eighties. She came through it okay, but Caroline got fucked up and had some problems.'

'Like what?'

John got up, stood in front of the sliding doors. 'Our stop. Next time you see her, Caroline, take a look at her wrists. Scars the length of the vein.'

They stood in silence on the escalator under the fluorescent light. John swayed a little. Walking outside, Ted said, 'Wow. Jesus, it's incredible how you get sucked into the moment all these people are living in. I don't know if I want it. I can't believe I remember all these names, but I do. I know who Caroline is, and Roger, and Go-Go and Malcolm and Mike the bike courier, although I haven't met him. I don't know if I want to know exactly what's going on all the time.'

'Dude,' said John as they climbed his front stairs, 'it's too late.'

Georgina's room looked different. Ted switched on the light. All the clothes were gone, the bed made. There was space in the closet. Ted stepped forward to look at the top of the dresser. The jewellery boxes were closed and the stack of business cards was gone. There was no note.

SIX

'ALLAN, IT'S JUST the opening,' shouted Derek into the telephone, gesturing for Ted to sit down. 'It just kind of lays there. Yeah. Just kind of lays there.' He was probably thirty, not fashionably dressed, with curiously old-fashioned bi-focals slipping down his nose. Ted had worn a tie for the interview. 'I think,' said Derek in his loud, nasal voice, 'you're using the verb "to be" too much.' Derek crossed his long legs. He wore an old man's cardigan. 'The fish is good, the service is bad, you know? You want a sentence that gets up and grabs you. Like the fish teases, the service niggles, I don't know, you know what I mean. Just pizazz it up a little. Pizazz it up. Just a minute.' He put one hand over the mouthpiece and rolled his eyes across the desk at Ted. 'I'll just be *one* minute,' he said in a stage whisper.

Ted nodded. He looked past Derek's head at the mirrored canyon of office buildings through the window. It was hot in the office. Ted dried his palms on his grey trousers. On Derek's notice board were a naked man and a sign that said Our Writers Are Everything.

'And Allan,' Derek shouted, 'You've got the word trendy here. I've substituted "drop-em-dead fashion", okay? And where you have downtown I've put "downtown and on the edge". Okay? And Al, stay away from "restaurant". You have it three or four times. I've got "eatery" instead. Okay?'

Derek hung up the phone, folded his arms over his crossed legs and looked at Ted. 'Edward.' He nodded sagely. 'I'm *so* sorry you had to wait so long.'

'Oh, that's – '

Derek held up a hand. 'You must excuse me.' He pulled a crumpled handkerchief from a pocket and dabbed at his nose. 'I've got one *fuck* of a cold. Now. Sorry it took me so long to look at your stuff.' He opened a file folder. 'Tell me. This essay in *Culture Angst*. What exactly is *Culture Angst*? I've never heard of it.'

'Well,' said Ted. 'It's an academic journal, really. They do a lot of ... ' He hesitated, focusing on the noticeboard behind Derek's head. 'Semiotics.'

Derek nodded. 'It's kind of neat, the stuff you said about soap operas. Of course it's not the kind of language you could use in *Cities*. Tell me, how did you meet Julia?'

Ted told him about John's friends, about Julia and Miranda in Penumbra. He made it sound as if he'd been there often. He hesitated before mentioning Max, since he didn't know his last name. 'And I don't know if you know a fellow called Max, used to publish *Haze* – '

'You know Max?' Derek was peering at him from over his bi-focals.

'Yes, in fact it was Max who first suggested that you might like the kind of, uh, material I do, I write.'

Derek looked down at the folder, nodding. 'Edward, I like your stuff. I like it. And I like the idea about the British music. That's a little exclusive, though. I mean we don't want to scare off any of our readers. We have to think of everyone, and we don't want to sound snobbish. You know what I mean? But what I *am* thinking of doing, which I think you might be *perfect* for, is a little light piece on some celebrities and their pets. You know, we'd run a photo of them in their work or home environment with their pets, with some interview. Maybe fifty words each, a spread of four celebrities, just ask them, you know, what the pet means to them and so on. Go for anecdotes. Now if that doesn't grab you we've been throwing around this piece on the trendy aldermen, or alderpeople I should say, the politically progressive ones, and why they wear what they wear. Not totally from their point of view, though, a kind of style analysis. With some kind of snide table or pie graph or something, you know what I mean? A la *Spy*. You know what I mean?'

SEVEN

TED SAT at the kitchen table hung-over with a cup of strong coffee and a pad of lined paper. He wrote,

Sunday, September 21
Dear Janet,

Sorry about not writing, but then you've hardly been exemplary in that department yourself, or whatever. I called a couple of times and left a message with Gayathri but I knew the chances of it reaching you were about as good as Gayathri's meditation that day.

No steady work here yet but lots of leads, and some little things. I've made my debut in the commercial world with a small article in a materialist magazine about some lampshades you can get in Rome for $2000 each. Very artistic lampshades, these; they're made of industrial rubber and rotting leaves by some nineteen-year-old artist who is apparently a millionaire already. The magazine has promised me more little bits like that. And I'm still working on the big piece about television, although I don't know where I would sell it, and the screenplay. I'm thinking of turning it into a play; John lives with a nauseatingly sincere actor called Malcolm who says all kinds of alternative theatre groups are desperate for material to perform, and it doesn't cost much.

At least I'm having a good time. I think the best thing I've done is buy myself a black leather jacket; a real biker's jacket, with zippers all over it. Can't afford it, of course, at this point, but I've always wanted one. Perhaps this new wantonness is John's influence. He has changed quite a bit; he's not working, and seems to be wasting a good deal of time. He's great for contacts, though.

I also seem to have been taken in hand by an extremely nice group, who don't at all fulfil our expectations of snotty Toronto turds. Yes, I hesitate to tell you, they are rich. And may well be politically compromised or downright immoral. But you know how I've always been attracted to people who know how to introduce you to strangers and make sure you have a drink at parties. Such simple things seem harder to come by in more sensitive groups. And I admit, I like the way they dress up at parties, too. Some of the men wear ties and the women wear dresses. We always used to think of that as conservatism, but I realize now that it's almost the opposite, a kind of anti-establishment defiance. The relentless jeans-and-sweaters of a less self-assured crowd are far more widespread among people our age; we are the status quo.

I know, I know, you're thinking they dress like their parents and their parents are crypto-fascists, and you may be right. I wish I could convince you how unsquare this all seems to me, but I'm sure if you saw them you'd still hate them so enough about them.

John shares a house with Malcolm and a girl (sorry, I can only think of her as a girl, although she's only a bit younger than me) called Go-Go, who goes to night clubs a lot. She works at the box office of a rep cinema and talks about recycling a lot.

Then there's a marvellous computer dweeb called the Mole whose friends can't say anything without a foreign accent of some kind.

Oh, I met an excellent Torontonian named Max on the train who seems to have a finger in every pie. Surprisingly intelligent, too. As soon as I get hold of him he should prove helpful.

Last night Malcolm the actor finally took me, as promised, to a party of 'alternative theatre' actors. Didn't introduce me to any directors, though, just some pre-Raphaelite woman in a big hat who found out I read books. Well, she started bubbling about the most marvellous book she'd read. She wondered if I knew it; she couldn't remember the title or the author, but knew it was about this famous old family, couldn't remember what century it was set in (I wonder if it ever registered in the first place); but she knew I would love it. She said it really focused her, really left her feeling centred, you know, *in* her body.

You talk to fringe theatre actors and you find that they all seem to think that they are cut off from their bodies in some way by an unfeeling, uncaring world, and the mission of art is to reunite them with their own flesh. They're constantly doing voice and movement workshops which seem to resemble the primal scream therapy of the seventies. Really puts you in touch with your body, man. Apparently directors are constantly admonishing actors to 'get out of your head'. There seems to be a tacit understanding that the cerebral is essentially patriarchal, racist and environmentally unfriendly.

I realize as I write this that you sometimes think like that, too. Or do you? Perhaps I have you wrong.

You know, I can't say I do miss the croissants every morning on the Main. I do miss you, though, and I wonder what you're doing. How did the belly-dancing class work out? Say hello to Shelley and the gang at the Womyn's Collective.

No. Listen, I want to end my letter that way because I think it would be salutary for us to start talking like that, but I just can't do it. You know I think it's unhelpful for us to go over what happened between us one more time, and I think it's best to make a clean break, but I can't resist telling you that I'm thinking about you and hoping you're okay and wondering a lot about the whole thing. It's not easy for me either. I'm sorry for whatever. Please write.

Love,
Ted

He reread this letter, folded it and put it aside. He knew it would take days before he would remember to go out and buy envelopes. He opened his diary, a bound artist's sketch pad. Most of the pages were blank. The last entry was from the previous May. It was all about the Western Canon. It ended:

> Lozere says we can still read Baudelaire with detachment, as a kind of sociological education, as long as we refuse to abandon ourselves to its sensual pleasure and thus its ideology. Must its pleasure always be corrupting? Janet won't even allow Baudelaire in the house. O toi que j'eusse aimée, ô toi qui le savais!

He turned to a clean page and wrote,

September 2 1
Hung over Sunday feeling. Two parties last night: Malcolm's alternative theatre crowd and then another with Miranda's crowd, some uptown apartment belonging to one Justin, whom I never met. Met the daughter of the chairman of the Bank of Canada. Just wrote to Janet.

He put down the pen and sipped his coffee, now cold. He heard heavy stomping in the living room and looked up to see Go-Go enter, in a tight tie-dyed dress and black drill boots.

She said 'Coffee!'

'Have some,' said Ted.

'Is there milk?'

'No. There's no milk.'

'Gross. I'll have tea.' She filled a kettle.

'Going out?' said Ted.

'I have to work at the theatre. There's a Goddess festival all day. Are we out of fennel?'

'I wouldn't know. Were you out last night?'

'Um. I was at Hole for a while for Oblivion night and I

thought it was all right but Sarah wasn't all about the death disco thing, so we went to Helium because they have Coma Saturdays now and it was really posey, which I am like *over*. Even Sarah gets there and she's checking all these groovy fashion looks and she's going uh, excuse me? Like, hair don't, kids.'

He watched her thick legs bulge as she stretched to reach the almond tea in a high cupboard. The kettle began to creak and sigh. She turned to face him, fingering teabags. 'What are you writing?'

'I just wrote to Janet. My ... '

'Girlfriend in Montreal.'

'Ex.'

She turned back to the stove. 'What did you write?'

'I said ... ' Ted closed the diary and touched the folded letter. 'I said all kinds of things I knew she didn't want to hear. I'm not sure why. I guess I wanted to piss her off.'

'Like what?'

'Oh ... I told her about Miranda and how I like going to those parties. And then I was bitchy about actors and all kinds of things she likes.'

'Why? What did she do to you?'

'Nothing. Nothing at all. I don't know why.'

Go-Go poured boiling water into a teapot. The room filled with the heavy smell of almonds. She brought the teapot to the table and sat down with Ted. She eyed him in a knowing way that embarrassed him. 'Why *do* you like Miranda's parties?' she said.

'Oh Go-Go.' He sighed, drumming his pen on the table. 'It's a long story. I can't explain. I can, but I'd have to tell you the whole story of what I was doing before I came here, and Janet and all.'

'Okay. That's fine. I just don't get how small talk – '

'Yes, small talk. That's it. That's exactly what Janet would say. She *hates* small talk. And you know why? Because she's hopeless at it. She can't do it.'

'Maybe she doesn't want to do it.'

'Oh I know she doesn't want to. Which is precisely what I see as a lack. A failing. She thinks you can just jump right into How We All Feel About Everything with everyone she meets. But you can't. It doesn't happen.'

Go-Go raised her eyebrows and pursed her lips, pouring almond tea into a mug. The smell was intensely sweet. Ted watched her bring the mug to her nose and inhale the steam.

He tried again, in a lower tone. 'Go-Go, it's just that you don't know how boring it was, where we lived together. I didn't know at the time, but it was. *You* can go out any time you want to Hole and the Aquarium and – '

'I would *never* go to Aquarium.'

'Wherever, I never even knew about these places, and nobody I knew at Concordia would ever have gone to any of them either.'

She watched him, listening.

'You know what our parties were like? There would be a group of us, our like-minded friends, and nobody would ever wear any kind of makeup or anything tight or even black, and we would be sitting around in a circle on the floor in someone's apartment, drinking white wine – *moderately* – '

Go-Go giggled. 'White wine?'

'White wine, but *moderately*, and we would be talking about abortion rights strategy or something, and the hostess would be disappeared in a bedroom with her best friend – '

Go-Go laughed again. 'Oh I know that scene. A Long Talk with her Best Friend.'

'Exactly. And everyone would talk about it in hushed tones – 'oh, Barbara and Jane are *talking*, finally' – and leave them alone, and maybe there would be some dancing on the carpet later – '

'To Nicaraguan music,' said Go-Go.

'Exactly. You see? And so when I meet someone like Max, or Miranda, or – ' He was about to say Georgina, but stopped.

'Or any of those people, it's like I'm someone who, who hasn't eaten food for a long time. For months. I haven't eaten for months and someone comes along and gives me sugary birth-day cake. I mean, I know a steak would be better –'

'A falafel would be even better.'

'Sure, that's what Janet would have me eat, and I know that would be better, but I'm going to eat the birthday cake any-way. You know what I mean?'

Go-Go smiled. 'Oh Teddy. We'll have to feed you.'

He looked down at his diary, closed.

'You want some tea?'

'Sure.' He rose to get himself a mug. 'I was at another Miranda party last night,' he said, reaching. 'Some friend of hers. And I met the daughter of the chairman of the Bank of Canada.'

'Oh, Suzie? Suzie Wilstonehurst? The bitch?'

'She called herself Suzanne. To me. And she didn't seem particularly bitchy. Although I imagine she could be. In fact she was so polite and friendly to everyone that it made her friendli-ness meaningless. I suppose that could seem bitchy. You know what I mean? I grew up with girls in the Maritimes who wouldn't speak to you if you weren't good-looking. That meant that if they agreed to go out with you they wanted to sleep with you. You knew where you stood. With chicks like this Wilstonehurst you don't know a thing.'

'And you prefer the Maritime girls?'

'God no. I prefer the Wilstonehurst. Janet would hate her.' Ted poured himself steaming almond tea. There was a silence. Go-Go was fiddling with a broken nail, frowning. 'Janet hates a lot of things,' said Ted softly. 'And it used to be really impor-tant. And here it all just fizzles away. She doesn't really like herself, so she hates things, and it's not all so significant here.' He sipped his tea, talking almost to himself. 'The one thing that I've never allowed myself to think is that she hates attractive women. And now I've said it. And I guess I wanted her to turn

her hatred onto me now – which she will, once she gets my
pricky letter. And I guess I want that. She won't even answer
this letter. And I'm guiltily relieved by it. I'd much rather not
have a letter to answer than continue to be comforting and supportive. I get tired thinking about it.'

Go-Go stood up. Ted knew he had said too much. 'I'd better go,' she said.

'See you.' Ted smiled.

She avoided his eye. 'Bye.'

Once he had heard the front door close, Ted opened his
diary again. He read 'Met the daughter of the chairman of the
Bank of Canada.' After it he wrote,

Beautiful, of course. Totally beautiful and poised and opaque.
I'm still feeling like an outsider among Miranda's set. I see
someone like this and I know she goes out with tall lawyers
with squash rackets, and that makes me feel like one of the
computer nerds, a scholarship boy. At least I've lost my
Maritimer's sense of defiance and bitterness.

And Miranda is being inexplicably friendly in a sexual kind
of way. I can't figure out why she would be interested in me.
She must just be interested in everybody. We had breakfast
together on Friday in some little pseudo-French bakery; it was
actually quite romantic. We talk at high speed but never touch,
when we're alone. Of course she touches everyone in public.

John was being hilarious last night. I do think he's drinking
too much but it's amusing all the same. On the way to the
party he was sitting in the front of the taxi mumbling, 'God,
I'll end up in the lake again, I know it.'

I say, 'What's that, dude?'

He says, 'I *won't* do it. I *won't* go in.'

We get to the party and Miranda is in black tights and black
hair and dark red lips. Absolutely deadly. She is flirting outrageously with Roger, the unshaven dudemeister and *soi-disant*

novelist with cowboy boots. He has a stunning neanderthal appeal for most of the women there, it seems. I think he's just a brute. M. keeps kissing him on the lips. What I didn't realize is that Miranda has been seeing Arthur the tall prep for years. Apparently they lived together at university, travelled through Europe together and so on. He and Roger are best friends. It all seems a bit sick to me. Arthur was there, of course, making dull small talk with me. I was remembering that first party at M's, when I was passing a bedroom on my way to the can and I saw M. and the dudemeister talking so intensely together in that bedroom. Yikes.

I love it, of course. A scene like that is exactly what I want.

Ted put his pen down and sipped his tea. Go-Go had left a scent of cigarettes and patchouli in the air. His stomach growled; he had forgotten to eat. He closed the book and stood up. He put on his heavy leather jacket and his glasses, picked up the diary and stepped into the autumnal street.

He walked through the Annex towards the bakery he knew was open on Harbord Street. A few yellow leaves were falling; among upturned tricycles haggard academic women were raking them up. There was a distant child's wail. Each woman looked at Ted suspiciously as he passed, pushing wisps of greying hair behind her ear. A smell of rotting apples hung in the air. Ted's throat was parched and his stomach upset; a muffin or cake would be about all he could handle.

He studied the narrow Victorian houses, terraced red brick cottages, and the dates on their historical plaques – 1887, 1890, 1888 – and had a vision of Protestant Sunday in suburban Toronto at the turn of the century. A thick smell of midday roast in each house, and patriotic songs played on an upright piano.

He found the bakery on a wide and empty street, and pushed open the glass door, the heavy buckles on his jacket clanking. There were no customers, but a slim girl with pale blond hair piled in a bun behind the counter. She looked at him and looked away, arranging cookies. He peered at the rows of pastries and muffins, studiously avoiding her body and face. When he ordered from her he looked up, briefly, to see that she was very young, a high school student, and blushing red, and delicately pretty. She fumbled with the sliding doors of the display case, blushing even more. Timidly, Ted smiled at her as he paid for his piece of poppy-seed cake, and she smiled back.

Outside, he stared through the window but could see nothing but his own reflection. He was unused to making women nervous, and decided it was the aggression of the leather jacket and its clanking buckles. She was very beautiful but a nervous teenager, which made him feel guilty, for he wanted at that moment nothing more than to kiss her.

He walked for half a block on the deserted street. There was a bench in the sun on which he sat and ate his cake. The odd cyclist passed. He grew drowsy, thinking of the fey blond girl, gone now as if from a fairy tale. He opened his diary, took a pen from his pocket and wrote,

Car j'ignore où tu fuis, tu ne sais où je vais,
O toi que j'eusse aimée, ô toi qui le savais!

EIGHT

October 4

Dearest Teddy,

Your dad and I are both *so* pleased that things seem to be going so well for you. I'm so impressed that you've published *two* articles – even just small ones – since you got there. We found the one in *Teen-o-rama* – that one, at least, you can get here! – and we both laughed. Mrs McGillivray called us all in a flurry because her daughter had brought it home – she was *so* excited!

And the play sounds very interesting. Will it bring in any money, do you think? I must say, Dad is worried about the instability of the kind of work you seem to be aiming for. He says you'll never know where your next paycheck will be coming from. I suppose he's right, but if you're *sure* that this can be profitable in the future then I'm happy to help you out while you're getting set up. The big cheque is from him, and I've included a small one of my own, which he doesn't have to know about.

Let us know how you get on, and how John is. It's been years since I've seen him. Why did he quit that excellent job with the bank? You know, Mrs Reynolds doesn't seem to know about that, so be careful if she calls! What does he do for money now?

Georgina sounds nice. Will she be going back and forth from Toronto to Japan? Isn't that expensive?

How is Janet? Does she come to see you in Toronto at all?

Things are rather hectic here, with all the preparations for the wedding. (I know, I know, it's not till June, but there is an *awful* lot that will have to be done.) Anna is still pretty calm, though, and still goes out every night with her friends. She says it's to enjoy the last freedom she has left!!! Your dad is so busy now, he doesn't have time to write, but he says hello. You know he really misses you a lot. We're thinking of making a little trip to Toronto in the spring. Maybe you'll have your own apartment by then.

Write soon!!

Love,

Mom

Ted folded this letter and placed it back in the envelope, from which he extracted two cheques. He held them close to his face to examine them, squinting; since he had stopped wearing his glasses the world was all a little distant.

Once he had deciphered the figures on the cheques he frowned, stared at them a moment longer, then put them in his wallet. From Georgina's futon he picked up the shiny packet he had put there that afternoon and pulled out its crepe paper filling. From the crepe paper he unwrapped a bright silk tie. It looked duller in the dirty room than it had in the shining York-ville shop window. And less blurry, close up. Flowers and Japanese characters. He fingered the soft fabric in amazement. He had simply been thinking about Miranda's birthday – she had been talking about them all going out to dinner – and then he had seen it and bought it. He held it up to his shirt, but remembered that there was no mirror in Georgina's room. He put it on a hanger and hung it on a nail in the wall.

He sat on the futon, angling his head and looking at the hanging tie as if it were a painting, then stood up and pulled down a shirt – a new one, washed silk – and put them both on. There was nothing planned for that night. The telephone had been silent all afternoon. He had met with the actors that morning to discuss the script but left once they started humming querulously and doing acrobatics to warm themselves up.

All they really seemed to want to do was dance. His play was set in urban apartments and restaurants; he would have to make sure Malcolm stopped them from moving around too much on stage.

His new tie knotted, he picked up his leather jacket and went downstairs. Go-Go was sitting at the kitchen table with nothing in front of her. She wore the black tights and loose tank-top that meant she was in a bad mood. The room smelled of cigarettes. Ted walked past her in silence to get the Leather Treat from a shelf. He sat down at the table with cloths and brushes and his jacket. In the late-afternoon light from the window her skin was pale and her eyes bright blue-grey. The silver palm-tree that always dangled from her right ear hung over a tiny red pimple on her neck. Her black hair hung over one side of her face. The loose arm-holes of the tank top exposed coarse underarm hair and the pale swelling of braless breasts. Ted tried not to look at them.

'Hi,' he said, busily wiping cream onto his jacket.

'Hi.'

'You okay?'

'Me? Sure.' She bit a fingernail.

'Mike coming into town tonight?'

She nodded. 'I guess so.'

'Ah.' Ted began vigorously to buff the leather with a brush.

'Not sleeping with me though.'

Ted looked up.

'I just don't think I can sleep with him tonight,' said Go-Go.

'You guys have some problems?' Ted asked innocently, resuming his brushing.

Go-Go drew her knees up to her chest. 'No. Things have always been pretty casual between us. I would hate to be someone's girlfriend, you know? We've always been – we're just friends who sleep together sometimes, you know? And we can feel free to see other people, you know?'

'And that's a good system? It's worked?'

'Oh yeah. I'm just not sure how much longer I want it to
... to go on. I'm not sure I like it any more.'

'And he likes it?'

Go-Go shrugged, pulled the box of cigarettes towards her.
'It's been fine for me, you know, if I need to screw ... ' She
flashed a curious look at him as she lit her cigarette. 'I meet
guys at the theatre, down at the Bev, and it's easy. I never let it
– I never wanted it to last more than a couple of nights, you
know? And I always thought that's what he was doing. But I
think now there's someone he's been spending more time with
than others.'

'Ah. She's a courier too?'

'Yes.' Go-Go sucked hard on the cigarette, exhaled with
force. 'I think so. They live in the same squat.'

'They live in the same house? Jesus.'

'It's a crazy environment there. He lets it go to his head.
And whenever he sees me he has some new theory, and if I dis-
agree with it I'm like some bourgeois cow. Complacent. You
ever had anyone who fucking *lives* on acid call you complacent?
That's what he called me last time. And I just don't need that
shit, you know? I don't want it and I don't need it. And I don't
have to have it.'

'No you don't.'

She smoked in silence for a moment. 'So where's he going
to sleep?' she asked, looking at Ted. 'I can't get hold of him
now. He may be on his way here.'

'Couch?'

She nodded. 'Except that would freak John right out. John
doesn't like him around at all, and if he came home – you
know, Mike kind of spreads his stuff out when he stays somewhere, and he always carries tools and parts and shit around
with him – '

Ted laughed aloud. 'And also – you're not really sure
what's going to happen when you see him?'

Go-Go nodded, staring at him and smiling.

'Okay,' said Ted. 'Easy. I sleep on the couch – no, no, I'm used to it, and so is John, it's no problem – I'm a guest here anyway, you know? – and Mike gets my room, George's room. That way if you guys really hit it off, there's a double futon in there and everything. And if not, you still have your own room.'

'You sure?'

'Absolutely. No problem.'

'Thanks. It *would* be perfect.' She was blushing, fumbling with the cigarette package. 'We could leave a note for him. I'm not going to wait around.'

'Good idea.' The sweet smell of the leather cream was mingling with the cigarette smoke and reminded Ted of something good and troubling, something vaguely guilty.

'What are you doing tonight?' she said brightly, looking at him.

'Well, no plans really. But I think I'll stay in.'

'Why don't you come down to the Bev? It's kind of fun on a Thursday night.' She reached over and put her hand on his shoulder, smiling. 'It's always the same crowd. I know most of them.'

Ted looked up from the outline of nipples moving under her top. 'Thanks. That's nice of you, but I'm actually waiting for a phone call, and I think I'll just chill out tonight. Haven't spent a quiet night for a while.'

'Sure.' She withdrew her hand. He watched her round thighs as she walked to the door on tip-toe. 'Thanks again,' she called from the living room. 'Have a nice night.'

Ted heard the front door open as she tripped upstairs. 'Doan FUG wid me mon,' came John's voice.

'Dude,' Ted called.

'Dude, you know it,' said John as he came into the room. Ted whistled. John wore a dark double-breasted suit, a loosened tie. 'Yeah, yeah,' he said. 'A little business. Nice tie. Going out?'

'Drinks with Uncle Bob?' said Ted.

'Bob's your uncle,' said John, sitting down heavily. 'Not his fault he's an uncle.'

'Any prospects?'

'Oh yeah. Megacash. Just on the horizon. Going a little slowly right now. We're being cautious. But in the meantime ...'

'Megadrinks with Uncle Bob.'

'Bob's your uncle. Hey, listen dude, got news that might interest you. Heard from Tina – '

'Tina?'

'Model, knew George – that old Georgie's heading for home this weekend. Going to stop off at her mother's in London and then tie up some loose ends in Toronto. Tina thought she was coming into town this very night. She spoke to her from some airport yesterday.'

Ted felt himself blushing. 'She's coming from Japan for a weekend?'

'Hey, they do that, they get money for that. It happens.'

'Shit.' Ted thought for a moment. 'That means she'll want her room.'

'Guess so. Doesn't mean you have to move out of it though, wah wah.'

'Yeah yeah. Shit. Well. I'd better clean it up then. You know Go-Go's expecting Mike too?'

'Christ help us,' said John, getting up. 'Put away the silverware. You going out?'

'Ah, no. I'd better just ...'

'Sit around and wait for Georgina?' John said from the door, and disappeared.

Ted heard him singing as he stumbled up the stairs. He sat for a moment, fingering his leather jacket and feeling the blood rush in his veins. He and Mike would have to sleep in the living room. No big deal. How long would she stay?

He had an image of a restaurant, some warm French or Italian restaurant with checkered cloths and candles, with

Georgina laughing as he told a story, his hand on the blood-red glass.

He ran up the stairs to her room.

At eleven o'clock Ted was sitting on the living-room sofa reading the System 7 update; it was a newsletter the Mole received regularly. In bold colours, it told of compatibility and enhanced multitasking. Built-in networking would never be the same. There was a utility you could buy from an online data-base, called Tiny Editor, whose file name was TED.

The Mole was still at the lab, or drinking Coke in one of his friends' brightly lit living rooms; Malcolm was almost never home; John had to go to a business meeting at the piano bar at Boss. Ted had promised to drop in later. Georgina's room was immaculate, the sheets clean and Ted's clothes stowed in suit-cases in the closet. A note for Mike lay on the banister in the hall, telling him that someone was borrowing Go-Go's room and he would have to sleep on the couch.

Ted looked at his watch. He was still wearing his silk shirt and new tie, but felt rumpled now. He put on the soft leather jacket, smelling new again. Its heaviness was comforting. No word from Georgina, and he could have been at the Beverley with Go-Go. He could have used a drink. In fact he had no proof that Georgina would be there at all. He saw her being pushed into a wad of people on a bullet train by a pudgy uni-formed official, a fragile skein of Western silk being bent to fit through Lilliputian doors, on her way to a morning shoot in a grimy industrial suburb.

The telephone rang. He recognized her voice. 'Ted!' she said, 'you're there. How *are* you?'

'Where are you?' he said. 'Are you in town?'

'Yes, oh yes. I was in London. But I – '

'Well come on over. Your room's all ready for you.'

'Oh, Ted, don't be silly, I wouldn't dream of kicking you out of your room. Listen, how *are* you?'

'Terrific,' he said. 'I'm wonderful. I can't wait to see you. And of course you can stay here. It's your room after all, and – '

'No, it's not, you're paying for it and I wouldn't dream of it. Don't be silly. Actually I'm just in town very briefly, it's kind of a whirlwind, and I don't think I'll be able to see you, it's sad really.'

'Oh. Where are you going to – how about tomorrow? Are you dropping in at all?'

'Well I might. I – maybe. I'd *love* to see you. I have so much to tell you.'

Ted ran his hand through his hair. 'Well, drop in tomorrow then. We'll have coffee.'

'I might. I'd love to. Listen, is John there?'

'No. Had to go out. He's at Boss, I think.'

'Well, listen, it's not important but I have to talk to him, I'll ... no, it's okay, don't tell him anything.'

'You sure? I might be seeing him tonight. Sure you can't meet us for a drink?'

'No, Ted, thanks, I'd love to but I can't. Don't bother him. Maybe I'll see you tomorrow, okay?'

'Okay, George.' And then they had said goodbye and hung up. Ted sat for a moment, then rose, fingering his leather jacket. He put it on and walked to the door, then stopped. He came back into the living room, took off the jacket and sank back down on the sofa. He studied Go-Go's purse collection for a moment, then the old print, then the ceiling.

He stood up again, thinking vaguely of going to Boss; he had always wanted to see it. The phone rang again. A male voice, far away, with music in the background. 'Go-Go there?'

'No, she's not. Is that Mike?'

'Uh, yeah, listen, are you going to talk to her? Because I have to tell her I'm not going to make it in. I'm not coming in tonight.'

'You're not, eh? Well. She's expecting you.'

'Well I'm not going to be there, man, got it?' The tone was

amused, verging on hostile. A man's laughter in the background.

'Well I don't know if I'm going to see her. I'll leave a note.'

'Thanks so much.' Sarcastic.

Ted hung up. He walked to the banister and crumpled the note he had left for Mike. He began looking for the notepad and pen when the phone rang again.

'Dude,' said John's voice, 'You coming out or what?'

'Where are you? Boss?'

'Yeah, but I'm leaving now. You didn't show up. George there?'

'No. She called. She's not coming. She's in town though. I wonder where she – hey, are you going to see Go-Go? Because Mike's not coming either. I have to tell her because she thinks he'll be in my room.'

'Your room. Got it. I'll tell her.'

'You're going to see her? Where are you going?'

'Penumbra. She'll be there. She always goes there after the Bev. You coming?'

'No, thanks, I don't think so, I'm totally wiped. I'm just going to crash.' Ted loosened his tie, picked up his jacket.

'Pining for the fjords, hey?' said John.

'Haw haw. Listen, you're sure you're going to see Go-Go, hey? It's important. And Georgina said she wants to talk to you. I think she'll call tomorrow or something.'

'No problem, dude. All systems go. See you tomorrow.'

Ted hung up. He suddenly felt exhausted. In Georgina's room he undressed and was quickly asleep.

There was construction outside the room where he had to write his exam, and his mother and father were sitting on the desk at the front of the classroom. He couldn't concentrate with the banging, the opening and closing doors; someone was in his room but he couldn't open his eyes; he was too exhausted to even pick up the pen in front of him and lift up the examination paper, which he knew to be easy, grade twelve chemistry which he was sure he could remember if his mother and father weren't there in the room.

He opened his eyes to find that his room was dark. Someone was in the room, fumbling with the door, trying to close it. He rolled over and heard Go-Go's muffled voice, muttering. 'Fuck's sake. Mister smooth.'

He tried to speak but found it too great an effort. He managed to grunt.

'Mister fucking too cool to go to the fucking bar where we fucking said we'd ... ' he heard her whisper. Her words were slurred and he couldn't make it all out. ' ... even fucking call me. Had a nice sleep?'

'Go-Go,' Ted said thickly, 'It's not – ' There was a thump as she swayed into the closet door. He heard her swear. He propped himself up on one elbow to watch her; she was struggling with her jeans, pulling them over one ankle and giggling.

'Shit,' he said, letting his head fall back. He felt like laughing. All he wanted to do was get back to sleep. 'Go-Go, it's Ted.'

'Fuck off,' came her muffled voice. He looked up again to see, in the dim light of streetlamp filtered through paper blind, that her sweater covered her head; she struggled to pull it off, cursing. The glow on her body from the blind was pink, and she wore nothing under her sweater; he saw the dull forms of breasts swaying. She pulled the sweater off with a gasp and stumbled onto the futon, giggling. 'Bastard,' she said, crawling under the duvet.

Ted froze as he felt her arms snake around him, the naked breasts against his flank. 'Go-Go, it's Ted, it's not Mike, it's me.'

Her hands stopped moving for a moment on his chest. Then she laughed, a choked little laugh. She thrust her nose, slightly wet, against his neck. 'Ted,' she said. 'Teddy bear. What a surprise.'

'You didn't get the message?' he said. He knew he should get up, move away from her, but he lay still instead, keeping his arms at his sides. She was kissing his neck. Her breath smelled of beer and cigarettes, and he could feel her flesh the length of his.

'Good old Teddy bear,' she murmured to his neck.

His body began to rouse itself. Getting up would be increasingly difficult if he didn't do it right now. It was nice to feel her warmth. Her hands rubbed his chest. With an effort he said, 'So you didn't run into John? He was supposed to tell you.'

She laughed again. 'John shmon. Sure, sure. Good trick.'

He sighed, keeping his body from relaxing. He stared upwards. 'Go-Go. No.' He pushed her hand from his chest and shifted away from her.

She made a petulant sound and brought her leg up over his thighs. 'Bastards,' she said softly. Her breathing was slowing.

'You're wasted,' said Ted.

'Wasted,' she said in a small voice, as if with great effort. 'You better fucking ...' She was drifting into sleep.

'Go-Go, don't sleep. Wake up.' He reached down to push at her thigh, but it was heavy on his leg. His hand's contact with the flesh excited him, and he withdrew it quickly. Waking her would be dangerous. She moaned with irritation, small and vulnerable against him. 'Are you ... are you going to be okay?' he asked softly.

'Uh-huh.' Her hand drifted onto his chest again, and she was asleep.

Ted stared at the dark ceiling. He wanted to shift his weight but was afraid of waking her. He let his arms relax. Her breathing beside him was deep and regular. Presently, he fell asleep.

NINE

BRIGHT PINK LIGHT like a gaze on his face awoke him. He felt someone's presence. He grunted and pulled his chest out from under Go-Go's head, pushing her hair away from his nose and mouth. She curled away from him, making childlike sucking sounds. Ted opened his eyes and saw the open door, Georgina's face. She stood watching them silently. Their eyes met but she didn't react. Her face was set in dismay. Ted was aware of the duvet, down around their waists, and Go-Go's pale breasts splayed across the mattress. He made a move to cover them up. Georgina turned; he saw her sundress flash out of sight and heard her bare feet running down the stairs.

He sat up quickly. Then he saw that Go-Go's eyes were open too. She stared up at him blankly, then smiled grimly and sat up, running both hands through her tousled hair. 'Well,' she said croakily. 'Hi.'

Ted stared at the dangling breasts, the pale brown nipples. He did not want to touch her. She noticed his gaze and pulled the duvet up to her armpits. 'Well,' she said again. She looked up at the open door.

Quickly, Ted stood up and shut the door. He got under the duvet again to cover his nakedness.

'Sorry,' said Go-Go.

Ted felt sorry for her. He put his arm around her bare shoulders. 'Sorry for what? You were a bit drunk last night. I couldn't wake you. You thought I was Mike for a while.'

She nodded, looking sad. 'Did anything ... did anything happen?'

'Happen? Between us? Oh no. No no.' He tried to smile.

He felt as if he had swallowed a broken clock. He felt the needles and cogs and shattered crystal shifting inside him. He patted her shoulder.

'Well.' She sighed. 'Sorry.'

'Don't be sorry.'

'Could you hand me my sweater?'

Ted nodded and reached to the end of the futon. He handed her the crumpled fabric, and she put it on discreetly under the duvet. He pulled on his shorts with his back to her, then handed her underpants and black jeans. She dressed demurely, her back turned. 'How do you feel?' he asked.

'Not so good.' There were circles under her eyes. 'Mike never showed up?'

'He called. At about eleven. Said to tell you he couldn't make it. John promised to tell you. I thought he might forget. Sorry.'

'No problem.' She picked up her socks and black boots, standing up. 'And Georgina's back. I feel kind of bad.'

'I didn't realize she'd be here. I knew she was coming today, but not so early. I would have told you.'

Go-Go moved to him quickly and pulled his face into her belly as he sat on the futon. She patted his shoulders and let him go. It was a hug. She smiled at him from the door and left quietly.

Ted put his shirt on. He supposed Georgina wouldn't be coming back at all now, before she left for the bullet trains and the coffin-hotels. Little cubes stacked like drawers, for tired businessmen. He wondered if she had ever stayed in one, if she had felt claustrophobic. Suddenly the dim room, the rumpled duvet disgusted him. He left without lifting up the blind.

At the kitchen door he hesitated. Georgina was sitting, reading the paper. She looked up.

'Hi,' said Ted. He opened the fridge, looking for juice. 'Kind of a bad scene last night.'

'Oh?' Her voice was cold.

'Yeah. Go-Go, Go-Go was kind of drunk, and – '

'Ted, I don't think I want to hear about it.'

He sat at the table with his juice. She wouldn't look at him. Her face was pale, her hair flat. 'No, listen, George – ' He was about to say 'you don't understand' but thought it would sound clichéd; 'it's not what you think' would be no better. 'I want to tell you about it. I want you to understand something. It was a very weird scene last night and it's not – it's not what you think.'

'Listen, Ted.' She was staring at her paper, trying to sound cool. 'It's your room while you're paying for it and you can do what you want there. You don't have to explain to – '

'Go-Go came into the room late,' Ted interrupted. 'She was drunk and she thought I was Mike. There had been some mixup about rooms and I had told her Mike would be in mine. In yours. I couldn't wake her up and I didn't want to leave. Nothing happened.'

Georgina looked up at him angrily. 'Oh Ted, give me a break. I have no idea why you think you have to explain all this to me and why you want to hide something which is perfectly fine and ... and natural, I think it's great for you. And for her, too, I think it's about time she found someone nicer than – '

There was a loud rapping at the front door. Ted ignored it. 'Nothing happened, for Christ's sake, I – '

Georgina got up. 'There's someone at the door.' She left him at the kitchen table. He prodded his abdomen with his fingers. He had just come out of surgery and his insides were held together with gaffer tape. If he moved he would do himself internal damage. The kitchen was filthy and smelled of old fruit.

A woman's voice rang out. 'Georgina, how are you! Why are you back?' Miranda. Ted went cold. The two of them, together, that morning, was too much. He couldn't face it. Georgina would be furious just at hearing that tone of voice. Even to him it sounded false. He looked at the sliding back doors. No one would hear him if he slipped out. Georgina was speaking softly; he couldn't hear her reply.

'Well,' Miranda's voice rang out. 'Great. That's great for you. Listen, I don't want to bother Ted, but I know *you're* not busy, tell him the party's to*night*, at Boss, you give him directions how to get there . . . '

Ted grimaced, imagining Georgina's face. Miranda sounded exactly as he imagined her mother would, giving instructions to workmen. His heart was racing. Fight or flight. He stood up and began tiptoeing towards the back doors. Georgina said something indistinct.

'Okay,' said Miranda coldly. 'Okay. Well perhaps you could manage to tell him to call me, if that isn't too much trouble.'

The screen door slammed. Ted hesitated with his hand on the sliding doors to the garden. Georgina's footsteps were on the stairs. He turned and emerged into the living room. Miranda was gone. He hesitated before pursuing Georgina upstairs. He would have to thank her for taking the message and apologize for Miranda. Her bedroom door closed and she was walking down the stairs again. 'I just had to get something,' she said, brushing past him. 'Miranda wants you to call her.'

'Thanks,' he said, 'I – '

But the door had opened and closed again; she was gone.

Ted sat on the sofa and looked at Go-Go's plastic purse collection on the far wall. He exhaled at great length and said 'Wheel sheeet,' as he had heard Mick Jagger say it.

There were footsteps upstairs. Ted remembered the Mole; he had agreed to go and look at a new computer program with him. That would be good. Spend the day with some nerdy guys, a fluorescent world of files and commands, abstract problems with solutions. They'd probably be able to show him something colourful and impressive. He would eat pizza and Coke with them. He tried to slow his breathing. Someone was coming down the stairs. He looked up, expecting the Mole, but saw John in his terrycloth robe. 'Dude,' said John. 'Missed an excellent night last night.'

Ted laughed creakily. It hurt as it came out his throat. 'I guess I did. I guess I fucking did.'

He followed John into the kitchen. 'Met the head of Submarine, the party agency,' said John, gulping juice. 'This incredible chick, used to be a model, now she goes out with this CFL linebacker. Dressed entirely gothic. Calls herself Petunia. Completely wacko.' He glared at Ted abruptly. 'Whatsamatter? Was George here?'

'Yes. She just dropped in to get something and left again.'

'Too bad. Everything okay?'

'Sure. Fine. You going to this Miranda party?'

John looked at him suspiciously. 'What did you do last night?'

'Nothing. Stayed home. Crashed early. It's dinner, at Boss, tonight. Is that expensive?'

John raised his eyebrows, exhaling. 'Expensive? Boss? Naw. Naw. Shit, you really are from Montreal, aren't you?'

'It's expensive?'

'It's the place, man, it's the suits and limos and Porsches. It's the serious scene. It's all the new money. It's one of Pellegrino's places. Construction money, stock market money, advertising ... You need a hundred bucks to go in there. At least.'

'Christ.'

'Hey, speaking of shady glitz, your friend Max called for you.'

Ted stood up too quickly, knocking a plate off the table and scattering crumbs. 'Max? He called here? When? Why didn't you – '

'Shit, I'm sorry, man. Yesterday morning. You were out. He wants you to call him. He says he has a really neat project you might want to get involved with.' He drank serenely from his glass of juice.

'Did he leave a number?'

John unfolded the newspaper. 'No. I thought you had his number.'

'John, for Christ's sake, you *know* I tried that number, it wasn't the right one.' Ted's hands were shaking. 'Man, this could be really *important*, and you know how much I need money right now, and I can't even fucking get *hold* of him now – '

'Hey, relax, dude,' said John, studying the newspaper. 'If he really wants you he'll call back.'

'For fuck's sake,' said Ted, furious. He strode out of the room. To get out, go somewhere quiet, maybe a library, read a book ...

The Mole was on the front porch, unlocking his aging CCM. 'Hello,' he said brightly.

'Hi,' said Ted shortly, walking down the steps.

'Hey, aren't you coming? Didn't you want to go to Dalrymple's? See the new Septra nine hundred AV he's got?'

Ted stopped walking, turned and looked at the Mole. He tried to breathe deeply.

'Ultra high definition flat monitor,' said the Mole. 'The screen, I mean.'

'What?'

'It's flat. Not convex.' The Mole looked like a teetering ghost. He had his usual brown cords and plastic bag.

Ted smiled. 'Flat, eh?'

'It's like a piece of window glass.' The Mole opened his eyes wide. 'Liquid cooled.'

'Liquid cooled? Well then. Sure. Let's go.'

TEN

DALRYMPLE'S REAL NAME was Peng; he was an engineering
student from Hong Kong. 'Why? Well, he's just such a Dalrymple, don't you think?' shouted the Mole, standing on the
kitchen table. Dalrymple smiled from behind his Coke can and
reflective round glasses, his creaseless face becoming only
rounder and smoother by the gesture. 'Dalrymple,' shouted
the Mole, 'is the Rolls Royce of CUNT!' Dalrymple shook his
head, smiling. He hadn't said anything yet to Ted, who sat at
the table with the animators, Theo, Rob and Rob, and their
pizza, laughing at the Mole's Starhawk impersonation. The
Mole had mentioned particle physics; Dalrymple was the whiz
on the biggest accelerator in Canada. He never said anything.

'Green light fills the room,' sighed the Mole, and collapsed
gracefully onto his knees, exhausted by his contact with the
astral plane. Ted applauded wholeheartedly with the others as
the Mole clambered off the table. He was safe there, in the
brightly lit room, with the bland taste of pizza and jokes he
didn't understand. 'Nerk nerk,' said one of the Robs, standing
up, 'How you making out, Phil?'

A pale little man had come silently into the room; he
rubbed his hands nervously. 'I think I've got it, if you guys
want to look at it.'

'Phil, man,' said Rob, walking out, 'The Terminator.' Rob
and Theo followed, trailing strings of melted cheese.

'Phil's the programmer they use,' explained the Mole.
'Whiz at computer animation. He makes the constructs,
they're the creative guys, they make art. He's been up all night
making this guitar. Take a look.'

Ted and Dalrymple followed the Mole into a room full of computers. Phil stood back as the three animators clustered around a colour screen with their pizza. Rob sat back, his feet in running shoes on the table, stuffing his mouth. He manipulated the mouse on his thigh. 'Excellent, dude,' he said to Phil, his mouth full. A three-dimensional chrome electric guitar rotated slowly on the screen. 'And the lettering?'

'Pull the file,' said Phil softly. 'They should merge.'

'Right on,' said Rob. Three-dimensional words floated around the image.

'Pull the guitar through them,' suggested Theo.

'Spin it to the left a little. They should really explode.'

'Excellent.'

'How about splitting the guitar in two? Then it reforms once the letters are formed.'

'Cool.' The images spun and metamorphosed. 'Excellent, Phil, thanks man,' said Rob without looking at him.

Phil nodded and left the room. Ted heard him unlocking his bike on the veranda. The Mole caught Ted's eye. 'He loves it,' said the Mole.

'Phil does?'

'Working all night on something the boys can use makes him happier than anything. It's his life.'

Rob was still manipulating the images on the screen. He began to intone in a solemn voice with a heavy American accent, 'I can see many, many motorcycles.'

In the same voice the Mole said, 'Mrs Kennedy's pink dress.'

Theo said, 'Something is rawng here, something is terribly rawng.'

Rob's voice rose. 'Mrs Kennedy jumped up, she cried – '

'o h n o!' said the Mole.

'The motorcade sped on,' all three animators said in unison, triumphantly.

'Bumbum!' shouted Theo, jumping up. 'Bumbum! Here

doggie!' A cat scuttled away from him. Two more hid under chairs.

'Cat's name is Bumbum?' asked Ted.

'That's Bumbum,' said the Mole, 'the others are Dog and Porky. Here Porky!' His voice went sweet. 'Come here and FUCK ME UP THE ASS!'

'Nerk nerk. Wheep!'

'Suhf's up boss!' Theo was standing up, ruffling Dalrymple's hair. He put on his aging Mandarin face. 'Going lunning today, boss?' he said in a heavy Chinese accent.

'No,' said Dalrymple, unperturbed, 'No tlaining today.'

'What are you training for?' asked Ted.

'Come here doggie, come here dog dog,' said the Mole, chasing cats. 'Dalrymple trains like a madman.'

'Just a little lunning,' said the physicist, his eyes invisible behind the bright glasses.

'Ten k today or what?' said Rob with his mouth full, intent on the screen. His hand was moving the mouse rapidly, constantly clicking.

'Actually,' said Rob, leaning forward to Ted, 'It's for the running of the bulls. Dalrymple's going for it.'

'Actually,' said Theo, 'It's a running with the bulls *triathlon*.'

'Iron man running with the bulls, with bungee jumping. You have to do it drunk too.'

'Except Dalrymple does it with split peas in his shoes, paying penance – '

'No no, reading a newspaper – '

'In black tie, and – '

'There's a dissertation also, at the end, on Lacan and – '

'Fractals, abortion, field theory – '

'Wheep! Wheep!' Rob was too excited now, simply jumping up and down and making technological noises. 'The motorcade – '

'SPED ON!'

Ted asked to use the phone. He had to disconnect it from an old-fashioned modem. 'Oh they don't use it,' the Mole had said, 'Just Dalrymple uses some kind of wake-up call for his console from it, and Rob gets Tiny Editor and the Sleazebar Forum off it. And Pet Shop, sometimes. They have the good modems connected to Pizza Pizza, so we can type orders right onto their screen, and of course we all use Hackers' Forum all the time.'

Ted dialled John's number. 'Hey dude,' he said. 'Sorry I kind of lost it earlier on. Having a bad day.'

'Yeah. No problem.'

'Listen, is Georgina still there?'

'Sorry dude. She got on a plane.'

Ted was silent. 'Listen. I'm thinking of going to this thing at Boss.'

'Uh-huh.'

'But I was wondering if I could borrow some cash for it.'

'You'll need a lot.'

'I know. But I'll have some coming in pretty soon. I get a cut of the box when this play comes through – '

'Dude,' said John, 'I'm happy to lend you money, but I wouldn't count on the play too much, it's a fringe production, you'll get a hundred people in there max, once you've paid – '

'Yes, but then there's the reading series I qualify for as a per-formed playwright, down at the Core Development Cultural Centre; I get a hundred bucks for one reading if I get in, and Miranda's set me up a meeting with Queal for next week – '

'Okay, dude, relax. No problem. I'll leave cash in your room.'

'Thanks dude. Thanks.' Ted sighed. He always felt tired these days. 'You're a pal.'

'No problem. Now, if you don't mind my asking, what are you going to wear?'

Ted got off the subway at Eglinton. John had told him to

just walk north until he saw the cars. He had never been to this part of town before; it was where John had grown up. John never talked about it. Go-Go had sneeringly said it was white, just white and nothing else. In the dark, Yonge Street seemed deserted and sterile. There seemed to be a disproportionate number of specialty food shops with baguettes and jam jars and italic lettering in the windows, all closed. In between them were dry cleaners, a dark Second Cup, an imitation British pub at the base of a mirrored office building. A cold wind blew directly at him; he could see the streetlights extending in a perfectly straight line for miles, disappearing over the horizon.

He walked aggressively in John's suit and shiny shoes, craning his head sideways to see his reflection in dark windows. He carried his own worn trenchcoat; he wished he hadn't brought it. Some voice from his childhood had told him he might be cold. The trenchcoat was absolutely inappropriate for the suit. He had hesitated between the single-breasted and the double; the double seemed so much more Toronto, and this one was perfect, the dark charcoal. And his new tie. Go-Go had helped him slick his hair back with gel. He felt positively Italian.

He looked at his watch and realized that he had left it in Go-Go's room. Immediately he began to look about him, squinting, at the tops of buildings, for a pixelboard time display. There was none, and he cursed the inadequacy of the street. In a *real* city, one would always be in sight of a pixelboard.

Ahead of him was a group of tired schoolgirls in uniform at a bus-stop. They carried gym bags; perhaps they had been at a game since school ended. His unfocused gaze was drawn to their unfashionable tartan ties and skirts, their textbook whiteness. Then their bare legs in the cold wind – the kilts seemed ridiculously short for girls their age – and their long hair. They watched him boldly; as he passed he saw they all wore makeup. One smiled to another and crossed her long, goosebumped legs; she was a woman, definitely, not a schoolgirl; Ted became aware of the ugly trenchcoat he carried. He looked straight ahead. It was uncharted territory up there.

Boss was immediately recognizable. A blank, two-storey façade like a factory wall, with a frosted glass door and a stream of stretch limousines and convertibles outside. Young men in windbreakers jumped into the cars as patrons abandoned them with the engines running. Ted hesitated, then remembered the suit he wore. He puffed his chest out and walked through the door.

A circus tent was his first thought. A vast, bright room, a ceiling at least two storeys overhead, bright geometric shapes like huge building blocks in gaudy colours — salmon-orange, purple, brown — a sea of tables and heads, dark-jawed Italianate waiters gliding around, frowning. Facing him, behind a sort of podium, was a tall blond woman in a purple silk dress. She seemed to be in a kind of spotlight, smiling at him brassily. 'Yes?'

He approached her, murmuring Miranda's name. Frowning, she scanned the papers on her podium. Her purple dress was cut very low. Ted tried not to look. 'One moment please,' she said, and gestured to one of the dark-jawed men. His face and suit looked sculpted. Ted remembered a poster in a history book, praising Mussolini's army. The two hosts murmured together for a moment, studying the list of reservations with great seriousness. She looked up, smiling. 'Would you care to check your coat?' She gestured to the counter to their right; behind it was an almost identical woman with even more cleavage.

The middle-aged man before Ted dropped a five-dollar bill into the coat-check woman's glass bowl. Ted sheepishly handed over the trenchcoat, avoiding her eyes. He only had twenties from John and he wasn't going to ask her for change. He followed the sculpted man through the tables; every face looked up at him expectantly as he passed. The men were all in suits, the women were tight-jawed and high-heeled; they laughed histrionically and kissed one another. Men sauntered between tables, red-faced, shaking hands. He saw with relief that most of the suits were double-breasted. The biggest bottles of champagne he had ever seen lined the walls; everything seemed exaggeratedly large. Very quickly he felt proud, as if he were growing in size himself. He wanted to talk, to be witty and acerbic.

The host led him to a crammed corner table where he recognized Arthur, Roger and Julia; Miranda wasn't there. They greeted him laconically; Arthur seated him next to a striking woman with a mass of black hair, introducing her as Lisa, and the mousy one in the corner seat with a name Ted instantly forgot. She looked like a physiotherapist. He turned to Lisa. 'Teddy,' he said, squeezing her hand. 'Rather like a circus in here, isn't it? I was handled by four people before I got sat down. Kind of like spa attendants. Actually I've never been to a spa in my life.'

'You haven't been here before?' She leaned forward in a cloud of perfume.

'No, I haven't been in Toronto long actually. Seems kind of American, this place.' Someone poured him a glass of wine. He felt extraordinarily confident. 'I don't trust this wealth at all, actually,' he said confidingly to Lisa. 'I get the feeling these people have made their money very quickly and could lose it just as quickly. Don't you agree? I mean, I can see this guy over here, don't look now, the guy with the gold bracelet – see it? I can see him losing his temper and bludgeoning his partner to death in the stairwell. With a baseball bat.'

'You think these people are gangsters?' asked Lisa.

'No. Not necessarily. Quite possibly. It's rather how I imagine an expensive prohibition speakeasy night-club to look. And they were always bludgeoning each other ...'

'I guess you'd rather some dark wood panelling waspy place, with hunting prints on the walls?'

Ted noticed the physiotherapist staring at him. He looked at

Lisa's dark eyebrows, her olive skin, and decided not to come on too strong with waspy. 'Well – '

'Don't know how to treat champagne, that's for sure,' interrupted Arthur, slightly drunk. 'You can't keep jeroboams standing up in a hot room like this.'

'It's all for show,' said Ted, nodding. Arthur seemed very judicious.

'It's a terrible waste,' said a voice from behind him. It was Andreas the filmmaker, dragging a chair and looking rather rumpled and tired. His ponytail was loose. Still he wore his silver-toed cowboy boots. 'Sorry I'm late,' he said, wedging the chair among them. 'Been shooting all day. Keep losing my fucking PA's. And I lost my fucking watch.' He sat heavily.

'Do you know,' said Ted, 'so did I. And on my way here I was looking for a pixelboard display, you know the ones on the tops of buildings and in the subway, to check the time, and when I couldn't see one I was actually irritated? I mean we've come to expect that every street has one somewhere.'

'Fully,' said Andreas, pouring wine inaccurately.

'And I realized that a mere two years ago I would never have expected them on *any* street, much less desired them, and even less been embarrassed by their absence. I mean it felt strangely provincial. I've come to feel that in a *real* city you'd always be in sight of a pixelboard time display.'

Andreas laughed. 'And the temperature.'

'Exactly. And preferably with a constant stock ticker running, so one can keep track of New York prices. And when the New York exchange shuts down, at night, it would switch over to Tokyo prices. At least that way we'd all have some sense of being *connected*, I mean you wouldn't feel this awful dislocation that you feel up in deserted suburban areas like this. I feel so inhuman up here.'

'Fully,' said Andreas, taking out a pen and notepad from his jacket pocket. 'That's good. I like it. Rich. Fully.' He scribbled in his pad, smiling.

'If it *is* champagne,' said Roger laboriously. 'It's a terrible waste.'

'Judicious, Roger. You're very judicious,' said Ted.

'I am, Teddy. I am. Teddy boy, you judicious man, you been doing any writing?'

'Too funny,' said Ted, 'I have. I was just doing an outrageously *weemo* piece on – '

'You're a writer?' asked the mousy one softly.

Ted nodded. 'Derek asked me to do this *weemo* piece on restaurant architecture, so I'm going to turn it into a piece on social spaces generally, you know, commercial social spaces, what is constant, what different values are reflected ...' He paused, thinking rapidly; he hadn't thought about it, really. He would have to improvise. Giddily, he began.

An hour later Miranda still hadn't arrived and Ted was eating the oysters he had had the good sense to order for the table, with disparaging remarks about Arthur's salad; someone kept ordering wine; and he had almost perfected the social spaces idea. The mousy one, who couldn't have been a physiotherapist after all, kept asking him very pointed questions, and murmuring to Andreas the filmmaker. Andreas was complaining about how he kept losing PA's, and this and the mousy one's questions – Karen? Janet? Couldn't be Janet – disturbed him, as it interrupted his flow of thought. 'Now take your Maritime tavern or cabaret, for instance,' he said over Andreas. 'Designed to be menacing. As few windows as possible. Decks stripped for action, so to speak. The facility for drinking as much beer as possible in the shortest amount of time, and physically,' he held up one finger, '*physically* intimidating.'

'Feel my hands!' said Lisa. 'Icicles? *Icicles!*'

'Can't get enough of this hydroponic lettuce,' said Arthur.

'Teddy,' Andreas said, 'Could you use some money?'

'Not at the moment. I'm on to something. Have you ever *seen* one of these places? I mean *imagine*, a sort of barracks with – '

'Because I could use a PA tomorrow. Just running around, gofer work, you know. It won't pay much, just a hundred bucks, for the day, and if we use you for more than that it could go up.'

Ted stopped his wine glass before his mouth. 'Andreas,' he said. 'You are a very judicious man. You are judicious.' They drank his health. Ted agreed to be on the set at ten the next morning.

Helium seemed darker and louder than most clubs; Ted couldn't remember exactly why they had ended up there. He sat on a worn Victorian sofa in the throbbing beat with his tie loosened and a drink in his hand which he couldn't finish; green smoke swirled around him. He didn't much care where Andreas and the others had got to; he knew there was another floor somewhere on which he had watched, for a few moments, a huge whirling gyroscope machine one could get strapped into, but it had frightened him and made him slightly bilious. And then there had been a live sex show, or something close, a sexual performance dance, with two women in bodypaint and a gay man on a dais, but without his glasses he had found it frustratingly blurry. He had wandered away and hadn't been able to find it again.

He had tried dancing for a moment but had found himself sweating and coughing in the smoke. Now he was remembering Boss. Miranda hadn't shown up at all, and they had never got around to ordering main courses, since they were all waiting for her anyway, and at midnight they had all left and he had still been parted with his hundred dollars. They'd had a lot of oysters, he supposed. Someone must have paid his entrance to the night club. He looked around. The woman in the garter belt and shaved head sauntered past him again, disappearing into the smoke and nagging him with a sense of sexual obligation – he should try to talk to her, at least. He stood up and danced for a moment, on the spot. He supposed he could be a good dancer if he tried. He wondered where he'd left the suit jacket.

'Teddy!' someone screamed in his ear, and her arms were all over him, on his neck, around his waist, inside his waistband. He felt Miranda's breasts against his back and almost toppled over. 'Teddy!' she said, pulling him back to the sofa and sitting him down, 'You are the *sweatiest* guy!'

'I am,' he said. 'Hello. You missed your party.'

'No I didn't,' she said, running her hands through his hair. 'I'm here now. This is my party.'

'Oh.' He waved to Julia and Caroline, who swirled around him, dancing in the smoke. Miranda kissed his neck. 'Hell,' he said.

'Come on upstairs,' she said. 'Let's talk.'

She led him by the hand through bodies and smoke, up some stairs into a sprawling, low-ceilinged room full of old sofas at odd angles, with low coffee tables between them. The pounding was just as loud upstairs, but waitresses in stilettoes circulated with trays. Miranda and Ted sank deep into a sofa. 'Now,' she said, putting one hand on his neck and the other on his knee. 'Tell me how you are.'

Ted was looking around. 'Lot of sofas,' he said. 'Kind of like the furniture section in Eaton's.'

Miranda laughed, swaying into him. He told her of all his new projects: the play, the articles, especially the new one on social spaces, which he was sure would be published before Christmas.

'What a success,' she said. 'And what about John? How's he?'

'Oh, John's fine, he's — '

'What's this I hear about him having a girlfriend? What do you know about that?'

'A girlfriend? John?' Ted shrugged. 'I wouldn't know.' He looked around. Dark forms were embracing on sofas close to them. Two tall men were watching them, motionless, from a shadow a few yards away, holding drinks. Miranda was rubbing his neck.

'John could be *such* a success, you know,' she was saying. 'He's such a *brilliant* man. I admire you guys. You have such – '

'Hey,' said Ted, sitting up. 'Who's – it's Arthur, and Roger.' Their faces were indistinct, but it was definitely them; they had been there for some time. He smiled and waved; Arthur lifted his hand, but his face was tense. Roger scowled.

'I know,' said Miranda without looking at them. She played with Ted's hair, then sighed. 'My man. The two men in my life.'

Ted shifted slightly, trying to pull away without being rude. 'I didn't know they were so close.' He smiled at the two men, who weren't speaking to each other, just watching intently him and Miranda. 'Miranda,' he said, 'how long have you and Arthur – '

'Oh, Ted*dy*. Let's talk about something that isn't *tiresome*.'

He looked ostentatiously at his wrist, but there was no watch. 'I'd better be going.'

'Oh. Teddy, why don't we meet sometime, where we can talk? Let's meet for breakfast tomorrow.'

'Breakfast. Tomorrow.' He stood up, looking for the suit jacket.

'At Moue? The French place we went before?'

'Rosedale. Sure. Ten? No, I'm working for Andreas. Nine?'

'Nine. Perfect.' She blew him a kiss, then stood, smiling at Arthur and Roger. Slowly, she swayed towards them.

The wind was stronger and colder on Bathurst Street. Ted hobbled into it; John's shoes were hurting him. He felt as if he had walked from a distant suburb. He wished he had remembered to retrieve his trenchcoat from the Boss coat-check; it might have had a subway ticket in the pocket. At least he had found the suit jacket, under two embracing men at Helium. It smelled of oysters. He had no idea how much it cost to dry-clean a suit.

He was walking past warehouses, empty gas stations. Every outline was blurred. He tried not to think of Miranda and Roger together. Or of Georgina. Perhaps Georgina hadn't left town at all. It didn't seem to make sense to fly in from Japan — the tiny, coiffed waitresses on JAL, the sushi snacks in styrofoam — to this wind over the streetcar tracks, Toronto, for two days. Of course she had been in London with her mother for a while first. It was encouraging, really, how upset she had been by the Go-Go episode. Perhaps she had reconsidered a sudden departure and had left a note for him at home. The wind cut his eyes and Ted cursed; he lifted his arm to wipe his nose on the suit's sleeve. Over the oysters, perfume: Miranda's hair.

Two lovers passed him, Italian teenagers, wrapped together and giggling. With envy, he watched the girl's shiny legs in black tights pass.

By the time he reached the house his head was filled with black tights, perfume and stilettoes; the spot where Miranda had been rubbing his thigh still seemed to tingle. He dropped his key on the front porch and had to fumble on his knees. In the dark entrance hall, the banister swayed to meet him; he bruised his shin. Lurching into the kitchen, he looked for a note on the table and for orange juice in the fridge, but found neither.

Go-Go's door was closed, but outlined in soft light from within. He passed her room gingerly, trying not to stumble. The overhead light in his room was too bright; he squinted looking around for a note from Georgina. The duvet was still rumpled from the morning. A faint odour of cigarettes and Go-Go's gel still hung in the room. She had been so sweet that evening, helping him dress. He stood still, trying to hear a sound from next door. Perhaps she had fallen asleep with the light on. He took John's shoes off and stood in the hall with his ear to her door. There was a quiet rustling of papers, her little voice humming a Bile Ducts tune. Ted knocked.

ELEVEN

MOUE WAS STEAMY WARM in the mornings, smelling of coffee and baking. It was raining outside. Around Ted, the brightly clean people seemed altogether too energetic, false, and older than him. They wore expensive casual clothes, mock-turtlenecks and canvas trousers with deck shoes; he imagined them all going off to work in urban planning offices. The matron serving coffee was more exaggeratedly, pretentiously French than Ted had ever seen her. He couldn't finish his espresso; it cut his stomach. He looked across the table at Miranda.

'Then we went to Area,' she said. She looked just as red-cheeked as the others. 'That was just before it became the totally hip place and collapsed, just a few people knew about it, and it was *great*. I didn't give a shit about it being pretentious or ... or anything. I was just happy to *be* there. It was really, really the best year of my life, that year. You all right?'

'Having trouble finishing this,' said Ted. 'Have a good time last night?'

'Oh wonderful. Didn't you?'

'Excellent. I just had a bit too much to drink.'

'Ted, you were *so sweaty*!' She laughed clear and high.

Ted made an effort to laugh, shifting in his seat. His stomach contracted. He hadn't shaved or showered and the musky smell of sex wafted up from under his clothes in waves. He said, 'I can't believe you didn't drink. Was I the only one drinking?'

She laughed again, so naturally. 'Oh yes. Yes, Teddy. Everyone else was completely sober and you ... do you remember putting the raw steak over your face? And the goldfish? Teddy, you were *so* embarrassing ...'

He shifted again. Go-Go on his fingers. 'Arthur seemed to keep up with me.'

'Arthur, *Arthur* was *shit*faced from – Arthur was drinking like he was *des*perate or something, he and Roger trying to keep up with each other like it was some kind of competition ...' She sighed.

'How tiresome,' said Ted, looking at her.

She looked away. 'Anna!' She waved brightly at a woman who looked like her, then looked down at the table. 'We were all drinking like crazy. I bet no one remembers Helium hardly at all. I can't even believe I found you guys there. Do you want another coffee?'

Ted shook his head. He took a deep breath. 'Miranda. You and I have coffee together a lot. We have coffee and drinks and lunch and – '

'Breakfast, that's what I *love* about you, Ted, you love breakfast as much as I do.'

'Right. I love it. I really love it. But I was just wondering – '

'Oh!' Her mouth was full of croissant; she put up a hand to make him wait. 'And Thanksgiving!' She swallowed. 'I meant to invite you!'

'What?'

'Thanksgiving dinner, with my family! Are you going back east, or back to Montreal, or do you have any plans? Because I figured it would be a really lonely weekend for you, it's a long weekend, and my mother always makes a big Thanksgiving dinner and we each bring a guest, always.'

Ted paused. 'Well. Yes! I'd love to. But what about Arthur? Don't you – '

'Arthur goes to his family in St Catherine's.'

'Well. Sure. That would be wonderful. I've never met your family. And you're right about that weekend; I always find it miserable.'

'Oh I'm so glad.' She smiled brilliantly and Ted smiled too, looking at her and astounded once again by the incredible

smoothness and colour of her skin. He could feel her body's
warmth right across the table.

He glanced at his watch, John's watch. 'Shit!' He stood up,
fumbling in his pocket for change. 'I'm going to work, can you
believe it?'

'I'll pay,' she said, still smiling, and waving him away.

He waved to her from the rainy doorway, and she smiled
back from under her sleek hair. She really was very lovely.

'Andreas and Jim, I don't want to see any jumping around.
We've got two cameras in each room, each one on a one-shot,
no panning, no movement, just slow zooms when I tell you,
you'll hear me over the headsets. I don't want to hear anybody
speaking on their headsets unless their red light is on, that
means I want you to tell me something. We're recording all
the time, remember. I don't want any fuck-ups. You fuck with
me, I'll fuck you up.' The man speaking was the one they
called Gord, a balding businessman with a moustache. He stood
at the head of the long table of polished wood with a china cup
and saucer in one hand, dressed in a cardigan and what looked
like silk and linen trousers. He glared over his coffee at the
technicians sitting the length of the table and leaning against the
wallpapered walls of the hotel suite. Gaffers with silver tape
and pliers on their belts, grips with hammers, cameramen with
long fingers, PA's with U of T sweatshirts. The table was spread
with a catered breakfast on a linen cloth: silver coffee pots,
white china plates, muffins, sliced melon and prosciutto, fresh
bread and jam, a basket of oranges and pears. The technicians
looked down nervously. Ted, leaning against a wall between
two fat hippies with beards and ponytails, looked across at
Andreas, who sat with two other cameramen.

Ted didn't understand a thing. There were Americans
everywhere, Andreas wasn't in charge, and this clearly wasn't
his movie. Andreas had greeted him enthusiastically and introduced him to Gord, who was from SensiMax Pictures in L.A.

This didn't make sense to Ted, as all the trucks parked outside the hotel were adorned with the logo of MarketNet Field Productions, which he knew to be a Toronto company. Gord had nodded absently and Andreas had disappeared with the other cameramen. Then there had been a meeting in one of the suites, with another middle-aged man, Dan or Dave, Ted didn't know if he was from SensiMax or MarketNet, and the PA's, Ted and the two athletic girls in sweatshirts. Dan or Dave, sitting awkwardly on the bed in his expensive casual pants, had been friendly, paternal and menacing, explaining what a press junket was and what they had to do.

Ted looked through the huge window at the skyline of office towers. The window, like every window on the top floor of the hotel, had been covered by a sticky orange plastic filter, but he could still make out the gleaming shapes, a silent orange sky. Every suite on the top floor was occupied with lights and equipment. Thick bundles of cables ran down each corridor, stuck to the carpet with silver tape. Ted sipped his coffee and felt nervous.

'PA's,' Gord said grimly, and Ted looked up. 'Your job is to get the reporters in and out of those rooms in exactly ten minutes each. You warn them when they've got thirty seconds to wind up their interview, and you cut them off. You don't take any shit. You've got about ten seconds, count 'em, ten, to get the last one out and the next one in. There's no fucking around. We've got two stars and the director, all in separate rooms, being interviewed simultaneously. Two cameras in each room. We're monitoring every interview, every camera angle, from the control room. We got ten monitors in there. We can hear every breath everybody takes in every room. You fart, we hear it. The star wants a coffee, you tell me through your headset, I'll get a coffee sent up. You see a makeup problem – especially sweat, they're going to be under the lights for about ten hours – you buzz me, then forget about it, don't worry about it after that, I'll get makeup sent in. You label the

videotape with the name of the film, the name of the star –'
Gord was counting firmly on his fingers. 'The name of the
reporter and the network. You give the labelled tape to the
reporter on his way out. Got it?'

When the briefing was over, the crowd wandered into the
wire-crossed hallway. The gaffers strode away; the cameramen
cracked their knuckles. Ted saw Andreas chatting beside the
elevator.

He approached. 'Andreas, excuse me, I'm confused.'

'Okay man,' said the other cameraman. 'See you.'

'Catch you,' said Andreas. He turned and smiled at Ted.
'Sure. Shoot.'

'This isn't your film.'

Andreas laughed. '*My* film? No. No, this isn't my film. This
isn't a film at all.' He laughed again, sticking his thumbs into
his belt. 'This is the company I work for.'

'MarketNet?'

Andreas nodded. 'Didn't I tell you? I'm sorry. I thought I
made this clear.' He looked at his watch, then down the busy
corridor.

'Aren't you making a film?'

'Me? Oh yes. But I'm not getting started for a while. That's
not until the spring, I think. You can certainly work on that
too, if you like. I just knew that we needed a PA today, because
we lost one yesterday –'

'Lost one?'

'One got fired, yesterday, and I thought I'd do Duane a
favour and come up with one for him. You don't mind, do
you?'

They had to flatten themselves against the elevator as two
ponytails passed, carrying a sound-mixing board. 'So Gord,'
Ted asked, 'Gord's an American, right? SensiMax is American?'

'Very good. It's for their picture that we're doing this. They
hire us to tape American TV reporters, entertainment show

guys from all over the States, interviewing the stars and the director. They invite the reporters up here. It's cheaper, everything's cheaper. The stars just sit in one room all day, giving the same interview. We sell Sensi ten-minute tapes they give to the reporters. SensiMax sends Dan and Gord to oversee; it makes them happy.'

'What's the movie they're publicizing?'

'I think it's called *Flight Into Shadow*. Julian Claude's in it.'

'Julian Claude? The English guy?'

'You'll get to meet him. And Kiki Jensen. You know what room you're in?'

Ted shook his head. Dan, the one in charge of PA's, came rushing down the corridor towards them. 'Edward,' he said, riffling through the pages on his clipboard, 'You're in three with Julian, this way.'

Ted nodded to Andreas and followed Dan down the bustling corridor. They passed a brightly-lit suite with two chairs in it, facing one another, and a video camera behind each chair. A small blond woman with bright red lips and a short dress sat in one, a vampire girl in black doing her hair. 'That Kiki's room?' Ted asked nonchalantly.

'That's her,' said Dan. 'You'll get to meet her.'

'Next, Robert Riccino, NYET-TV, New York,' Ted called, reading from his clipboard. He pressed his digital stopwatch and moved to the door. The sound man relaxed for a moment, cracking his knuckles, but without taking his headset off; the two cameramen looked up from their viewfinders. The last journalist, an enormous peroxide blonde from Detroit, was still shaking Julian Claude's hand; the star didn't move from his armchair, looking up at her, smiling, with his legs crossed in the same relaxed position he had managed since eight that morning, four hours before. Interview number twenty; Ted was behind. His bladder was bursting.

He handed the videocassette to Angie Bodax, InfoTainment

Morning, KNOT Detroit, as she brushed past Robert Riccino, on his way in. In a second the vampire girl – everyone just called her makeup – had Riccino in his chair, dusting his face, while Robbie the sound-man with the Metallica T-shirt clipped on his mike. Already the plastic-faced talk-show host was chatting with Julian, and Ted was taking his next round of abuse over his headphones.

'Edward,' the voice began.

Ted clicked the red Talk button on his radio unit. 'Ted,' he said, reaching behind to unstick the shirt from his sweating back. 'Over.'

'Ted. Ted, you don't have anything *like* that kind of time to get them in and out, I clocked you at twenty seconds that time, last time you were at fifteen, you want to be here till midnight or what? And Bobby, what was that, I mean what the fuck *was* that *bonk* at the end of that one?'

Bobby the sound man talked softly into his headset; Ted heard the conversation clearly. 'Julian tapped the mike with his hand. Must have been wearing a ring.'

But the control room wasn't interested; the cameraman was being warned about avoiding a reflection in the corner of the painting behind the star's head. 'We set all this up beforehand, Jimmy,' Gord's grating voice continued. 'You must have cheated a little. I can see camera two in the reflection. I'm not impressed. Keep it to the – Jesus. Edward. Ted. Jesus. Look at his face. Just *look* at his face.'

Ted looked up from his clipboard to see the droplet of sweat on Julian Claude's perfect forehead roll slowly down, gathering pink powder and leaving a pallid, crooked trail. The star was laughing at Robert Riccino's banter, unaware. Makeup had just left. Ted pressed his talk button. 'Makeup. Makeup.'

'It's done, Ted, she's on her way.' Gord's sigh came over the headphones. 'All right. Let's keep on it. Dan and I are doing a tour of all your rooms for the next interview. Just checking in to watch. Then we take a break for lunch.'

Bobby was signalling to Ted that his levels were okay, and Ted signalled to the cameras to wait. The vampire girl arrived with her toolbox and flattened down Julian's forehead. Once she had left the room, Ted signalled for the cameras to roll, and punched his stopwatch.

'Julian Claude,' said Robert Riccino, smiling, '*Flight Into Darkness* must have been more than just a film for you. It must have echoed some of the most stressful times of your life, brought forth ... ' The interviewer stretched his hand towards the star. 'Ghosts. Tell me about those echoes, those parallels, those ...' He made the gesture again. 'Ghosts.'

'Robert,' said Julian Claude, 'in a way, you're right.'

Ted listened to the interview with his eye on the stopwatch. It was the same interview, the same questions he had heard at ten-minute intervals, with slight variations, since eight that morning. Claude seemed just as fresh and animated in this one; he never tired of it. Twice, he had called for coffee, and the sweat stains were appearing more regularly on his forehead, but the casual pose, the earnest enthusiasm for the film remained the same. Ted's hand shook; he was hungry and he needed the bathroom, but Julian Claude, under the lights and faced with an uninterrupted stream of wide-smiling cretins asking him the same prurient questions about his personal life, his divorce, the months in the Ford clinic, showed no fatigue.

'And is that,' asked Robert Riccino in a different tone, 'who you're seeing now?' The interviewer crossed his legs with an air of triumph.

'You know,' said Julian Claude, motionless, 'I don't recall who I'm seeing now,' and smiled.

Ted made his thirty-second signal to Riccino, who wrapped the interview up smoothly. As Ted turned to the pile of video-tape boxes behind him the door of the suite opened violently. Dan, the American from the control room, burst in. 'Fine, Jimmy,' he said to camera one. 'Just fine until the last thirty seconds. And then you had to fuck it up, didn't you?'

'What, Dan? You mean the —'

'How are you doing, Julian?' Dan said unctuously, approaching the star. Both Claude and Riccino stood and stretched, smiling at Dan. They all seemed to know each other. Dan patted Claude on the shoulder. 'You doing okay? Tired? No? One more interview before lunch, and then we're past halfway. You're doing great.'

Ted peeled off the adhesive label on which he had written Riccino's name and network; as he stuck it to the cassette he dropped the transparent plastic box he was to put it in. Dan jerked his head irritably.

'You got the next one lined up?' he asked, looking at his watch. Riccino was waiting at the door for his videotape.

'Yes, Dan. Just labelling this one.' Ted jammed the cassette into the box and handed it to Riccino at the door.

Dan intercepted it, taking the box from Ted's hand. 'What's this? What do you think this is?' He was pointing at the label through the clear plastic.

'The label?'

'The label. Is on upside down.' Dan looked at Riccino, shaking his head. 'I'm sorry about this, Bob.' He handed him the tape. 'That's great,' he said to the room at large. 'It's great. One upside-down label. One upside-down label coming up.' He and Riccino left the room together.

Ted ushered in Pamela Singer, WXKQ News, Baltimore, and she rushed over to Julian Claude. 'Oh *Julian*,' she said, sinking into the chair opposite him. 'It's *so* good to meet you.'

Lunch was excellent: cold meats, rare roast beef, fresh bread, salads, fruit, muffins, bottles of mineral water, all laid out on linen cloths and china plates. The technicians, in dirty jeans and T-shirts, ate energetically. They talked about stereo systems and cars, and the best route into the city from Brampton. Ted listened.

He was on his way back to suite 3 when the tall man with

the ponytail stepped out of the control room and stopped him. 'You Ted?'

Ted nodded.

'Come over here a second.' He took him into an alcove near the elevators, out of the busy corridor. 'Um.'

Ted stared at the angular face.

'Ah, it's like this,' said the man. 'Gord and Dan aren't happy with your work, so, ah, you needn't come back this afternoon.'

'Needn't come back?'

'No. Don't come back. Sorry. You'll get your daily wage anyway.'

'I'm fired.'

'It's sort of like that. Don't worry about it though. Happens all the time.'

'Uh-huh.' Ted looked up and down the corridor, at the laughing figures who hadn't been fired. 'What was the problem.'

'I really don't know,' said the man, looking at his watch. 'Could have been anything, you know. It happens like that.'

'The videotape label, I guess,' said Ted.

The man shrugged. 'Good luck,' he said, walking away.

Ted hesitated, then moved in front of the elevators. He pushed the button. Andreas's hand was on his shoulder.

'Leaving?'

Ted nodded.

'I heard you're not coming back. Listen, it's no problem. Don't worry about it. I'm sorry.'

'No problem,' said Ted.

'Listen,' said Andreas, 'I've been meaning to ask you about Thanksgiving. My family always gets together at my parents' place in Caledon. It's in the country, really beautiful there.'

TWELVE

ON THE STREET outside the Four Seasons the wind had picked up. Ted turned his collar up and walked towards where he thought a subway might be. The wind brought a new cold with it, a damp cold, more wintry than autumnal. Even the habitually bright Yorkville streets seemed grey and shuttered. A woman in a fur coat stepped out of a car in front of him, hurrying into a salon, scowling. She was exaggerating, really, it was too warm for a fur coat, and the image irritated Ted. He felt exhausted and nauseous, and stunned. He half expected the woman in the coat to turn and dismiss him. The whole of Yorkville had fired him. Best not to think about it.

He rubbed the stubble on his chin, and Go-Go's scent filled his nostrils. He wondered if she would be at home. Best not to think about that either.

A man was looking at him from across the street. Ted turned; the man seemed to be smiling at him. He was tall, about Ted's age, with short hair and an expensive dark raincoat. Something about him looked familiar. He waved. Ted slowed down, and the man crossed the street towards him. 'Ridley,' said the man loudly, pointing at him.

'Sorry?'

'Ridley? No. Southern. You were at USO?'

'Yes,' said Ted.

'Forsdyke,' said the man, shaking Ted's hand firmly. He was good-looking in a bland way. 'Dick Forsdyke. I remember you. You used to do the literary stuff for the *Gazette*.'

'That's right. Ted Owen.'

'Owen! Of course!' Dick Forsdyke angled his head and

smiled at the sky as if he couldn't have asked for more from the day. He was still grasping Ted's hand. 'Good to see you. We met once at a Students' Representative Council Meeting. It was over that whole *Gazette* cafuffle. You were –'

'You tried to impeach the whole staff.'

Dick Forsdyke laughed, letting the hand go. 'That's right. I remember the whole thing. What a riot. Things were pretty tense for a while, right?'

'Right.' Ted looked down the street. He could see the subway entrance.

'Ted, Ted. Based in Toronto now? What are you doing these days?'

'Well, I haven't been here long, actually, but I'm working as a writer.'

'A writer?' said Forsdyke. 'You know, Ted, that's fascinating. *Fasc*inating. I've been doing some writing myself. I've just published a book, with Rob Phibbs, we co-wrote it, myself and Rob, you never knew him at Southern, no? We've just published a report on excellence in Canadian companies. The hundred most excellent Canadian companies, not just in terms of profits, but in terms of service, employee benefits, and of course excellence of product, everything taken into account. You may have seen the book around. It's been doing quite well. And you know, Ted, we found some incredible things.'

'Really?'

'We really learned a lot, about Canada, as a country. And about excellence in business. One of the things we found was that –'

'I'm writing about architecture,' said Ted hiking up his upturned collar so his chin was buried. 'And a play.'

'A play! That's fascinating. Ted, I'll have to get your number before I go. We'll have to talk. I'm so interested in that sort of thing. You know, Ted, one of the things we found was that Canadian companies really have a lot they can *teach*

American companies, not just learn. You know, American companies tend to think that a company's value is found in those things that are quantifiable, assets and so on. But then they make mistakes.' Forsdyke paused, looking around him and nodding his head. He put his leather-gloved fingertips together under his chin. 'They make mistakes.'

Ted watched a seagull wheel overhead. 'They make mistakes.'

'We found one American company – and we tell this story in the book, if you glance at it – that bought a small, successful pharmaceutical company because they had several patents in the previous years. So they bought it and it started to do badly, it produced no more patentable pharmaceuticals. What was the problem?' Forsdyke spread his arms wide.

Ted coughed. 'Well, Dick – '

'Well, they checked the producing scientists' names and they found that three out of the five patents granted to that company in its first years had been the work of one scientist – and he had just left the company, just before the takeover. That's what they hadn't checked when they sized up that company. They hadn't realized that the power of a company, a company's excellence, comes as much from the *people working for it* as from anything else. Isn't it incredible, that they didn't check that?'

'Jesus Christ,' said Ted. He whistled. 'Incredible, Dick.'

Forsdyke beamed, immensely pleased. He put his hands to his waist and chuckled, shaking his head. 'Ted,' he said, 'terrific to see you.' He shook Ted's hand again and gave him his card. Ted gave him his own number and they separated; he left Forsdyke still watching the empty Yorkville street, smiling widely and waving after him.

He held onto the railing on the stairway down to the subway. A warm wind blew upwards from the tunnels, bringing its familiar smell of heated metal. The platforms were almost empty; he sat gratefully on a bench, smelling Go-Go again. An image from the night returned: her giggling, wriggling out of the black tights, the pale flesh.

Ted said 'No,' aloud, to dispel the memory, then glanced about him. An old black woman leaned against a pillar some metres away. He stared back at the track, shaking his head. He tried to remember what he knew of Dick Forsdyke; there had been a graffito on the library wall one year that read 'Forsdyke iS a pRick.' He laughed briefly, then looked around again.

It was either Forsdyke, the film, or Go-Go, to think about. Not much of a choice. There had been such awkwardness. Such a loss of cool. She had known what he wanted as soon as he had come in, moving aside on the rumpled bed for him to sit beside her. Then her cigarette breath, the spandex top. He winced at the image of his roving hand between her legs, the wiry hair. He supposed it had all been over rather fast. His body had felt weak and flabby afterwards, as if they were stuck together with grease or dirt. The feeble expulsion of bodily fluids.

The train thundered alongside; the slamming doors made Ted wince again. The post-operative feeling had returned. Inside the aggressively lit train, he thought of Mike the bike courier, an emaciated, unshaven male face.

A pretty punk girl in black drill boots sat opposite him. He looked away. All he needed was a nap, and he would feel better.

The house was dark and cold when Ted came through the front door. He found the thermostat under a handbag on the living-room wall, and turned it up. Cautiously, he stuck his head into the kitchen: empty. The house was silent. He took his shoes off before he walked upstairs.

Go-Go's door was wide open, her room empty and dim. With relief, Ted shut his own door, undressed and fell onto Georgina's futon.

He was dreaming sporadically of parties when he heard her

door close. He opened his eyes and sat up, smoothing his hair. The room was dark, the sky black through the window, and Go-Go was moving about on the other side of the wall. He turned on the lamp and lowered the pink paper blind. Dressed but shoeless, he stepped into the hall to listen at her door, which opened suddenly. She flinched.

'Hi. You're back early.'

'I was fired.'

'You were *fired*? Oh my God.' Her face looked tense and preoccupied.

Ted told her the story of the press junket for as long as he could. She listened sympathetically. Then he told her the story of Forsdyke the prep, but she didn't laugh. Once he finished, neither made a move towards either bedroom, which would have been more comfortable and friendly than the corridor. They were both silent for a moment, standing apart and looking at the floor. Ted's stomach growled. He looked up at her worried face, the worn black T-shirt. The faint odour of cigarettes sickened him. 'Are you hungry at all?' he asked.

She smiled, then shook her head. 'Yes. But I'm on my way to the theatre.'

'Ah,' said Ted with relief.

'But maybe we could meet up afterwards.'

'Ah. Sure. Sure. What are you thinking of?'

She shrugged. 'I don't know, maybe we could just meet for a drink or something after I get out.'

'Sure. That would be fine. It's just that ... '

'It would be too late for you?'

'Well, how late would it be? It's just that I'm really wiped.'

She nodded. 'Yeah. It would be late. Not until midnight. Don't worry about it.' She turned into her room.

'Sorry,' said Ted. 'I'd like to, but I just won't be able to stay up until then.'

'It's okay, really,' said Go-Go from her room, her head in the closet.

From John's room, the phone rang out. 'Phone,' said Ted energetically, and scrambled up the stairs.

He found the phone on the third ring, under a sleeping bag. 'Hello.'

'Yes,' said a young woman's voice. 'Ted Owen, please.'

'Speaking,' said Ted, sitting heavily on a pile of clothes.

'Ted? Hi. This is Annette McEachern calling, we met at Boss? The night of Miranda's party?' From downstairs, Ted heard Go-Go's door and her feet tripping down the stairs. She was leaving already.

'Sorry?' he said. 'At Boss?'

'Yes, the night that Miranda didn't show up? I was sitting next to Arthur? I have brown hair ... '

'Ah yes! Annette!' She was the mousy one, the physiotherapist. 'Annette, I'm *so* sorry, of course I remember you, I ... ' The front door slammed as Go-Go left the house. 'Did I ... did you come to Helium after with us?'

'Helium? No, no. I think I left before you did. Anyway.' Annette's voice was much brisker than he remembered it. 'I'm calling you from CQET-TV, I work for the Janni Bolo show – '

'Sorry, what show?'

'Janni Bolo, and we're putting together next week's tapings, I'm working kind of late and I thought it would be easiest to call you at home.'

'Of course,' said Ted. 'No problem.'

'And we want you to be on a panel. We're having a panel of people to talk about architecture, a lifestyle expert, a homemaker, and maybe an architect, if we can get one, but we're looking for a woman otherwise it's no good, and our host, of course, Janni, and we need one other. Now I remember you talking about the article you're writing for *Cities*, is that correct?'

'Well, yes, it's for *Cities*, but I should say that it's not exactly – '

'It's about bars and restaurants, is that right?'

'Um.' Ted hesitated. 'Yes.' He saw a television studio, lights, perhaps Miranda watching. 'Yes,' he said decisively. 'Partly. Commercial social spaces generally, actually. Mostly I'm interested in which environments people pay to be in, to relax. I've travelled quite a bit, and seen the spaces different cultures – '

'Excellent. That would be excellent. Janni wants the discussion to be about how architecture influences people's day-to-day lives, you know, ordinary people. You know, buildings these days don't seem to be about *people*, you know? They seem to be very cold, and impersonal. People can't ... '

An awkward silence. Relate to them, Ted thought.

'Relate to them,' said Annette. '*That*, that's really the *issue*. And with your expert knowledge – now we don't want the conversation to get too technical, I mean I know the way you can talk, that's why I was impressed when I heard you, you can talk in a way people will under*stand* you, you know what I mean? We want this to be on a level that ... on a very *accessible* level, if you see what I mean.'

'I understand. How much – '

'The whole thing is about a ten-minute spot. Have you been on T V before?'

'How much does it pay?' said Ted. He leaned back into the pile of clothes.

'We don't pay. But it's a great plug for the magazine.'

Ted considered this. The magazine was not aware of the article. Which was unwritten. 'That's okay. I don't need a plug.'

'Oh really? It's a great opportunity to – '

'No, really. That's okay. But I'd love to – I'd be willing to do it. But could you tell me something about the show?'

'It's the Janni Bolo Show, on C Q E T.'

'Yes.'

'*Janni Bolo.*'

'Yes. But, actually, you see, I've never seen the show.'

'Oh! You've never *seen* it. Okay.' Annette paused interminably, then gave a nervous laugh. 'Okay.' She exhaled forcefully. 'It's a daytime talk show, with a live studio audience. It's national. You must have seen it sometime.'

'I'm sure I have. Okay. When are you taping?'

'Tuesday at ten a.m. Our studios are in Etobicoke. Of course we'll send a taxi for you.'

THIRTEEN

'PERHAPS TED WOULD LIKE some more turnip,' said Mrs Bentley, eyeing Miranda. Seen through the candles, her hair was just as glossy and black, her skin just as clear, her buttoned silk blouse just as pristine as Miranda's: she was certainly beautiful as well, and looked much younger than Mr Bentley, who sat silent and grey-faced at the head of the table.

'No, thanks,' said Ted, before Miranda could pass him the silver tureen. Miranda's smile seemed unusually fixed.

Mrs Bentley looked at her watch again. 'I do hope Andrew isn't *too* late, because the later he starts, the later he starts back to school, and the roads will be busy tonight.'

'Mummy, he'll be *fine*,' said Alison, the younger, engaged sister. 'And this is de*li*cious.' Stuart, her fiancé, beamed at her across the table.

Mrs Bentley senior, the immaculate grandmother, said, 'Alison darling, if you don't mind my asking, have you still got the side table?'

'Oh! Granny gave me the most gorgeous little side table from the Florida house,' said Alison to Miranda. 'We're thinking of putting in the living room, aren't we, sweetie?'

'Because it's very nice,' said the old lady, her grey hair swept back from her imposing face, 'if it's in a safe place, with the brass lamp on it, the French lamp. Very nice. If you take care of it. I *do* hope you'll take care of your things.'

'Oh, yes, Granny, we —'

'If you have nice things, because there's no point to having nice things otherwise, is there?'

Ted took another enormous mouthful of turkey and looked at

the few remaining fingers of red wine in the single bottle on the table, wondering if one served oneself. He looked over the candles at Stuart's dark jacket and tried not to think of his own tweed; he should have asked John for the suit again; then up at the high ceiling, the crystals on the chandelier sparkling with orange light from the flames in the fireplace behind him. He tried to focus again on the murky landscape on the far wall, behind Mrs Bentley's head; he was sure it was a Jackson, but couldn't make out the signature. More interesting, at least, than the Forrestall next to it or the Krieghoff, God help us, near the fireplace, to one side of Mr Bentley's bowed, solidly eating head.

'Alison is *very* good with things, Mummy,' said Miranda's mother crisply.

'How are things at the firm, Stuart?' said Miranda.

Stuart smiled as if addressing a television camera. 'Very exciting, right now, really, quite ... quite interesting. I'm doing a lot more litigation now.'

'Which was always your interest, wasn't it, Stuart?' said the old lady.

'That's right, Mrs Bentley. Other people seem to laugh at it.' Stuart held out his hands, smiling indulgently. 'But I find it very stimulating.' He sat back as if considering his words. 'Very enjoyable.'

'That's good,' said Miranda.

'That's really *very* good,' said Granny. 'And it's stable, isn't it? I mean there will always be litigation to do, won't there.'

'I hope so,' said Stuart.

'And are you a student, Ted?' said Miranda's mother.

'Yes,' he said immediately. 'No, not any more. I was until very recently. In Montreal.' Ted saw Mr Bentley's clear grey eyes flicker upwards for an instant, then set again on the slowly diminishing mound of beige, brown and orange food. 'I've just finished a master's degree.'

'Tell them what it was about, Teddy,' said Miranda. 'It's *so* interesting.'

Ted finished the mouthful of wine he had been saving. 'Ah, it was about all sorts of things. A mulitidisciplinary program.'

'What do you mean?' said Mrs Bentley senior.

'Well, we sort of combined a study of film, literature and what you could call mass culture, because we were studying, really, theories of culture. Interpretive approaches to different things. I suppose the approach was more important than the thing itself.'

'How very interesting.'

Mrs Bentley narrowed her eyes slightly. 'When you say mass culture, do you mean you studied things like television, and cartoon books, anything?'

'Exactly.'

'In the same way you studied literature?'

'Exactly the same way. That was the idea.'

'I see.'

Ted stared at the wine bottle with longing. Miranda smiled sweetly. Alison and Stuart smiled at each other. For a moment there was no sound but the tinkling of silver and china. Ted imagined that he could hear the soft tearing of fowl flesh.

'No, but Teddy, tell us what your real interest was,' said Miranda. 'I find this fascinating.'

Ted cleared his throat. 'I was particularly interested in psychoanalytic theory and, and feminism. How you can use psychoanalysis to interpret gender roles.'

Mrs Bentley was looking at him again. 'And is that what you're writing about now?'

Ted had an urge to laugh. 'No.' Then he found that he was laughing, loudly and freely. 'I don't believe in it any more.' He laughed louder, without understanding why, except that he was suddenly utterly certain he had no further interest in psycho-analysis or feminism. 'I think it's all complete nonsense,' he tried to say, gasping. He looked at Mr Bentley, who was smil-ing at him. Ted had another urge then, to fart and dance naked on the table.

'Ted's going to be on TV next week,' said Miranda, 'as an expert on culture.'

'Three weeks,' said Ted, controlling his laughter. 'The taping's next week.'

'TV?' said Alison. 'That's so neat. What show?'

'Janni Bolo,' said Ted. 'I think it's a daytime talk show, for –'

'Janni Bolo!' said Alison. 'That's so neat! That's *so neat*. How did you get on there?'

'Well,' said Ted, 'they just called me and –'

Mrs Bentley got up suddenly. 'There he is,' she said moving towards the kitchen. From outside came the purring of a European car engine, powerful enough to be a sportscar, and the popping of gravel under tires. A car door opened and closed; soon there were footsteps in the black-and-white tiled entrance hall.

'Hullo everybody,' said Andrew as he came into the dining room, still carrying his duffelbag. He leaned to kiss Mr Bentley's forehead. 'Hello Daddy. Where's Mummy?' He moved around the table, kissing every female forehead and shaking Ted's and Stuart's hands firmly. He was taller than Ted, and wore a school blazer with a crest, a striped school tie, and a rumpled blue button-down shirt, untucked. Blond hair protruded from under his baseball cap, on backwards. 'Hullo Mummy,' he said, embracing her as she brought in his food. His face was fine, freckled, perfectly featured yet open; he smiled constantly.

Ted could feel his own features creeping imperceptibly and unstoppably into their Sackville Gas Station Attendant mask, where they froze.

'Sorry I'm late,' said Andrew. 'Glad you started without me.'

'Are you driving out to school tonight?' asked the old lady as he sat down to eat.

'Yes, Granny. I have school tomorrow morning. I'll be *fine*.' He grinned, winking at Ted.

'How's the car running, Andy?' said Stuart.

Ted served himself more vegetables and sauces. Stuart and Andrew talked about overhead cams. Alison, Miranda and Granny worked out the matter of the invitations to the reception.

'Now, Miranda made these,' said Mrs Bentley, setting down the pumpkin pies.

'They're *gorgeous*,' said Alison.

'I didn't know you baked,' said Ted.

Miranda smiled demurely. Ted had a sudden hallucinatory thought that she had metamorphosed entirely, been replaced by a doppelganger, a replicant.

'Miranda's always baked,' said Alison gaily. 'Remember the time she made those cakes when Mrs Gideon and Stella were staying with us?'

'Alison,' said Mrs Bentley softly.

'It's all right, mummy, Miranda doesn't mind me telling, it was just so *funny*! Miranda, do you remember, Mrs Gideon said she wouldn't —'

'Ally, don't,' said Miranda.

Something in her tone silenced her sister. Ted looked up. Mrs Bentley was staring at Alison sternly, with pursed lips. Miranda was looking down at her plate, Andrew and Stuart were looking at her nervously. Mr Bentley was eating.

They all ate pumpkin pie for a moment, relaxing a little when Miranda picked up her fork and ate as well.

Ted looked across at Mrs Bentley senior. She was peering closely at her silver dessert spoon. Then she put it down and looked up at the ceiling, beatifically. 'I sincerely hope,' she said pensively, 'that in Heaven there will be *things*.'

'Ted,' said Andrew loudly with his mouth full, 'Ted, excuse me, just a minute.' He swallowed. 'Were you at university with Miranda?'

'No, no. We met here.'

'What university were you at? Because I'm applying to places now. I'm in my last year.'

'Oh. Southern. I did my undergrad at Southern Ontario.'

'Oh yeah?' Andrew smiled widely. 'That's where I'm thinking of going.'

'You'll like it there,' said Ted.

Andrew nodded. 'There's a fraternity there that Daddy was in.' He smiled down the table at his father, who looked up and nodded sagely. 'He thinks it would be a good thing to continue the tradition. I like that idea.'

'You'll like it there,' Ted repeated.

'But I'm in no rush, you know? I'm thinking of going travelling first, taking a year to see Asia. I'd like to see India, Thailand, Indonesia, Bali I hear is beautiful, maybe Tibet. I think you learn so much travelling, at least as much as you do in a classroom. And I think it's really important to see other cultures, you know, see as many cultures as you can.'

There was a tinkle as Alison's fork hit her plate. She pushed her chair back and stood up. Her face was crumpled and tears shone on her cheeks. 'Excuse me,' she said in a choked voice, and rushed out of the room.

No one said a word. Ted looked around, bewildered. Miranda was looking down, pushing a small piece of pie around her plate. Mrs Bentley stared straight ahead. Stuart looked dolefully after Alison. It was then that Mr Bentley spoke for the first time. 'Ted,' he said in a gravelly voice, 'may I interest you in some more wine?'

'Have some more turnip, Ted?' asked Andreas's mother, holding out the bowl. Under the bright overhead light her red face shone.

'It's all from the garden, Ted,' said Fred, Andreas's father, 'even the chickens. Anna made everything except the desserts, Sherry brought the desserts. But it's made with our pumpkins.' Like his wife, Fred was in his late fifties and like his wife he wore elastic-waisted trousers and a plaid shirt. He beamed. Sherry's baby screamed, Sherry clucked and shifted her,

Sherry's husband Don laughed and took the turnip bowl from Ted. The single bottle of wine the seven of them had consumed seemed to have left everyone slightly giddy.

'Such a beautiful drive up here,' said Ted. 'Beautiful colours, red maple, orange, that bright, bright sumac. I've never seen such foliage in Ontario. Reminds me of New Brunswick.'

'I saw the new deck, Dad,' said Andreas. 'Looks great. Who did it for you?'

'Oh, Bob and I did it, you know Bob MacLeod from down the way? Rented an excavator, for the foundations and the storage underneath. We got advice from Wilson, the architect in Collingwood, of course. Only problem now is the earth settling under it. We'll see. Have to wait till spring till we really finish it off, I think, I don't want to be worrying about ice expanding in the hole and the earth settling and whatnot, for a while anyways. So it will sit looking ugly for a while. But the snow will help that.' Fred looked excitedly out the window.

Ted cast his eye over the plaid-upholstered couches, the wood-panelling walls, the brass knick-knacks on the mantelpiece. An overhead light burned in every room. For the first time, he looked directly at Ellen, Andreas's girlfriend. When she had swirled into Andreas's car on the way there he had seen only the mass of dark hair and the hoop earrings, and been aware of a dark, oily scent that reminded him of the fashionable boutiques he used to avoid on St Laurent. Femininity had pervaded the dark car, and he hadn't wanted to look at it.

It seemed natural to Ted that twenty-five-year-old filmmakers with ponytails and cowboy boots should be accompanied by intensely sexual women in a way he had never been, but he still didn't want to look at it. Now he looked at her and saw with reluctance that she was indeed attractive, although Janet would have found her cheap: she wore a black spandex top. Pale skin and enormous dark eyes. She was staring abstractedly at Sherry's baby, as she must have been doing all evening, for she had hardly spoken. Her eyes flickered upwards, catching Ted's; she smiled briefly and vaguely.

'And you've seen the new truck?' asked Andreas's father.

'The red one?' said Andreas heartily. At that table, with his silk shirt, cigarette and ponytail, and Ellen at his side, he looked like an apparition from fiction, an alien being stepped from a cinema screen into the world of mortals. Yet he spoke in their language. 'I thought it looked new. Looks great. Four wheel drive?'

'Yup. The driveway, in winter –'

'Fred, pass Ted the dressing,' said Mrs Gunnarsson.

'Mom, the dressing's excellent,' said Sherry. Don agreed loudly, his mouth full.

'Ellen, you're not very hungry, are you? Sure you don't want some more chicken? There's light meat left.'

The pumpkin pie came and was devoured – sweeter than the previous night's version at Miranda's – and some weak coffee was made. The family slumped in a complacent discomfort, red-faced and smiling, under the overhead light. Ted wanted to shade his eyes. A second bottle of wine had not appeared.

'Andy,' said Sherry, shifting the baby, who seemed to be sleeping, 'Are you guys still living in that old warehouse?'

Andreas nodded, smiling with what seemed like grim amusement. He sighed loudly and glanced at Ted as if to tell him something, then at Ellen, who smiled back at him.

'I don't know how you stand it. Isn't it dirty?'

'Cold in winter?' asked Don.

'It's the security I worry about,' said Mrs Gunnarsson. 'Just about anybody could climb up that fire escape and break through one pane of glass, why half of them are broken already.'

'Not quite half, Mom,' said Andreas wearily.

'I don't know how *you* can stand it, Ellen, dear,' said Andreas's mother. 'Is there a real bathroom?'

'Oh yes,' said Ellen softly. 'Down the hall.'

Mrs Gunnarsson shook her head in dismay.

'Now,' said Mr Gunnarsson, standing slowly and holding up one finger. 'We have some liqueurs, since it's a special occasion, if anyone would like any ... let's see.' He opened a door in the sideboard and bent painfully, pulling out various bottles.

Sherry asked for Tia Maria; Mom said she'd have a little Bailey's. Ellen took a demure shot of Grand Marnier.

'People bring these as gifts, you know,' said Mr Gunnarsson, bringing out dustier bottles. 'Some of them have been in here for years, I guess. We just never seem to get around to drinking them, hey Mom? Now what's this?' He held a darker bottle. 'Cognac. No idea who brought this. Anyone want any?'

Ted glimpsed the gold lettering on the label, a word that began cour, and said, 'Yes, please, I'll have some of that.'

Mr Gunnarsson put the bottle between Ted and Andreas, with two tumblers. 'Help yourselves.' Andreas grinned sideways and winked. He produced cigarettes for himself and Ellen.

'Now, Andy,' said Mrs Gunnarsson, once they were settled. 'Tell us about this new film. What's it to be called?'

The table seemed to stiffen. Sherry and Don exchanged glances, and she stood up with the sleeping baby. 'I'd better put her down,' she said, and left the room.

Andreas narrowed his eyes in the cigarette smoke. 'This one is called *Napalm Whore*.'

'*Napalm Whore*.'

Andreas nodded, sipping Courvoisier from his tumbler.

Softly, timidly, Mrs Gunnarsson asked, 'And is it similar to your last one, similar to *Cock Boy*?'

'*Cock Boy* was in the Festival last year, you know,' said Mr Gunnarsson to Ted.

Andreas coughed. 'Ah, no. No. It's quite different.' He looked at Ellen with an expression of patience. She smiled.

'And will you be starring in this one too, Ellen?'

'We don't know yet, Mom,' said Andreas. 'It's quite different.'

'And what will you do once this one is finished?'

'Well, you know, Mom, we're in the very early stages of this one. We haven't even started shooting yet. I'm just thinking about that right now. Once we get this shot ... I've got some other ideas.'

There was a brief silence, until Mr Gunnarsson said, 'I *liked* *Cock Boy*. It was a good movie. A good film.'

There was a long silence. Don the husband murmured agreement, staring down at his plate.

'Thanks,' said Andreas.

'Well,' said Mrs Gunnarsson with relief, 'Anyone for more coffee?'

FOURTEEN

'WITH NO EDUCATION and he drinks, he's a drunk,' said the taxi driver. 'After fourteen years. Can't understand it, but then there are things in this world you just can't understand. You think you can, but you can't.'

Ted looked at his watch again. All eight lanes of traffic, four in either direction, had slowed to a stop. He could see the coloured polyhedron logo of the television station spinning on a distant tower, separated from them by a mile of overpasses and warehouses. It seemed to be on a different highway altogether. The taxi seemed filled with exhaust, or perhaps simply with noxious fumes from the taxi driver himself, his grey-brown ski jacket, and a bag of some kind of fried food sitting on the front seat. Perhaps it was all decomposing more rapidly than normal, as they spoke, releasing substances harmful to the ozone.

'I'm kind of late,' said Ted. 'I'm supposed to be on TV in a few minutes.'

'Uh-huh.' The driver slowly turned his red eyes onto Ted, nodding his head wisely. He opened his mouth. Ted tried not to look. 'I mean would you?'

'Sorry?'

'Would you leave a man, I mean you understand what I'm saying, a woman or whatever, I mean would you go with someone, *be* with someone, who was illiterate, and he beats you too? After fourteen years, an illiterate drunk who beats her?'

'No. No I wouldn't.'

The traffic began to stagger forward in five-yard increments.

Ted's breakfast moved around in him.

'Mind if I smoke?' said the taxi driver, waving the hot lighter.

'Actually, yes, if you don't mind,' said Ted. 'I'd rather you didn't.'

'Oh yeah,' said the man, waving the lighter uncertainly. 'Oh yeah.' He put the glowing lighter on the dashboard. Ted watched it jiggle as they jerked and stopped.

'Can't understand it. Because I thought we got along. You know. We talked and all. Talked a lot.' Absently, the man picked up the lighter and lit his cigarette. 'Not enough, I guess. Not enough.'

Ted tried to breathe deeply and then tried not to breathe at all. The TV station seemed unreachable by the route they were taking. They were already parallel with the revolving tower logo.

'But then there's just no point in trying to understand everything in this world. You think you can understand everything, but you can't. You just can't.'

'Do you think we'll make it by nine-thirty?' said Ted.

'Huh?' The man looked around again, wide-eyed. Suddenly he jerked the wheel and accelerated. They cut across three lanes with a squeal. Ted grabbed a handhold as they roared onto an exit ramp. 'Sure,' said the driver, accelerating. 'No problem.'

When they parked beside the beige brick warehouse of CQET-TV it was nine-thirty-five. A security guard watched them, speaking into a walkie-talkie, as the driver laboriously wrote out Ted's receipt for thirty-five dollars.

'Thank you,' said Ted, grabbing it.

The driver made some kind of whimpering noise.

'Sorry?' said Ted, half out the door.

The man was shaking his head violently. 'We used to talk a *lot*. Talk up a storm. Not enough, though, I guess. Not enough.'

'No,' said Ted. 'Sad really. Thank you.' He closed the door.

'Hey!' the man shouted, through the window. 'Hey!' He tapped furiously on the glass.

Ted opened the door again. 'Yes?'

'You going to be on TV?'

'Yes. Right now. I'm late.'

The man held up a skeletal finger. 'Hang on.' He fumbled with some scraps of paper. Then he held one out to Ted, a blank receipt, with a ball point pen. 'Just your autograph.'

Inside, the building was cavernous, a series of hangars and corridors filled with lights and cables, and largely empty. No-one stopped Ted as he wandered; occasionally women in lurid makeup rushed past him. He stopped a security guard who gave him directions to find a green room, which struck Ted as poetic. Going down a corridor he passed a room full of people, and poked his head in. It was a sort of lounge, with pink walls (Dusty Rose, he thought, Daiquiri Sunset) and several dressed-up men and women sitting tightly on sofas, drinking coffee from bright pink Janni Bolo mugs. There was a large television screen showing the Janni Bolo show. 'Um,' he said.

'Yes?' said a clipboard woman.

'I'm looking for a green room,' said Ted.

'This is it,' said the woman bafflingly, and then she was taking down his name and handing him a bright pink coffee mug and introducing him to the others on the panel: a thin man with heavy glasses and heavy shoes, who turned out to be a genuine architect, and a women's rights group woman with hair cut short but apparently at random, possibly in an imitation of Scottie dog fur.

Janni Bolo was present only on the screen in front of them, walking around the studio audience with a microphone in her hand on knotty little legs and spike heels. She wore a tight mini-skirt and much jewellery, and seemed supported only by a floating mass of glossy hair. Her legs looked like ropes.

Then he was sitting in the bright makeup room and having slime rubbed on his face. There was another monitor above the mirror, and a closeup of Janni Bolo appeared, so large as to make Ted recoil. Her face, framed by enormous gold earrings and a gold necklace, was deeply lined and leathery, caked with dark makeup. He could almost smell the perfume from the screen.

From the sofas in the next room he heard an assistant asking the architect questions. 'Are there any more women in the profession now than say five years ago, or last year? Would you say modern architecture is more of a male mindset than a feminine one?' This made him even more uneasy, though he couldn't say why. He tried to remember what the real name for Scottie dog was. Some kind of spaniel.

'Edward?' said the clipboard. 'Let's go.'

The three panellists followed her down a dark corridor, and then were suddenly in a painful glare. Ted shaded his eyes so that he could see the studio audience, sitting on banked seats like bleachers. First he registered simply that they were fat, every one of them, like a rack of slugs, then that they were mostly women in early middle age. The silence was ecclesiastical. Their faces were pale smudges over rows of bright sweatshirts and silk blouses: fuchsia, royal blue, several in a sort of radioactive green; Ted tried to make a mental note of the colour. Narrowing his eyes, he made out a few skinny ones in the front rows, emaciated teenage girls with terrible acne and an obviously dangerous lack of iron in the bloodstream, and then a couple of wizened little men in acrylic sweaters, cowering as if beaten. As the panellists' microphones were attached, the audience stared in attitudes of penitential sadness.

Ted could hardly see anything under the glare. Someone was sitting him down and attaching his microphone, and then Janni Bolo was on them in a floral cloud, smiling and tottering on her rope legs in gleaming black tights. Ted shook her hand; it was like grasping a knot of beaded necklaces.

Two elephantine cameras glided around disconcertingly, manned by jockeys with headsets. They all seemed to be nosing too close to Ted, sniffing at him. Next to one, a technician was counting down on his fingers under the big black lens, and the red light on top flashed on. Janni Bolo turned to the audience, lifted her microphone and announced, 'Women and Architecture. What's the connection? What's the difference? Who cares?'

Ted's stomach seemed to slip away from him. He looked around wildly. The architect and the Scottie-hair woman seemed perfectly composed. Women and architecture?

'Maurice Mecklenburgh is an architect with Mecklenburgh Schwitzer and Williams, author of numerous ...'

Ted's head spun. His knuckles hurt from squeezing the arms of his chair. Women and architecture. He tried to gather the fragments of what he had intended to say about social spaces. Convention of positioning of bars, function of certain oddly-designed nightclubs, idea of the deliberately menacing. Nothing about women.

'Theresa da Silva, director of the Oakville Women's Resource Centre and author of *The Flesh Within: Women Survivors of Facial Reconstruction Talk about Love*, and Edward Owen, a playwright and a specialist in the sociology of architecture.'

The audience applauded.

'Theresa da Silva,' said Janni Bolo, 'do you think the kind of modern *architecture* we're seeing these days –' she said architecture as if she were saying *infantilism* – 'is this kind of stuff a male kind of way of seeing things?'

'Well, Janni,' said Scottie hair, 'you know at our women's centre we see a lot of very creative women, and I think in fairness you can talk about a sort of, what you could call a *compassionate* way of seeing, of envisioning things and a *non-*compassionate, and what we find is –'

Ted felt his focus slipping away. He fixed his gaze on the audience, on a balding little man with his hands folded in his lap. The man was staring down at the floor of the studio with an air of such utter hopelessness he seemed about to cry. Ted strained his eyes to see if the man's lip was quivering. He couldn't make it out. The man's chin was sinking perceptibly lower.

Theresa da Silva was interrupted by Janni Bolo. 'Maurice Mecklenburgh, now you're a practising *architect*, what do you have to say about all this?'

Maurice Mecklenburgh didn't look happy. He crossed his legs, waggled his foot and folded his arms. 'I assure you,' he said loudly, 'that these considerations are not at all relevant to the architect's profession.' His face glowed a deep red, like embers. 'Architecture,' he said, even louder, 'architecture, like all the arts, is subject to historical trends. When Alberti, for example, first wrote out his masterwork –'

Immediately, Ted sensed a shift in the audience, a tension. The expressions were turning from melancholy to distracted, as if they smelled farts. They didn't like this. Rapidly, Ted began changing his ideas about social spaces. Women in bars. Treated like sex objects. Bad. Change bars somehow.

'Beautiful,' shouted the architect, 'entirely beautiful. Take Pal-LA-dio, even –'

No, no, thought Ted. Wrong. Look out. The fat faces were now distinctly bitter, Brueghelesque. They had all suddenly turned drunk. Soon they would be howling and biting people. Janni Bolo was grinning.

'Just a minute,' said the fur hair. 'Just a minute here. This is a perfect example. Just look at the way you're talking. Elitist. Totally elitist.'

Sudden applause. Ted tried to concentrate. What kind of dog was a Scottie? Retriever? No.

Then Janni Bolo was talking again, pacing back and forth at the front of the stage. 'An article in the *New York Times* recently reported that sixty-five percent of American women feel they don't have places where they would feel comfortable going alone for a drink or a coffee. Don't you find that? Maybe we'll get some audience feedback here.' She tottered off the stage and began holding out her microphone to the pale faces.

As various inaudible women stood up to talk, Ted began to relax. He understood the game now: it wasn't a conversation, but you had a few seconds to say a little piece, and your piece was supposed to represent your type. It didn't matter if it followed logically on what was said before. He wondered what his type was. New generation. Looser values. Someone who goes to bars.

A makeupless natural blonde in a fuchsia silk blouse was standing at the microphone. 'Theresa,' she whispered, 'I was wondering if, with your experience, you'd agree that women have trouble expressing their sexual needs?'

As dog fur answered, Ted fixed on a grey-haired woman with enormous breasts whose nipples were faintly visible through a sweatshirt. Then he went back to the little bald man's hunched shoulders. The man was staring at the speaker with doleful compassion.

'Thank you,' whispered the fuchsia blonde, and sat down.

'Edward Owen,' Janni Bolo said, 'now, Edward, you're a member of the younger generation, what do you —'

'Oh, come now, Janni,' said Ted heartily. 'I'm not a member of the younger generation. I'm twenty-six.'

Laughter. Good. A red-lit camera loomed in his face.

He was about to say, 'Keats was twenty-two when he *died*,' but remembered the architect's reception and stifled it. He said, 'The younger generation are the teenagers. And the teenagers are very important. We should be asking them for their opinion on these matters, more often, because — ' He wavered. The little bald man was staring at him intently, a fire in his eyes. 'Because they're our future,' said Ted firmly.

Much applause. The bald man particularly enthusiastic. Ted plunged onward. 'Anyway, Janni, I'm particularly interested in *social* spaces, you know, like bars and night-clubs and coffee places, you know, places where you – where women can just relax, you know, and what I would most like to see in these designs is, is indeed something a little more feminine, something that would make us all feel a little more human, and, and you know this is something my generation feels, we feel these are our values, this is a contribution we can make, and what we would like to see is an attitude that would make women not feel so much like *sex objects.*'

Huge applause. It seemed to last half a minute. The architect glared at him, his face an inflated eggplant. Dog hair stared stonily forward.

'Thank you,' said Janni Bolo. 'We'll be right back.'

The red light winked out. In the applause, the cameramen straightened and stretched. Janni Bolo dropped her mike and smiled at them all. 'Wonderful.' A technician was removing Ted's lapel mike.

'That's it?' he said.

'Thank you so much,' said Janni Bolo.

'If you don't mind,' said the clipboard woman, pulling on the back of Ted's chair, 'we have to move you kind of fast, to get the next guests on.'

In the dank hangar next to the studio, the clipboard said, 'Thanks again, terrific,' and disappeared behind a metal door. The architect strode off down a concrete corridor full of cables. Scottie hair looked around, bewildered.

'Well,' said Ted. 'Thank you. I mean, nice to meet you.'

She blinked at him. Ted turned and walked purposefully in a random direction, leaving her standing between a vast metal door and a bank of poles and lights, her hands in the pockets of her mauve cotton sack dress.

He found the pink green room again and had his makeup removed, and then he found the carpeted front lobby. As he entered, the studio audience was filing through, appearing from another door. They were being herded by assistants towards the glass front doors but first had to pass a table in the middle, where two security guards were dispensing, to each person, a rolled-up tube of paper and a pink Janni Bolo coffee mug. They each took their gift silently.

Ted hung back to watch the procession. It reminded him of documentary films he had seen of famine relief stations in Africa. Clutching their mugs and posters, and struggling with many other brightly coloured and voluminous bags, the studio audience shuffled out the front doors and onto a Janni Bolo Shuttle Bus.

Standing next to him, also watching the ceremony, was a short blond woman smoking a cigarette. She held a coat and a briefcase. He looked at her again and realized it was the mousy person who had booked him on the show, the one he had met at Boss. He couldn't remember her name. 'Hey,' he said. 'Hi.'

She turned. Her eyes were red, her face sallow. 'Oh, hi, Ted.' She held the cigarette between her teeth, put her arms behind her back and began doing some kind of stretching exercise with her neck and shoulders. 'Kind of tired.'

'You're going home?'

She nodded. 'Okay. Coast is clear.' The lobby was emptying.

Ted walked with her through the glass doors, and shuddered as they stepped into a cold wind on the potholed parking lot. The highway ran alongside the lot, raised on massive concrete posts. The sky was grey, but the rain had stopped. There was a thunder of traffic from the overpass.

Grunting and farting, the Janni Bolo Shuttle Bus began to pull away from the building, and pallid faces peered out the windows. As it passed, two of them recognized Ted, and pointed. Ted waved, and the entire bus waved back, smiling and pointing.

The mouse was fumbling with keys next to a car. 'You live downtown?' she said.

'Yes. Right downtown.'

'I'm going to Pickering.'

'Oh. Well.' He watched the shuttle bus move onto the ramp, towards the overpass, and shivered. 'What do the audience get?'

She opened her car door. 'What do they get? What do you mean?'

'I mean for doing this. What's in it for them. Beside the mugs.'

'They get a poster too.'

'That's it? A mug and a poster?'

'Yeah. But it's –' He voice was drowned in the wail of a passing eighteen-wheeler.

'What?'

She shouted, 'It's free for them. Plus transportation. We send the bus to pick them up in various suburbs.' She threw her bag and coat into the car.

Ted nodded. He looked down to see that he was standing in a puddle. He stepped out of it, shaking his shoe. 'So what do they get out of it?'

'What do they *get*?' She laughed shortly, threw her cigarette away. 'It's TV. It's magic. It's magic for them.'

Ted nodded. He looked around at the parking lot, the roaring highway, the brown brick wall of the building. It was flat and long like a supermarket. He turned up the collar on his coat. 'Well,' he said. 'Thanks for this.'

She waved and started the car. As she pulled out of the lot Ted realized he had forgotten to obtain his taxi chit for the ride home. 'Terrier,' he said aloud. 'Scotch terrier.'

FIFTEEN

November 15

Dear Mom and Dad,

I got Dad's cheque on Thursday; thanks a lot, again. I should have some more money soon. My friend Max, who seems to make a lot of money in various media here, is apparently back in town and called here to offer me a job. I'm not sure what it is yet, but knowing Max it will undoubtedly be interesting. Unfortunately I wasn't here when he called, and I haven't managed to reach him again.

Yes, Mom, don't get all excited, of course you can see the TV show I did, I'm not trying to hide anything from you: it's on next Friday at ten a.m., but it's just not really that interesting.

It did go rather well, though, so I should be doing more TV appearances soon, I imagine, which will probably be career-useful, don't you think, if people see them?

And yes, Mom, Thanksgiving was fine. I was invited to two separate family dinners, so I ate well.

I must stop now. I'll write again soon. Thanks again.

Love,

Ted

Sitting on Georgina's futon, Ted reread this letter, then folded it and put it in an envelope. His eyes were stinging furiously from the new contact lenses. He cursed and rubbed them again. They began to water. Loud laughter came from downstairs; soon he would have to stop skulking and go down and greet Go-Go's friend Mike, who had arrived unannounced with a gang of bike couriers. The living room was covered in sleeping bags and bicycle wheels.

He stretched and put on his shoes. As he came down the stairs, blinking, his red eyes streaming water, he smelled cigarettes and bodies. A young man was saying, 'No, no, this chick, man, is like evil. We met her and Steve in Miracle Mart and I'm like hi, how are you doing, and she just doesn't say a word. She's just staring, like boring into my head, you know, like a drill, zzz-zz-zzz-zz! And I just turn around and get some, I don't know, bacon or something, and I can just feel her eyes in the back of my head, like she's putting the evil eye on me. Evil.'

'Bacon, man,' said another supine cyclist. 'I love bacon. Like in a BLT?'

'Hi,' said Ted, stepping over a backpack. Go-Go and Mike were sitting on the sofa, enlaced.

'Hi, Ted,' said Go-Go softly.

Mike glared, said nothing, spinning a bicycle seat by its alloy seat-post. There were three other couriers, in spandex shorts and torn T-shirts, sprawled on the floor. With the new contacts Ted could see every tiny detail of their appearance as if it were outlined in black. Two had long hair, two had shaved heads, two had nose-rings and one had a small animal bone piercing one ear. One had a goatee and a metal stud through his lower lip. No one moved.

'Excuse me,' said Ted, making towards the kitchen.

'That guy last night,' said the one with the bone. 'I could tell he thought he was going to score with that chick. But he just totally wasn't going to score.'

'That guy,' said the goatee, 'he's okay to be around, but sometimes he's so fucking ... I don't know. You know?'

'I was just totally ready to totally fucking go to sleep.'

Ted poured some water in the kitchen and retreated to his room, where he tried to read. It was a book Go-Go had given him on witchcraft and it seemed mostly to be an attack on thinking 'with your head' instead of 'in balance'. He hoped John would come home with something for them to do. He closed the book and reached for the battered postcard lying beside the bed. He stared at the technicolor image: a snow-capped mountain. He turned it over and read its message again. It was dated from two weeks before.

Dear Teddy,
It's Friday morning and I can't get even my regular miso because it's a special flower petal day and everything's closed, so I'll have to go downtown and pay for American cereal, which I hate to do. What new clothes have you bought? They take this parade so seriously, I wish I could hear your jokes about it. I might be back soon. Can't wait to see you. Will you take me for coffee in the Bakery?
Love XOXOXO Georgina

There was a stomping on the stairs; voices approached, Go-Go's petulant and Mike's sarcastic. Ted couldn't hear what they were saying. Her door opened and closed and their voices were suddenly clear in his room. He looked at the heating duct that joined the two rooms, next to the futon: they must have been sitting right next to it, up against the wall.

'Listen,' Mike was saying, 'I don't know what you're hinting at but if it's what I'm thinking it is, then okay, do what you want. What I don't get is ... I don't get how you think you can give *me* any shit about, about shit that I do. Fuck man. Like you do what you want and I do what I want, fine, cool, if that's what it is.'

'Well, that's what you always say you want, isn't it?' came Go-Go's voice. 'Fine. If that's cool, cool. But you don't seem to think it's so cool.'

Ted didn't move. He knew he should get up, make a noise so they could hear how close he was.

'Well, fuck,' came Mike's voice. 'It's cool.'

'Okay. So why are you being so shitty? I don't even know why you're here, if you don't want to ...'

'Well, fuck. What do you expect. If you'd talked to me or something, or if I had any fucking idea what was going on, or for how long ...'

'Mike, nothing. There's been hardly anything.'

'Great. Great. Hardly anything. I feel so much better. What the fuck does that mean? What the fuck is going on here? And who, *who* the fuck are we talking about?'

Ted began to get up, then stopped. Any move he made now would be audible to them. He shifted slightly on the futon.

'Mike,' Go-Go was saying. 'It doesn't matter. It was nothing. It's over.'

'Is it someone at the theatre?'

'No. Mikey.'

'Someone in the house? John?'

'Oh, John, don't make me laugh. Listen, I think it's really great that you care so much. I'm really flattered. How's Trixie, or Treena or whatever she's called?'

Ted heard a rustle as one of them stood up in the next room. 'Listen,' came Mike's voice, more distant. 'I don't need this shit, okay? You do what you want.'

'Okay.' There was a silence, then more movement, then a low murmuring. They must have been standing together in the middle of the room. Ted stood up, then stopped moving as he heard a giggle, probably Go-Go's. Mike was talking in a low voice. Suddenly he said loudly, 'Him?'

Go-Go laughed again.

'That guy? I thought it must be that guy, but I just couldn't believe it. I *knew* it was that guy. Shit. Mister Holt Renfrew fashion? The guy ... that guy could be a lawyer or something.'

Ted stared down at his shoes, standing motionless in the middle of the room. He heard Go-Go saying, 'Shh.' Then, softly, 'The clothes are new. When he first got here he looked like a prep.'

'He go to Southern with John?' said Mike. 'Figures. Those guys all dress like they're about to ... go camping. Then they get rich and they dress like they're fat. That guy isn't fat. He doesn't need to dress like that.'

''Mike ...' Her voice grew faint, but sounded plaintive. Ted heard the words 'before' and 'okay'. Then, '*Want* it to be so fucked up. Do you?' Mike's reply was inaudible. Go-Go continued, 'I really don't. I want it to be okay. I don't want to do this shit.'

Mike muttered something else and left the room. Ted heard him in the corridor, then on the stairs. He heard Go-Go move towards her door, and close it. Then her room was silent. Ted bent towards the heating duct to listen. For a moment he was convinced she was standing in absolute silence, but then came a rustling of bedclothes and he heard what he expected, a repressed sniffling.

As Ted straightened, a pain in his stomach caught him. He realized his stomach had been cramping for some minutes; now it was churning. He stood a little stooped on the futon rubbing his belly, his face contorted. His contact lenses felt like sandpaper on his corneas. The knot in his abdomen was surely a reminder of his evil. He tried to breathe deeply and relax. He could smell stale clothing from the plastic milk crate in the corner. He would have to leave the room, even if it meant Go-Go would hear him and realize he had overheard. She might as well. Served him right. 'Shit,' he said through his teeth, exhaling. 'Shit you are.'

There were heavy steps on the stairs. For an instant Ted pictured Mike, coming to get him with a Kryptonite lock, but then he heard the singing: it was the deep voice of John, pretending to be a woman on the verge of orgasm. 'Je *suis*, je *suis*, je suis pour le Common*wealth*,' he chanted, gasping between words. His accent was atrocious. As he mounted the stairs he changed to a computer voice. 'In-som-ni-ac,' he growled. 'All. Systems. Activated.'

Ted's belly gave a twinge and relaxed slightly. John said 'Em. Martha. Marvellous Martha. Em-em-ememememmm.' He stopped before Ted's door. 'Now which asshole is behind *this* door?' he shouted.

Ted didn't reply, looking at the heating duct.

'You naked?' John said. 'Jerking off? You got your big diaper on or what?'

'Come in dude,' said Ted. There was no reaction from the other side of the heating duct.

'Okay,' said John, entering and closing the door behind him. He looked Ted up and down. 'Uh-huh. Yoga?'

'Belly,' said Ted, rubbing his.

'Belly. Okay. Um, abdomen, torso. Nipple. Your turn. Elbow. Go.'

'Feeling a bit tense,' said Ted. Next door, Go-Go's door opened and closed behind her. Ted heard her running down the stairs. 'Shit,' he said, grimacing.

John looked at him curiously. 'Something wrong with Go-Go?'

Ted nodded. 'I guess she's having problems with Mike.'

John laughed. 'Wouldn't worry about that. It's what makes them happy. They fuck each other up for fun. Trust me. They've been doing it for years. Months, anyway.' He looked at Ted again. 'Something wrong with *you* and Go-Go?'

'No no. Just a bit tense about my meeting tomorrow. With Queal.'

'Now who's this again now?' said John in his Maritimer voice.

'Augustus Queal, runs the City Core Development Program Reading Series. Since I have a play being workshopped, you know the one Malcolm's organizing, which they really think they're going to perform, Malcolm and his friends, in the Fringe Festival, I qualify for a reading in their sort of 'up-and-coming' category. Queal says he's really into promoting local writers, giving unknowns a chance and so on. I was thinking of taking a scene with only three of the characters in it, we could use me, Malcolm and Ursula to read, and do a read-through of just the one scene. You get a half-hour public reading in the Dufflet Centre, in the Spinder Auditorium, which is huge, it's a great space. It would be great. And they do all the publicity. Derek got me a meeting with Queal to talk about the play and my background and so on, and I hear he's something of a tough nut.'

'Kul,' said John.

'What?'

'Kul. Kul.' He was being a surfer again. 'Hope it works out. Teddy, what's this play about, anyway?'

'Oh,' said Ted, looking about the room, 'young people in a city.'

'What happens to them?'

'There are bad people and you get confused, because you don't know what's bad about them.'

John pondered. 'What do they do that's bad?'

'They fuck you up. Then the hero starts learning how to fuck people up, because he's trying to be cool, and he fucks up this innocent chick. Then he can't figure out if he's bad or not, too.'

'Kul.' John nodded. 'And Ted, this hero, he's a white, middle-class, educated guy in his mid-twenties?'

Ted smiled. 'I thought I'd try it for a change.'

'Kul. Anyway, I came in here to tell you about the new club. Opening Friday night, that's tomorrow. I think I can crack us an invite. Nobody knows about it yet. But they say it's going to be the coolest people. They say it's going to be a reincarnation of Spleen. It may even belong to Max, although he can't own anything in his own name these days.'

'Who says this?'

'Oh everyone knows. You may want to go. Maybe you'll run into Max there.'

'Excellent,' said Ted. 'I'll go. I have my actors' party to go to first. But yours will be late, right? Where is it?'

'I don't know yet. Nobody knows. I'll have to get back to you.' John turned to leave.

'What's it called?'

John turned back, a crooked smile on his face. He said slowly, with an air of triumph, 'Nobody even knows *that*. It's going to be *very* cool.' He left and went upstairs, singing, 'Je suis le professeu-sseu-sseur de gymnasti-ti-tique ...'

SIXTEEN

TED SAT in the reception area of the City Core Development Program, outside Augustus Queal's office. The secretary made an uninterrupted clicking at her computer keyboard. When the phone rang it made that subdued electronic chime – *deedle doodle deedle* – that left these offices so much quieter than the ones Ted had worked in as a teenager. There were no more typewriters, no more ringing bells. It was like a library. The carpet was grey; there were posters made from blown-up dust jackets from books by Canadian authors. Ted hadn't heard of any of them. A Chinese-food delivery man came in, carrying garlic-smelling packages. 'That way,' the secretary pointed, without looking up. When the man left, having delivered his packages somewhere in the corridor she guarded, she looked up at Ted. 'Gus will see you now. Go on in.' She pointed.

Ted took his script and walked in the direction she indicated. As he rounded the corner he heard the shouting. 'It's our name and it's how we make our money,' came the nasal voice, strangely slurred or muffled. 'We gave you permission to make the tape in our space, and yes, the reading itself had our name on it. But I did *not* give you permission to release a tape with our name on it. Nobody asked me for permission about this. Nobody talked to me.' The voice sounded almost hysterical.

Then Ted saw the office: a mass of papers and books piled on a desk, around it, on the two small chairs, and fast-food wrappings: doughnut boxes, pizza boxes, big plastic Coke bottles, and the two newly opened bags of Chinese food. An obese man was sunk behind the desk, shouting into the phone, digging with stubby fingers into a carton of fried rice. He was talking with his mouth full. 'We'll just have to initiate legal proceedings,' he was saying. He wore round glasses, and veins bulged on his balding forehead and on his enormous neck. His face was bright red. Ted couldn't tell how far his bulk actually extended behind the desk; his head seemed afloat on it, moored in a turgid sea. Ted waited in the doorway until the man had slammed the phone down. 'Yes?' said Queal, looking at him with hostility.

Ted moved forward, extending his hand. 'Ted Owen. I'm the playwright Derek told you about.'

'Just a minute,' said Queal, picking up the phone. 'Yes? Yes?' Ted sat down. 'Hello Don. No. No, I'm sorry Don. Those are the conditions. You signed the contract, you saw them right in front of you. No other public readings for six months after your reading at the Dufflet. I don't care how much they pay. Just a minute.' Queal took a bite of a dough-nut, then punched another button on the phone. 'Yes? Yes? No. No I won't reconsider. Tell him Legal Aid is there for people like him. Just a minute.' He prodded the phone again. 'Don? Don, listen. Do you know who we have reading here this season? Let me tell you.' Queal's voice rose even higher; his fingers scrabbled frantically in the rice carton. His forehead bore a shiny film. 'Let me tell you. We've got two Medicis, one Goncourt, three Commonwealth Best First Book, one Booker, one Aer Lingus and *five* Governor Generals this season, and you think I'm interested in making a special allowance for *you*?' He slammed his palm down on the desk. Ted jumped. Queal hung up the phone and looked at him. 'Ted Owen.'

'Yes.'

'We have no room left in this playwrights' series.'

'No room at all?'

'Not this season. Not a chance.' Queal was breathing heav-ily, still angry at the unknown caller.

'Oh.' Ted looked at the script in his hands. 'I understood

... Listen, I have the script here, it's going to be performed in a month, less than a month, and I think it would really suit the reading format, it's quite entertaining, perhaps I could simply leave it with you, or better yet read some of it to you – '

Queal grunted, gasped. 'Leave it with me.' He extended a greasy hand.

Outside on the bright street, Ted wondered if he should have surrendered the script. All the way home on the subway he pictured Queal's office, the script under a carton of French fries, or Queal maniacally tearing it up and eating it.

When he got home he realized he really didn't have anything to do until the party that evening, with the actors. It was at the house of Malcolm's friend Ursula, an angular German. He would have to break the bad news to them about the reading, and then try to talk to them about how the rehearsal process was going. So far Malcolm had led them through various visualization and conceptualization exercises, and they all seemed happy. At every meeting, Malcolm had proudly told him, at least one broke down into confessional tears. Ted wasn't sure if they had got to the script yet.

He was taking his coat off in the hall, straddling the pile of photographic lights and poles, when Go-Go came at him. She just walked out of the kitchen, leaned against the banister and stared at him. Her face was red. 'Hi,' he said.

'I don't know what you think happened between us,' she said.

Ted breathed deeply. 'Hi, Go-Go. Hi.'

'What do you think happened between us? Or are you too afraid to even talk about it?'

Ted nodded. 'No. We should talk. Let's talk. How are you doing?'

Go-Go slipped past him and walked up the stairs. Ted followed her. 'Let's talk, ' he said.

He followed her into her room. She sat on her futon and

stared at him sullenly. 'Listen,' he said. 'I didn't think we should talk while Mike was around. I didn't want to screw things up between you.'

'Thanks,' she said, taking a cigarette out of a packet.

Don't smoke, thought Ted, please don't smoke, I can't stand it. 'I didn't realize you were upset about anything.'

Go-Go began to cry. Ted sat awkwardly on the edge of the futon, put a hand on her outstretched leg. 'I'm sorry,' he said weakly. 'Listen, I thought it was clear, what happened between us. The way you talked about picking men up in bars, and the way you talked about your relationship with Mike, I – '

'Don't,' said Go-Go through tears.

'Don't what? I knew you were going out with Mike, you knew I – I knew he was coming into town soon, is he still in town?'

'He left this morning.' Go-Go puffed on her cigarette.

'Oh. Were things okay?'

In a calmer voice she said, 'Things were better, by the time he left.' She gave a choked laugh, wiping her eyes. 'I guess he realized he liked me more than he thought.'

'So he knows something happened between you and me,' said Ted.

She narrowed her eyes in the smoke. 'You know he does.'

Ted looked at his hand lying weakly on her leg. 'Right. And he wasn't pleased?'

Go-Go smiled. 'He was surprised. And it turns out his chick, Tracie or something, in the squat, has moved out. So now he's really pissed off. But I think it made us both think.'

'That's good. That's good. I've always thought it's silly to leave things open like that. You've got to know where you stand in a relationship. I think that's good, then. I bet things will come back to normal again soon.' *Cockbuggerfuckshit*, he said to himself, *bumfartpoop*. 'I guess I thought we both knew where we stood.'

'I figured that,' said Go-Go, her voice wavering again. 'I

figured that out when you didn't touch me for three weeks, then you stopped even trying to see me, and now you avoid me.'

'I don't avoid you.' She was crying again, silently. *Fuckshit-bumshit, fuck*, thought Ted, *fuckfuckfuck*. He wanted to take her and kiss her or flee.

'Ted,' she said, 'I like Mike, I really do. I like him a lot. And I really want things to work out between us. But it wasn't just because of him that I wanted us to ... that I thought you might ... '

'Right,' said Ted, stroking her leg and dreading the unequivocal statement he would have to make. Suddenly and equally predictably he was deeply bored.

She pushed his hand off. 'I fucking like you. I fucking thought you might like me too.'

Ted was silent, looking away. He said, 'I'm sorry,' but now he was irritated, bored with contrition. He glanced at the open door with yearning. 'I'm sorry. I really thought something might work out between us too, but right now I'm kind of fucked up, I've got a lot that seems to be going on and a lot that really isn't going on and should be, and I guess I – '

'I guess you're in love with Miranda,' said Go-Go suddenly.

Ted's boredom contorted his face, and before he knew it he had said, 'Yes. Yes I am.'

Go-Go forced a laugh. 'I knew it. It's always chicks like that. Fucking Georgina – if Georgina had been living here you would have fallen in love with her instead.'

Ted rose angrily. He felt trapped in the room, interrogated. 'I did,' he said. 'I am in love with her. Too.'

Go-Go's sullen face crumpled completely. She drew her knees up and put her head down onto them and sobbed. Amazed, Ted bent towards her, put his hand on her shoulder. 'Get out,' she whispered. 'Get out.'

He straightened and withdrew his hand. 'Oh Go-Go, I'm sorry, I – '

'Get out.' Her voice was firm.

Ted retreated to the door. He stopped with his hand on the handle. 'Go-Go, listen – '

'Would you just fucking get out please?'

He stepped out of the room and quietly closed the door behind him.

'New Brunswick?' said the red-haired one with a pillbox hat like Malcolm's. 'You're from New Brunswick? I set my hair on fire in New Brunswick once.'

'What were you doing in New Brunswick, Jenny?' said Malcolm.

'I was shooting a film. In Halifax. You remember Krishna Wilson's film, Shitstick? I was the dead girl on the bicycle.'

'Halifax,' said Ted, 'is in Nova Scotia.' He felt himself swaying slightly as he said it. He was on his third or fourth beer, he wasn't sure.

'Krishna still with Buddha/Dada?' asked another actor, the tall manly one.

Ted looked around at the crowded apartment. Actors with long hair, with crew cuts, with denim jackets and leggings and military fatigues, standing, sitting crosslegged, hugging, acting. Some South American music was playing in a heavy pall of smoke.

'So are you in the business too?' It was Jenny, the dead girl on the bicycle, looking at him.

'In the acting business?' said Ted. 'No. Not at all.'

'Oh come on,' said Malcolm, wrapping his arm around Ted's shoulder. 'Ted's being very modest. He's the one who wrote this play we're rehearsing now. And he's been working in film.'

'Film?' said Jenny, 'what film?'

'I wasn't – '

'Ted worked on *Flight Into Shadow*,' said Malcolm. 'With Julian Claude.'

'Julian Claude?' said Jenny. 'The English guy?'

'Yes.'

'So did you meet him? What's he like?'

'Ursula!' said Malcolm, in the German fashion. Oorsoola. 'Our host,' he said to Ted.

Ursula was approaching; she was also tall, but bony and pinched. Her straight blond hair hung to her shoulders. 'Hello sweetie,' she said with a heavy accent, kissing and hugging Malcolm. 'Hello, Ted.' She extended a long Klimtian hand.

The red-haired dead girl on the bicycle broke away and slipped effortlessly into the even thicker crowd in the bright kitchen. Voices greeted her joyously there.

'Ursula,' boomed the tall man, Dave or something. 'How's rehearsing with Lori these days? Flaky or what?'

'God,' said Ursula, rolling her eyes, 'Don't even, don't even talk to me about it.'

'She still into the apex of emotion thing?'

Ursula turned to Ted. 'I'm rehearsing a play with a director who is a little inexperienced. She has this idea that all the characters don't communicate, see, so they can't look at each other, they must look at the point where the lines of emotion cross, on the stage, she calls it the apex, the apex of emotion. So I'm talking to you but I can't look at you, I'm saying ''I love you I vant to fuck you'' but I've got to look over here, at this apex, the fucking apex.'

'Sounds terrific,' said Ted. 'You have such a lovely accent.'

'Rasputin!' said Ursula loudly. 'Rasputin! Off the couch! He scratches the furniture. He's not mine.'

'Those Krishna's cats?' asked Malcolm, bending to pet one.

'Yes. Rasputin's the pretty one, that one's Metatext.'

Past Ursula's head, in the crowded kitchen, Ted could see the dead girl on the bicycle whispering in the ear of another woman. They were both looking at Ted.

'Colin!' said the tall actor.

Another actor who looked almost identical – short hair,

denim shirt – was coming towards them. Dave greeted him enthusiastically. 'Good to see you,' said Colin. 'Listen. Message for you from Richard.'

'Which is?'

'Which is, he's busy. Busy, busy, *busy*. But he's got all your messages, and he would definitely like to get together with you.'

'Ah,' said the tall one.

'You know he's moving out, right? There's been a whole *thing*.'

'Ah. With?'

'Yes,' said Colin.

'I see.'

'Beer, anyone?' asked Ted, moving towards the kitchen. Malcolm followed him. The kitchen was packed, bright but hazy with smoke. He penetrated the crowd around the fridge and grabbed another beer. The group was all listening intently to Jenny; she was telling a story with great emotion. 'They're beautiful, and so warm for walking, not so warm for your bike with the wind, but they're so *soft* and beautiful,' she was saying.

'You need mitts for a bike, really, in the winter, not gloves,' said Malcolm.

'Right, well, anyway I didn't really *need* these but they just *felt* so good so I got them. And all I knew about angora was cat fur, you know like an angora cat. I mean I knew it couldn't be cat fur but I just didn't think about it. I'm so *stupid*. And then Darlene told me it was rabbit fur and I'm like ...' She made a face of horror, clutching her neck and sticking her tongue out. 'I just hadn't even thought about it. And suddenly I'm walking around with like rabbit fur all over me and I'm thinking oh my God, how did they trap this rabbit? This rabbit probably spent the last hours of its life mangled in some sort of trap.' Her voice began to quaver. 'And then I thought, maybe, because I love the gloves so much, I guess, I thought maybe they shear the rabbits without hurting them. Do you think it's possible? That they get it off without hurting them?' She looked at Malcolm.

'Sure,' said Malcolm in his deep voice. 'It's entirely possible.' He put his hand on her shoulder and started massaging her neck. His knotted arm emerged from his short-sleeved shirt; the black skin shone. Ted was envious. 'They probably don't hurt them at all. Don't worry about it. Your shoulders are like steel. Let it out a little.'

'I don't really see how they could do that,' said a short man, shaking his head and staring down at his beer. 'It wouldn't seem possible, to shear individual rabbits. Nope.' He sighed. 'They just kill 'em,' he said dolefully.

'Jason, don't,' said a woman.

Jenny wiped a tear from her eye. 'That feels so good,' she said to Malcolm, sniffling. 'I just can't stand to feel like I'm some kind of murderer, walking around with them on. I would throw them away but they're so expensive. I would give them to Goodwill but then somebody *else*, some *street* person would probably be walking around with dead rabbit fur on their hands, and that's the last thing *they* need.'

Ted didn't understand this last part but Malcolm seemed to; he gave her a big hug. Ted took his beer back into the living room and found Ursula. She was talking to a small group about childhood games. 'Red Rover is the one where you have to run at a line of people?'

'No no. British Bulldog.'

'I loved that one.'

'I *hated* it.'

'Ursula?' said Ted. He took her aside and told her about his slim chances at the reading series, but she didn't seem worried.

'Well,' she said, 'a play-reading is never very interesting anyway.'

Ted found his coat, thanked Ursula, said goodbye to many unknown people, but couldn't find Malcolm. Someone pointed down some stairs to the basement. With his coat on, Ted stepped gingerly down the stairs, then looked around the dark basement room. Malcolm and the red-haired Jenny were sitting on an old sofa, both sideways, as Malcolm massaged her neck and shoulders. She was crying. Ted stood still for a moment. Malcolm was talking in a low voice. 'You've got to make your pain into a positive experience,' he was saying. 'You've got to own it. You own this pain.'

'Malcolm,' said Ted. 'See you.'

Outside, the night was densely black and cold; Ted's nostrils froze as he entered it. On a deserted corner he found a payphone and called John's answering machine as instructed. 'All. Systems. Activated,' came John's recorded voice. 'Special dudes dial the secret code. All the rest of you can leave a message. Marvellous Martha.' The beep came with unexpected suddenness as Ted fumbled in his wallet for the piece of paper. Shivering, he found the crumpled slip and opened it. In John's handwriting, it read '7-3-9'. Ted punched in the numbers. The tape whirred and clicked, and John's voice returned, this time fruitily British. 'Red leader heah. Come in red units. Red leader heah. Red Four, the intelligence report is in. Rendezvous point is a warehouse behind seven one nine Adelaide East, upstairs, enter by truck loading bay. Rendezvous at oh oh thirty hours. Red leader ovah.' Ted hung up, stepped out of the phone booth and hailed a taxi.

SEVENTEEN

'HOLOCAUST,' thundered the gravelly voice from the speakers, three walls of black boxes. The empty dance floor reverberated with the pounding of synthesized drumbeats, overlaid with a roar of fuzz, some kind of tribal chanting and a siren. The voice sounded Dutch or German. Perhaps Belgian. Why not Belgian?

Ted took another sip of his six-dollar beer and peered through the mist. With his new contact lens x-ray vision he caught another glimpse of the bondage girl, over at the opposite bar, her garters and cleavage. His groin seemed to contract, and she had vanished again.

He looked at his new watch. Midnight, and of course no John, no Miranda, no Max, no one. Ten bucks to enter, to find this vast cold room, six-dollar beer, these elaborate lights and black walls. There were lots of dark nooks and crannies, recesses hiding plush couches and low tables, all unoccupied except for one dim corner where a couple of scarily half-naked heavyweight lesbians could be dimly perceived, one on the other's lap, fondling each other's crewcuts and nose-rings. Ted resisted the urge to move closer and watch. Perhaps male prurience wasn't being invited.

The last blast of mist cleared slightly and he saw the three fetish girls again, their thighs and bellies, lingerie and latex, high stiletto boots, leaning against the other bar disconsolately. They looked embarrassed.

One had her back to him; a black G-string separated her large white buttocks so they quivered with every shift. Her straight black hair was cut like Cleopatra's, too shiny and perfect to be anything but a wig.

This was exciting in an uncomfortable way, so he looked away, at the only other women there, a table of suburban girls dressed as MTV stars, in diaphanous shirts and baggy jeans, who had tried dancing, earlier on, then subsided to a table to drink sodas.

There were only two men in the room: an obviously drugged bartender in a floppy wool toque, doing lonely pirouettes behind his bar, and the fetish girls' gay male friend whose leather jockstrap only succeeded in further exaggerating the emaciation of his legs, his pale little buttocks, his sunken and absurdly hairy chest. He swayed beside his friends, dejected and obviously embarrassed.

'HOLOCAUST,' growled the Belgian, his accent making him sound strangely educated. He probably was. Ted felt the soles of his feet vibrating with the floor. The throbbing was so loud as to be inaudible, only feelable. Probably he was supposed to be on special K or fantasy to appreciate it. He drained the beer and reached behind him for the second one he had providently ordered on entering. It was cool and wet in his hand, much like the previous ones.

A strobe light flickered intermittently. Ted drunkenly waved his hand before his face, watching it move without him in isolated frames. 'Proprioception,' he said aloud. No proprioception. It breaks down. He wished he had actually tried ecstasy, at least. He began to frown, thinking of all the things he hadn't done. He looked at his watch again.

Then a small group had entered; someone he knew; but his heart sank: it was blond Arthur in a ridiculously colourful ski-jacket and beige trousers, and a man and a woman in similar outdoor gear. Ted half expected them to be carrying pitons and paraffin lamps. They looked around happily, undismayed by the desolation, and clustered around the bar, where the bartender served them sullenly. The fetish girls shifted away from them, haughty.

Ted stood. Where Arthur was, Miranda couldn't be far

behind. Taking his beer, he crossed the floor and slapped Arthur's back. 'I don't think it's going to happen,' he shouted in Arthur's ear.

'Teddy!' Arthur shouted back. 'This is Greg, and Jeannette. Teddy! It'll happen! It's early yet! What time is it? Midnight? We're way too early! Give it time! It'll happen!'

'Miranda coming?'

Arthur shrugged. 'Oh yeah. She'll be here. She'll be here when it gets going.'

'ACID,' chanted the speakers. 'ECSTASY.'

Ted looked at the blond fetish girl, now two yards from him, who was looking at him, and smiled. She smiled back. Immediately Ted felt angular and ill-fitting, as if all his muscles had suddenly constricted. He jammed his hands in his pockets and looked away. 'I was hoping to see Max here,' he bawled to Arthur.

'He'll be here.' Arthur was nodding sagely. Arthur always knew that all was in order.

'Seen John tonight?'

Arthur shook his head. 'He'll be here.'

'John invited me. Here.' Ted swept his open hand around, suddenly angry, gesturing at the cloud of billowing smoke on the deserted floor. He began to feel panicky. He couldn't remember why he was here or why he was so drunk. His breathing was coming too fast. This was the kind of time when his father's face would materialize before him, asking about his financial provisions for retirement.

'Hey,' Arthur was screaming in his ear. 'Caught you on Janni Bolo. You were great. Really great. Good going.'

'Thanks,' shouted Ted, surprised. 'I didn't think anyone would see it. It was a joke, really, wasn't it?'

Now Arthur looked surprised. 'No, man, it was great, seriously. I think you sounded really serious. I think you showed those other guys where to get off.'

'I saw you too,' shouted the girl, Jeannette, moving to his

ear. 'You looked *great*. Terrific. You've obviously done TV before.'

Ted nodded, smiling. He felt a little better, though mystified. He turned again to the blond fetishist, catching her eye deliberately, and smiled. She smiled back, but still he remained nailed to his spot too far from her to talk, in the noise. She exuded some strange kryptonic force which paralysed him. 'Must reach power source,' he said to no-one.

'COME ON,' chanted the speakers, 'FUCK ME.'

He sipped his beer. It would be all right if he could really go all the way, he thought, really pick up latex-wrapped strangers in bars, but he couldn't because he kept looking at his watch and thinking that some people his age had babies and mortgages and *college funds*, incredible thought, how had they, what lives did they lead?

He tried to sip slower. The dance floor now seemed pitched at an unnatural angle. The throbbing beat was becoming metallic, a shower of fine needles on his head. 'FUCK ME. TRANCE.'

Suddenly the Cleopatra-wig woman was at his side, leaning over the bar, ordering a drink. Scotch, straight up. She swung her hair over her shoulder, almost swatting him with it, and a wave of distinctly troubling scent came with it: sweet oil, alcohol on her breath, female underarm. She was looking at him, smiling.

'Hi,' he said.

'How are you?' she shouted.

'Fine,' he shouted back, idiotically. He would have to do better than that, improvise in an artistic manner. He drew himself up and yelled, 'I don't even have an RRSP.'

'A what?' she mouthed. He could hear nothing but the thunderous banging, now overlaid with some kind of Arabic wail. The girl was standing closer now, dancing a little. For a moment he thought his hand was going to stroke her naked buttock, but then he thought he was going to fall over and his hand held onto the bar. 'No,' he screamed. 'Never had one. I've made no provision for my old age.'

She took a step back, staring at him with a face of alarm, then looked back at her friends imploringly.

'Can I buy you a drink?' he shouted.

She shook her head, looking terrified. 'Excuse me.' She moved away, three metres down the bar, to whisper with the others.

Ted put on his Affable Cretin face: he smiled and waved, nodding idiotically. He turned to look at the entrance just as Miranda made her entrance, hand in hand with Roger and his cigarette, and with Julia and tall Andreas behind. She wore cowboy boots and a flared black skirt that lifted high and flapped as she ran towards Ted and Arthur, with long, athletic strides, squealing, to embrace them both.

'Teddy!' she screamed, her hand behind his neck, 'but this is awful! Where's John? This is atrocious!'

'Horrendous,' said Ted with immense relief. 'Unsurpassed. Death, horror, cataclysm. I don't know.'

But she had withdrawn her hand and turned back to Arthur, with whom she was whispering earnestly. He was nodding judiciously. Roger hung back, smoking. He nodded at Ted.

The speed of the whumping beat seemed actually, if impossibly, to have increased, along with the volume; Ted felt as if his head were being driven over by a train. It began to be fun. He took a few uncertain steps back and forth in front of the bar to feel it fully. He could feel his skeleton rattling. If he just accepted it, it would determine the direction he took.

Perhaps this was dancing. He looked around proudly. People, dressed in black, some with flared sixties trousers, were beginning to dribble in, in twos and threes, although the place remained empty. One stick-thin woman wore a dark amorphous blob like an ice-pack on her head; an oversized floppy velvet cap, half Renaissance and half Doctor Seuss. 'Sam I am,' Ted shouted in the noise.

Two of the fetish girls had begun to dance, slowly and sensually, ignoring the music; a little performance piece. Miranda and Julia had gone off in search of a washroom. Ted smiled blandly at Arthur. He shouted, 'I suppose you have an RRSP.'

Arthur didn't hesitate. He nodded enthusiastically. 'I contribute right up to my maximum every year. Mutual funds are best, of course. And then I roll them into fixed-interest term – '

'Business good, or what?' Ted couldn't remember what Arthur did.

'Reasonable,' said Arthur, his head bobbing again. 'Moderate to reasonable. If you need help with RRSP's, I can tell you who I – '

'Tiger! Tiger – ' Miranda was shouting in his ear. She had bounded up to them, had a hand on each neck. 'Teddy! You guys have to come and look! It's incredible! I've found something!' She was breathless, and began tugging on them to follow her.

Taking her hand, Ted followed her bouncing skirt to the back of the club, through the smoke, past the nuzzling lesbians, and down a corridor that smelled of burning oil. Ted could feel Arthur close behind him. Miranda turned a corner and stopped before a laden coat rack. She put a finger to her lips. 'Watch,' she said.

The corridor really was dark, illuminated only by the red glow of an exit sign. Ted peered at the mass of coats. Then he perceived movement. One clump, behind the coat rack, was actually a person, two people, under coats, grappling. Miranda gripped his arm and pointed. They were moving regularly, rolling and grunting. Through the coats Ted saw a flash of red-glowing skin, a hairy thigh, a mass of dark hair, a red female belly. Arthur laughed loudly, then turned and trundled off down the corridor. 'Just now,' hissed Miranda in his ear, smiling viciously, 'I saw a *penis*!' She laughed and laughed.

Ted shook his head. 'Terrific,' he said. 'Marvellous. Too good.'

'Julia and I came here to talk,' said Miranda, withdrawing her hand. 'She got – '

Ted couldn't hear the rest of the sentence. The music had changed to what sounded like a series of fatal accidents on an assembly line. The coat rack was shaking, its hangers making a rhythmic clanging, either because of the beat or the palpitating mass of coats behind it.

Miranda was still talking. ' ... and now she's left.'

Ted was staring at the swinging coats. He began to make out squeaks that didn't seem to be coming from the speakers. 'She what? Who?'

'Julia!'

'She got – '

'FUCK ME,' blared the speakers. The coats were swinging wildly now; through them, Ted glimpsed a pair of tense male buttocks. The squeaking was definitely female.

'MAD,' shouted Miranda. 'She got MAD.'

'Mad? Julia? Why?'

' – down the fire escape!'

Ted looked around wildly, at the closed fire door under the exit sign. 'She went down the fire escape?'

Miranda curled her finger at him, moved towards the fire door. Ted took a last look at the naked female leg now snaking from underneath the coat rack, then turned and followed.

'She was upset,' said Miranda, opening the door. Cold, damp air entered, and the night sky above a parking lot. They both stepped out onto an iron fire escape, drawing deep breaths. 'Keep it open,' she said.

Ted propped the door open with a piece of rusted metal. Miranda lit a cigarette, leaning over the iron balustrade. Ted watched his breath form clouds in the night. The thumping of the club was audible but muffled, free of menace. 'Why was she upset?' said Ted.

Miranda sighed. 'She and I have a lot to talk about.' She bit a fingernail, something Ted had never seen her do. Ted shivered in the cold. He looked down at the garbage in the parking lot, trying not to think about the fact that Miranda had invited him out here, alone, onto this isolated fire escape, and that no one knew where they were.

Quickly, he cast a glance over her legs in black tights, the black motorcycle jacket, the twist of dark silk that held her hair in its smooth ponytail. Almost reluctantly, concentrating on each movement as if it were an incision in a complicated surgery, he reached out and put his hand on her shoulder, then moved closer to her, looking at her neck.

Absently, she reached up and patted his hand, then pulled it down to her side, where she entwined her fingers with his. Quickly, he put his nose into her neck, cautiously reaching around her waist with his free hand.

She stroked his head and murmured something. He moved his lips to her mouth, and she jerked her head away. 'Teddy!' she said sharply.

He stood straight up, feeling himself blushing.

'Don't be silly,' she said, brushing his hand off her waist.

'What don't be silly? What do you mean don't be silly?' Ted moved to his corner of the balcony. His face was on fire. 'Sorry.'

'Oh Ted, no.' Her voice had softened. 'Silly.' She gave a short laugh. 'What did you think?' She moved closer to him, put her hands on his shoulders. He stiffened. 'Don't be silly. You didn't understand. That's not what I meant.'

'I guess not.'

She laughed again. 'Don't be dumb. Things are very ... ' She kissed him on the cheek, then backed off. 'Come on.' She slipped through the open door.

Ted stayed rigid on the fire escape. He tried swinging his arms back and forth, but hit his knuckle hard against the railing. 'Fuck,' he said loudly, and felt better. 'Fuck off. Fuck you. Fuck off.' He was breathing quite fast. 'Fuck you.'

He sucked on his knuckle. 'Christ.'

He gave Miranda enough time to rejoin Arthur and the others, then walked quickly through the door, along the dark corridor past the coatrack, back into the pounding club, still only a quarter full. He walked past Miranda and Arthur, waving goodbye, retrieved his coat from the morose, half-naked check-girl, and pushed past the bouncer who was trying to tell him there was no re-entry policy. On his way down the urine-smelling warehouse stairs, the thumping of the dance floor receding behind him, he almost bumped into John, who was wheezing as he mounted the stairs in his suit and trenchcoat, his tie loosened.

'Whoa!' shouted John.

'I'm off,' said Ted, moving past him. 'Sucks. No one's there. Miranda. Where the fuck have you been?'

'Wait, dude,' John called after him. 'It'll pick up. It's early yet.'

Ted reached the ground floor, leaped off the loading dock into the dark alley behind the warehouse. He could hear trains nearby. He breathed deeply, and walked towards the street.

'UN Probes Incident,' read Ted, and had to read again, for it made little sense to him, and John had just shuffled into the kitchen. Ted lifted his eyes over the top of the newspaper. John was in his old terrycloth robe, making toast noisily.

'Dude,' said Ted.

'Dude,' said John hoarsely.

Ted tried to read his headline again. Some light was penetrating the grimy window, casting a pale band over the crumb-strewn table, and for once the kitchen was actually pleasant. Ted felt agreeably hung over, slow moving and placid, as if he could concentrate now. But he was having trouble with this one particular headline. It seemed impossible that anyone should make so much noise just making toast. He put the paper down. 'Stay late last night?'

John shook his head. 'It was just starting to happen when I left.'

Ted snorted. 'I'm sure it was.'

John sat down, facing him across the table, with his toast. 'Have a good time?' He picked up the business section.

'No,' said Ted. 'Not really.'

'You left too early. Max was there, just after you left.'

'Oh for Christ's – fuck off.'

John was smiling into his newspaper. 'No, he wasn't.'

'You scared me. But it is his club?'

'No. That wasn't the right club. I got the wrong address.'

'I see. The right club is the one you didn't know about, but it was happening, somewhere, right?'

John shrugged.

'Did you have a good time?'

'Fine.' John yawned, gazing at the newspaper. 'What happened to you?'

Ted looked at him, his puffy eyes and grey face. John was looking downwards, not eagerly at him as he should, and looked older, not at all confident. Ted relaxed a little.

John looked up at him slowly. 'Something wrong?' he said, without a foreign accent of any kind, the way he and Ted used to speak late at night at Southern.

Ted nodded. 'I had a kind of scene with Miranda.' He messed with his cereal. John said nothing. 'I felt as if she were making fun of me or something.'

John nodded. 'She try to kiss you or something?'

'No. I tried to kiss her. She's kissed me many times. I guess that's different.'

'Yes, it is.'

'I was embarrassed.' Ted felt sad again, and slightly cold in his T-shirt and sweatpants. The kitchen was actually filthy, really, when you considered it.

John was munching his toast.

'I guess I've had a crush on her. And, you know, she invited me to Thanksgiving with her family and all. And I'm sure she knows it, has known it. And something happened a while back, the night of her birthday.'

John looked up, but without surprise. 'Yeah?'

'How long has she been with Arthur?'

'Several years. Four, five.'

'Five *years*?'

John returned to his newspaper, impassive.

Ted rose, thinking of making coffee. With his head in the empty fridge he said nonchalantly, 'Anyway, Miranda sat me down on this sofa, and it was very dark – we were at Helium, it was after that party at Boss where I got oyster juice all over the suit, and we'd all had way too much to drink – and – fuck.' He had pulled out a coffee tin and opened it; it was empty. He put it back in the fridge and sat down at the table. 'Anyway. Miranda sits me down at this table, I mean this low couch, and she's doing her touchy-feely thing and I notice there are two guys watching us from close by, and they've been there all along. It turns out it's Arthur and Roger, together, and they're very grim about watching us together there. And I sit up and say hey, it's Roger and Arthur, and she says I know, without even turning around. She knew they were there all along. And I realized that she sat me down there just for their benefit. Was she having an affair with Roger?'

'They were seeing a lot of each other, yes. I imagine something was happening.'

'And Arthur and Roger are best friends?'

'Well,' said John, sitting back and clasping his hands behind his head. 'Miranda always makes sure the three of them go out together. That way neither of them can get mad at her in front of the other.'

'Yeah. Yeah. Great. Good plan.' Ted rose again, thinking of toast. He fumbled with plastic bags. 'I guess my only role was to make them both jealous of someone other than the other one, then. Excellent plan. I'm sure it worked, too.' He put the one remaining heel of bread into the toaster. 'I wonder how nasty she can get.'

'Oh Miranda's not nasty,' said John vigorously, shaking his

head. 'Miranda's not nasty. She does these things instinctively. It's in her genes. She doesn't know what she's doing.'

'Uh-huh.'

'Well,' said John, 'I don't know. I'm very ... we live in a mirandaphilic world.'

Ted leaned against the counter, reflecting. 'Well. I can't judge. I've been a prick too.' He felt himself blushing.

John looked up at him with a faint smile.

'To Go-Go,' said Ted quickly, turning to the burning toast. 'I slept with her that night. And it was a mistake. I don't really want to go on sleeping with her, and she figured it out pretty quickly, because I was a prick about it, and she's been upset, and it's fucked up things with her and Mike, which I feel *really* bad about.'

'No you don't,' said John. 'That's not what you feel bad about. You feel bad about fucking up one more Ophelia.'

Ted laughed. 'Yes, it's not. Anyway. That thing has fucked things up with me and Georgina, too – do you mind me telling you this?'

'Dreadfully,' said John, rustling the papers.

'I'm sure it's no surprise to you that I have this thing about George.'

'Perhaps not.'

'Well, I had this real crush on her. And the night she was in town, Go-Go came in drunk and, it's a long story, she thought Mike was sleeping in my room, and she got into bed with me and wouldn't get out. But nothing happened. We both slept there, and who should arrive unannounced in the morning but George, to find us both sleeping there. And I was embarrassed.' Ted sat down with his toast. 'Probably pissed her off.'

'Hard to tell what will piss George off,' said John distantly.

'Anyway. I'm sick of this shit. I'm not going to follow Miranda around any more, that's just sick shit.'

John was looking up at him with curiosity.

'I've figured her out. I always thought there was something I didn't get, something great. But it's just shit. It's quite boring really, for them especially, what they do all the time. I really don't think those people have anything I don't have. Or anything I want, more importantly. So I'm going to stop.'

'Stop what?'

'Everything. Being with pricks and being a prick.'

'I see. And go out West and live on Vancouver Island?'

Ted laughed. 'Not quite. But I am going to apply for a job.'

'Oh, Teddy.' John groaned, pushing the newspaper away. 'Not this shit again. How many times do you have to have it proved to you? Jobs. Are. Bullshit. They're for cretins and losers. You get a job you just have no time for anything else, you never make any money because you save it away for houses and children and other assorted idiocies, and you're miserable one hundred percent of the time. What are you going to – '

The phone rang and John picked it up. 'Ted Owen? May I tell him who is calling?' he said smoothly. 'One minute.' He put his hand over the receiver and handed it to Ted. '*Next* magazine,' he said blandly, reaching with his free hand for the newspaper.

Ted laughed again. 'Not Margaret Atwood? Or just Malcolm, by any chance?' He took the phone and said into the receiver, 'Kick out the jams, motherfuckers. I put this together too.'

A woman's voice said tersely, 'Ted Owen?'

'Yes.'

'Hi. This is Sophie at *Next*, I handle the "My Threads" section, do you know the section?'

'Oh, Sophie, I'm sorry, yes. Yes I do know the section. Sorry about that.'

'No problem. I saw you on Janni Bolo the other day and was really impressed by what you had to say about architecture, now –'

'Thank you,' said Ted.

'You're welcome, and since you have the book coming out

about it, and because, frankly, because we know you've done some work recently with Julian Claude, you'd be a perfect subject for the section. Does it interest you at all?'

'I, yeah – what does it involve, again?'

'Oh, very little. We send a photographer to wherever you want to be photographed, it only takes an hour or so of your time, and you don't have to dress up at all, you just wear what you normally wear. And I'll take some notes on where you got it and where you get your hair done and so on, and we end with a little plug about the forthcoming book.'

'The book?'

'About architecture.'

'Oh yes. My forthcoming book.' Ted grinned at John. 'And you publish a photo of me?'

'A full page, yes. It's really excellent publicity for you. And for the forthcoming book.'

'Well, the book – yeah. Yes. The book. Well,' said Ted, 'yes, certainly, I'd love to do it. How much does it pay?'

'Oh, we don't pay. It's publicity for you.'

'Yes. Thank you. Well. You pick the date.'

'Well, whenever's convenient. Next week?'

EIGHTEEN

A WEEK LATER, at ten in the morning, Ted stood in his room before his new mirror, half thinking of what he was wearing and half listening for Go-Go's step in the hall. He kept expecting for her to arrive home suddenly – she had been away for days, he didn't know where – and snub him, spit into his room as she passed. But she was away, probably in Montreal or something. So things were obviously better with Mike, which was comforting.

He tightened the tie again. Floral silk, on a mustard shirt – exactly the colour Max had been wearing when he had first met him, on the train – and dark trousers. It looked dressy, of course, much more dressy than he would 'normally' be – against *Next*'s instructions, but what the hell. His parents would be pleased to see him respectable. And the tie was really him. No more tweed jackets and brown shoes.

The phone rang, and he ran up to John's room to answer it. 'Hello?'

'Hi dude.' It was John, with music and women's voices chattering. 'Getting dressed up?'

'Yes. Where are you?'

'Miranda's. What time's your shoot?' Loud women's laughter, Miranda's, echoed from behind his voice.

'My shoot. My one photograph. Not till one-thirty. I'm a bit nervous for some reason. I don't like having my picture taken. So I was going to walk around till then, have a coffee somewhere.'

'What you need,' said John, 'is a drink. Which is what I'm having right now. Miranda invites you for a brandy with her and Isabel, and her friend Louise, whom I really think you might want to meet.'

'No thanks.' He paused. Then, apologetically, 'It's ten in the morning, I'd better not start drinking. I have to make some phone calls this afternoon.'

'Uh-huh,' said John, distracted. Shrieking laughter rang out again.

'Why would I want to meet Louise?' said Ted.

'Well, I think you'd be interested in her. She's a grad student at U of T, doing something like what you did at Concordia. Feminist studies of some sort, in political theory. And she edits this small literary journal, *Seafire* or *Seamoon* or something. I told her about your play and she seemed interested. Very brainy, you know. Your type.'

'My type.' Ted looked at his watch. 'Who else did you say – '

'Miranda, Caroline, this Louise and Petunia, from Submarine. You'd love her. She's wild. By the way, have you seen Go-Go today?'

'No. I haven't seen her for days. I assumed she was in Montreal. Why?'

'Nothing. It's just that she's not in Montreal. Mike called last night. He's been trying to reach her, doesn't know where she is. I don't know.'

'Huh. Strange,' said Ted, looking at his watch again. He did have time to kill. 'Strange. Listen, I'll come by for one drink. What's the address again?'

'Orgasms!' shouted Miranda from the kitchen, and then there was a clatter and bang as she dropped something, probably the sheet of cookies, and more of Petunia's hysterical laughter. Isabel jumped off the stately old couch with her mug and ran into the kitchen, slipping on the polished wood floor in her socks and slopping brandy from the mug.

Ted turned back to Louise. 'Tell me again why all translation is patriarchal?'

She laughed, pushing a hand through her short hair. She was pretty, very pretty, in those round tortoise-shell glasses. Her skin was clear and glowing, faintly freckled. 'Oh, it's that whole domination thing, absorption, absorption of the text.'

Ted nodded. 'You're saying it's like a conquest.' He turned to John, wanting to draw him in, but John only smiled, lifting his mug of brandy slightly. He had seemed happily silent and glazed on the other couch for a half-hour. Ted looked back at Louise, poised delicately in a comfortable stuffed armchair, her slim legs in grey tights folded under her. 'The text as foreign country, to be assimilated. You see it as imperialist.'

'It's more like an absorption, an *eating* and digesting, to excrete in a processed form. Our culture sees everything as eatable. It's the text as food.'

Ted nodded, taking another sip from his mug of brandy. His belly was beginning to burn, his head growing fuzzy. Louise's language was coming easier to him now, coming back to him through a thick mist, along with all his memories of days spent arguing in student cafeterias with an upset stomach. 'But in that *all* writing is a re-writing, surely, all writing a layering of influences, previously written phrases, then surely all writing is a form of translation, of digestion? I mean you're never going to get away from the palimpsest of intertextuality, from –'

'Yes,' said Louise, 'but it depends on what you call it, on your attitude. If you call it someone else's work, then you're not being honest.'

'But of course we all know, when reading a translation, that we're reading the translator him or herself, of course. No one is unaware of that any more. I think the naive reader is a myth.'

More shrieks emanated from the kitchen, along with a definite smell of burnt chocolate. '*Burnt* orgasms!' sang Miranda's voice.

Petunia wafted back into the living room, all six gangly feet of her swaying, her white thigh-high patent-leather sixties boots clattering on the floor. Ted looked up at her: she really was amazing. She wore flower-power tights, a miniskirt of some synthetic material, and a historically perfect Twiggy haircut. The boots had zippers up the sides. She sank onto the couch beside John, and began stroking his hair. Ted remembered how John had described her: the force behind Submarine, the party agency. The woman made a living organizing parties.

John smiled. 'When do we eat?' he called to the kitchen.

'I think I'm getting a headache,' said Ted.

'Got a headache, take a pill, right? ' said Petunia in a sing-song voice. Everyone laughed loudly, including Louise.

'Not me,' said John. 'I hate to give in.'

'But when a real headache does come along,' said Louise. Everyone laughed again.

'Okay, stop,' said Petunia.

'I take Anacin,' said Louise.

'I don't get it,' said Ted.

'Oh, come on,' said Louise. 'You know it.'

'It's an ad,' said John.

'Oh,' said Ted. 'I don't have a TV.'

Louise put down her mug and stared at him. 'You don't have a TV?' She seemed genuinely surprised, and pained. 'Oh that's a mistake. That's really a mistake. You mean you don't watch Deep Space Nine?'

'No.'

'I don't believe it. You must be the only person I know.'

'Ta daa!' Miranda was at the doorway, also in tights and socks, holding a tray of chocolate goo. She set it down on the coffee table and sat down. Isabel followed, and with loud expressions of delight the three women pulled at the mess, extracting dripping clusters of chocolate and nuts, eating and licking their fingers. John took one and slurped without comment. Louise refused. Ted tried one but felt sick half-way through it. He put it down and looked around for a cloth, holding his sticky fingers upwards on his knees.

Louise kept looking at her watch.

Ted said, 'I'm sorry, but I have to get back back to this eating thing. I was going to say, what's wrong with eating and digesting? We do that when we read, surely, anything, everyone does, even women. What's so patriarchal about it?'

'Oh come *on*, you guys,' said Isabel, with chocolate smeared all over her mouth.

'Bo-ring,' said Miranda. 'Booring!'

'The attempt to impose meaning on everything,' explained Louise, serious and patient, 'regardless of its openness – you know Eco's use of open?'

'Yes yes,' said Ted quickly. 'Polysemy.'

'Regardless of polysemy, openness, is essentially a patriarchal project, because that meaning is always politically – essentially class, gender, defined.' She sat back and sipped her herbal tea.

'Christ,' muttered John.

'So all criticism is essentially domination,' said Ted.

'All criticism as we know it, yes. It's eating. It's one massive restaurant review.'

'I suppose you hate restaurant reviewers,' said Isabel.

'Now restaurant reviewing,' said Louise, smiling, 'is an archetype of literary criticism. It's a microcosm of the whole patriarchal project. Have you ever met a restaurant critic who was a vegetarian?'

'They can't be vegetarians,' said John, his mouth full. 'Most restaurants serve meat – '

'Most people eat meat,' said Ted.

' – and they have to eat what the restaurant serves. It's simple.'

'And most restaurants,' said Louise smoothly, 'all restaurants, in fact, are capitalist enterprises. They serve meat. Restaurant reviewers discuss the ingestion of the meat. All – '

'An orgasm,' said Miranda, licking her fingers with long strokes, 'is only a real one if it's messy.'

'Really sticky and gooey,' said Petunia, swaying.

'But wait a minute,' said Ted. 'If everything is patriarchal – eating, criticism, capitalism – then the phrase is meaningless. It's like the Freudians who say everything is sexual. It makes the fact unimportant.'

Louise began to answer, but Ted sat back, distracted by Petunia as she crossed her long, booted legs. She looked terribly bored. He was tired too, and suddenly drunk. He felt himself quickly subsiding, as if all his briefly mustered interest in the argument was escaping from him with a hiss.

The phone rang, upstairs, and Louise stopped talking abruptly. She jumped up and ran towards the stairs. 'My phone call,' she said, and disappeared.

'Uh-oh,' said Miranda, looking at Isabel. 'Carlos.'

'Carlos?' said Ted.

'Her new man,' said Isabel. 'He's Colombian.' She smiled salaciously. 'He was supposed to be here an hour ago.'

'She'll be in tears in a minute,' said Petunia.

'A minute?' said Isabel. 'She'll be on the phone for an hour.'

'Is he screwing her up?' said Miranda.

'Oh my *God* is he screwing her up,' said Petunia. Ted wondered, briefly, what Petunia's real name was. Probably something aristocratic, like Miranda. Claire, maybe.

'He flirts with everyone he meets,' said Isabel.

'More than just flirts, dear,' said Petunia. 'Did you know that when they first met he gave her a phone number, and every time she called it his room-mate said he was out or in the shower or something, and he would call her back. And then it turns out he's married, and he never was living with this room-mate –'

'Is he still married?' said Miranda. 'I thought he was getting divorced.'

'Oh my dear, of course he's *getting* divorced,' said Petunia. 'Aren't they all?'

Isabel laughed loudly. 'And now his friend won't even transfer the messages. She gets to see him less and less, and she just found out last week that he was back in Colombia, for a holiday, and he hadn't even told her he was going. Now she thinks there's someone else.'

'Besides the wife?' said Ted.

Isabel and Petunia nodded, sipping their brandy. Ted did the same. 'What does Carlos do?' he asked.

'A bunch of things, right now,' said Petunia. 'I think he's got work in his friend's body-shop.'

'Wasn't he a professional baseball player or something?' said Miranda.

'Soccer, dear. Baseball is the Dominicans.'

'What team d'he play for?' said John.

'Oh it was years ago,' said Petunia. 'I'm not sure.'

'He's a fantastic dancer,' said Isabel. 'He makes some money winning competitions in bars.'

Ted looked at the staircase up which Louise had vanished. 'What was the name of Louise's journal, again?'

Petunia pointed to the coffee table. 'That's it, there.'

Ted found a crumpled place mat on the table and wiped his hands. From under the tray of chocolate orgasms he pulled a small, square-bound book. The cover said *Moonfire 6*, and in smaller letters, 'Knowing the body of knowledge: no knowledge; all body.' He opened it at random, and read

She is the blank page
He writes her out of herself
And so each thing in saying it, the not-saying, once again.

He closed the book. Louise was coming down the stairs. She sat again, silently, looking drawn.

'Carlos coming over?' said Isabel.

Louise shrugged, her lower lip trembling. She played with the frayed hem of her sweatshirt, looking downwards.

'Lou,' said Miranda, 'I hate to see you like this. Is this really worth it?'

Louise spoke in a small, strangled voice. 'He'll be here any minute. He was calling from the pay-phone on the corner. He was just a block away. At Ramon's.'

Ted looked at John, who was smiling blandly, his eyes half closed. John caught his eye. 'So Teddy. That what you're wearing for your *Next* photo?'

Miranda sat up. 'Oh is it today, your thing? How fun. Is that what you're wearing?'

'Sure,' said Ted.

'But they'll think you're a lawyer or something.'

Ted shrugged. The doorbell rang. Everyone was still for a moment, then Louise got up and went through the door to the entrance hall. Ted heard the door opening, then murmured conversation. 'I don't think I look like a lawyer.'

Louise came in, hand in hand with a tall man with a chiselled face and shining dark hair, cut short. He wore baggy jeans and a loose black silk shirt. Ted was not good at discerning which men were good-looking and which weren't, but he knew at once that this one was beautiful. The man smiled warmly, extending his hand to everyone. 'Carlos,' said Louise, 'Miranda, Petunia, Isabel, and John. And Ted.' Carlos sat easily, smiling and greeting, extending his long legs, his open-necked shirt billowing. 'How you doing,' he said to Ted, squeezing his hand and looking him in the eye.

'I'll just get ready,' said Louise, and went up the stairs again.

'How've you been, Miranda?' said Carlos with a Spanish accent, leaning back and folding his arms.

'I'm marvellous,' said Miranda slowly, smiling and looking at Carlos in a way that made Ted want to look out the window.

Pale sun on naked trees, a quiet street, a dusting of grey snow like ash. Miranda was talking about the work she had been doing – set-dressing an American film which suddenly ran out of money, how she hadn't been paid – and Carlos was laughing.

'How's the job?' said Miranda.

'Not bad,' said Carlos. 'I learn a lot about cars. I don't care about cars. I don't give a shit about them.' He clasped his hands behind his head and laughed, and Ted found himself laughing too. Carlos looked at him. 'And what's your line of business?'

Ted took another sip of brandy and shivered. 'Nothing, right now. I'm not even looking for work.'

'Oh nonsense!' shouted Miranda. 'Ted's a writer. Honestly, writers always say that. He's even a celebrity. He's off to have his photograph taken by *Next* magazine in less than – '

'One hour,' said Ted. 'Yes. That too. Nonetheless, I do nothing.'

'*And* he's just been working on this huge American movie with Julian Claude – '

'Julian Claude?' said Petunia. 'The English guy? The gorgeous one? You're a friend of his? He is gorgeous, isn't he?'

'Well, he's looking a little old now,' said Ted casually. 'He's still perfectly charming though.'

'A writer hey?' Carlos whistled. 'Beautiful. Miranda, you want any music?' He pulled a cassette tape from his pocket. 'How about some music?'

Miranda leaned forward and took the tape. 'It's awfully early for salsa, Carlos. All right, but I don't know how to work the machine. It's in the kitchen.'

Carlos leaned towards her until their faces almost touched. 'Why don't you show me?' he said softly.

Miranda blushed and stood. The two of them went into the kitchen.

Petunia said, 'No. No. I don't think you can wear that for your photograph. You don't want them to think you're like what John used to do, do you? Or what? I mean I don't really know what you want but I'm not really all about that look. We're over it.'

'John was like one of those master-of-the-universe shit-heads,' said Isabel. 'Weren't you, Johnny?'

John gave a glazed smile from his couch.

Petunia hooted. 'Johnny was one of the master-of-the-universe shitheads who sold thirty grand in one phone call, you know, and everybody was like mega-intimidated, you know, like did I mention fuck you?'

John began to burp. 'The motorcade sped on,' he said in burps.

Petunia turned to Ted. 'I think you want to show them your hipper side.'

'You don't dress like that normally, do you?' said Isabel.

'Sure I do,' said Ted.

'What about your leather jacket?'

'I have it here. For getting there. But I wasn't thinking of wearing it for the photo.'

A blast of Latin dance music surged from the speakers, all trumpets and fast drums. Carlos reappeared, holding his hands high and swinging his hips. 'Come on!' he clapped, and pointed to Petunia, who shook her head. Isabel rose and tried some steps with him. He held her hips close to his, her one hand high. They were laughing and swirling when Louise came down the stairs.

'I'm ready!' she called over the music. She clutched a small canvas bag, but hadn't changed her clothes. Carlos let Isabel go and sighed. He went to the kitchen to turn off the music.

'Nice to meet you,' said Ted to Louise. 'We should talk longer someday.'

'Yes,' she said, not smiling. Then everyone was saying goodbye, and Carlos and Louise had left. The apartment suddenly seemed dead quiet. Miranda re-emerged from the kitchen.

'Jesus,' she said, sinking into a chair. 'That fucking guy ...'

'He make another pass at you?' said Petunia.

'As soon as we got into the kitchen. But it's as if he doesn't really care. It's as if he has to. So you don't really let it bother you.'

'God,' said Isabel, shaking out her blond hair. 'If I were Louise it would drive me crazy.'

'It does drive her crazy,' said Petunia, looking at Ted. 'Really crazy. I've got an idea. Clogs.'

'Who?' said Ted.

'Oh, *great*,' said Louise. 'Great idea. I bet *Next* really doesn't expect writers to be so cool. As to wear clogs.'

'You would look great in clogs,' said Miranda, nodding.

'You think?' said Ted.

'Oh, *perfect*,' said Isabel. 'Perfect idea, Pet.'

'And then they won't know if you're really a club type or what. Just hint enough to let them wonder.'

'And wear some daring shirt. Like wear mesh or something. Timmy at Skywards has the coolest mesh shirt, and it really makes it look like he has muscles and everything.'

Ted laughed. 'Sure. Isabel, if I had a mesh shirt and clogs, I would wear them just for you.'

'I have a mesh body suit that would fit you,' said Miranda. 'And Jeffrey left his clogs here when he went back to New York.'

'Who's Jeffrey?' said Ted.

'Come on,' said Miranda, rising.

Ted stood and found he was unsteady on his feet. He took the brandy mug upstairs with him.

When he shuffled back downstairs he wore a pair of baggy men's jeans – Jeffrey's, again, and far too big for him – big black clogs, Miranda's low-cut mesh bodysuit, which was loose in the chest and uncomfortable in the groin, and his leather jacket. 'Just to show your tough Maritime side,' Miranda said. He felt sexier than he ever had. He turned, stumbling, before the mirror on the landing.

'Perfect,' said Petunia and Isabel when they saw.

'Excellent,' said John. 'Right on.'

'I'd really better go or I'll be late,' said Ted. 'Thanks for the drinks and the orgasms. And thanks for your sartorial advice. The motorcade –'

'Teddy,' said Miranda, 'you're beautiful.'

He put his winter coat over the jacket, and Miranda's cat-eye sunglasses – 'You have to *act* like you're a star,' she said – and stepped into the crisp afternoon. His nostrils froze. As the door closed behind him he thought, for a second, that he heard a peal of female laughter.

NINETEEN

TED HAD THE BEGINNINGS of a headache as he stepped out of the taxi in front of John's house. A stone-grey sheet had covered the sky, and the watery sun was close to the horizon. Vague shadows criss-crossed the street. He tripped in the bulky clogs, giggling, as he ascended the broken stairs to the front door. Malcolm's bicycle was attached to the balcony.

He hooted as he came into the front hall. 'Hoo-ey!' He took off his coat. 'A star is born!'

'Hey dude,' came John's voice from the kitchen, sounding subdued.

'Hey Ted,' came Malcolm's deep voice.

Ted shuffled into the kitchen, still wearing the cat-eye glasses. Malcolm and John were sitting at the kitchen table, talking in low tones. 'What do you think?'

'I've seen it, dude,' said John. 'You look beautiful.'

'Looks great,' said Malcolm, looking at his fingernails.

'You guys should have seen my professional modellism,' said Ted, sitting down. 'They wanted pouty, I gave them pouty, they wanted feline, I gave them cat, they – hey.'

John and Malcolm weren't smiling, but looking at the table. 'Nothing,' said John. 'Something's up with Go-Go.'

'What something's up with Go-Go? She's in Montreal.' Ted took off the glasses and looked at Malcolm.

'That's just it,' said Malcolm, leaning back and folding his arms. 'She's not in Montreal, and no one knows where she is.'

'Her parents just called, from Vancouver,' said John. 'They're worried about her.'

'And Mike,' said Malcolm. 'He was expecting her in

Montreal last weekend and she never showed up. Then she was expected this week at her uncle's house in Barrie.'

'She's done this before,' said John, 'and it was a bad scene.'

'A very bad scene,' said Malcolm softly, stretching his arms behind his head.

'What?' said Ted, feeling his headache start to increase. 'What bad scene?'

'Oh, a couple of years ago,' said John.

'Go-Go's come a very long way since then,' said Malcolm.

Ted rubbed his temples. The kitchen was growing dark. There was a thunderclap from outside.

John stood up and leaned against the counter. 'She knows Mike from this year when she dropped out of school – '

'What school?' said Ted.

'She was at Ryerson. Fashion design.'

'Okay.'

'Okay. She was at Ryerson, she dropped out, couldn't stand the world of fashion.'

'Pretentious and posey,' said Ted. 'Body-image obsessed. Oppressive to women. Got it.'

'Right. In fact, she was having a lot of problems with her weight at the time. One month she'd be so skinny you'd think she was dying, the next month she'd balloon ... you know the scene.'

'Anorexia bulimia scene. Got it.' Ted looked at John. 'Janet had it.'

'Right. So she – '

'As you probably knew.'

'Right. Yes, I figured that. Anyway, after Rye-high Go-Go didn't want to work anywhere that was, you know, upscale, anywhere white, which meant competitive, anywhere that had anything to do with fashion or films or restaurants or money or hanging out in cafés. She hated all that.'

Ted nodded, looking at his clogs.

'So of course she couldn't find any work, and moved into this squat.'

'At that time,' said Malcolm, 'she was doing a lot of drugs. It was like everyone in this house was into drugs, so it was the scene, and she ...'

'What kind of drugs?' said Ted.

'Just chemicals, mostly. Acid, mostly, I think,' said John. 'And bennies, for when they went to clubs – they were going to places like to Holocaust and Hole, remember those places?'

'And then ex came along,' said Malcolm, 'and then heaven ... anyway, she got out of it, and that's when she moved in here.'

'And she's been really fine with drugs,' said John, 'even when Mike's around. But ... I'm just afraid that if she's been kind of depressed lately, kind of fucked up, as you say she might have been ... '

Ted nodded.

' ... then she might have ... she might be pissed off with the world again, you know? And what ... ' John paused awkwardly. 'And what *you* represent and so on.'

'What *I* represent!' Ted laughed, feeling his stomach constrict.

John shrugged. 'Anyway, we're just afraid she might be back at the squat, or ... who knows.'

'It's just that the squat,' said Malcolm, his voice sinking to a velvet murmur, 'the squat ... is a *very* bad scene.'

'Why?' said Ted, standing up. 'Where is it?'

'Well, for a while she was in a warehouse at Bloor and Lansdowne, and then in an apartment at Jane and Finch, and then ... '

The front door opened; the Mole came into the kitchen in long, gangly strides, his trenchcoat glistening wet, gripping his plastic supermarket bag of computer disks. His glasses were completely fogged. He took them off and blinked at the others. 'She's not at Julie's,' he said, putting the glasses on again, then taking them off. 'I can't see anything.'

'Is it raining?' asked Malcolm.

'Freezing rain. It's like sleet or something. It's shit.'

'Julie didn't know where she was?' asked John.

'Hasn't heard from her for weeks. They had a coffee date last week and Go-Go didn't show up.'

'Christ,' said Ted, exhaling.

'Got to check the modem,' said the Mole, rushing out and up the stairs.

'I've got to go work out,' said Malcolm, looking at his watch.

'See you, dude,' said John. 'I should get dressed.'

'But wait,' said Ted, agitated. 'We should look for her. If she's in one of these places, they could be dangerous. She could be . . . we should look for her.'

'Look for her?' said Malcolm, in the doorway. 'Look for her in squats at Jane and Finch? Later, dudes.'

'We don't really know she's there, dude,' said John gently.

'And Go-Go's no wimp,' said Malcolm. 'She's strong. She's built back her strength lately. She can take care of herself.'

'Yeah,' said Ted. 'You been doing some take-responsibility exercises with her, Malcolm? You been helping her through her pain? I did some of that myself.'

'Whoa, dude,' said John.

'What's that supposed to mean?' said Malcolm.

'Nothing,' said John and Ted simultaneously. 'Forget it,' said Ted. 'I'll – '

'I've got to go work out,' said Malcolm, turning.

Once he was gone, John said, 'For fuck's sake, guy, he's a fag.'

Ted was shaking his head. 'I don't believe that whole fag thing. Yes I do. But I mean chicks use that fag thing for some weird kind of flirting they won't do with straight guys, and I'm sure they get some kind of kick out of it. I don't understand it. Anyway. It doesn't matter. Why should I give a shit about it.' He rubbed his face again, trying to loosen the skin tightly wrapped around his skull. 'Listen, I don't think we can just abandon her. I want to look for her. I want to find where she is.'

John sat down, looked at his watch. He looked up at Ted. 'I suppose you want to go right now.'

Ted nodded. 'We could – if you don't want to come, I'll do it, but I want to find her. You give me Mike's number, I'll ask him where to go ...' Ted moved to the window, stared at the darkening garden.

'It'll be dark soon,' said John quietly, 'and it's pissing bad shit.'

'You don't have to come,' said Ted, kicking off his clogs.

'I'll call Mike,' said John, standing.

Half an hour later Ted and John were on the corner of Bloor and Lansdowne, in the fluorescent light streaming from a doughnut shop. A man with matted hair and glazed eyes watched them from inside the shop, his mouth working. The freezing rain had turned to wet snow, big soft flakes that coated their jackets and melted on contact with their hair. Neither wore a hat. John was untwisting a piece of paper that had become crumpled in his pocket. Ted was looking around wildly. 'Three oh four Keller,' John read. 'But it's in an alley off that. In a warehouse. There's supposed to be an old black Mercedes parked there that never moves. Nobody owns it.'

'Which way?' said Ted. An enormous black woman in a terrycloth beach hat was approaching them, waddling slowly towards them through the tattered carpet of snow.

'I think south,' said Ted.

'Which way is north?' said John.

'You looking for something?' said the big woman, who was now close. She breathed heavily; her eyes were bloodshot. 'You need something?' There was a small, wiry black man in a warm-up suit a few paces behind her. He stopped and watched them.

'No thank you,' said Ted.

The woman moved closer. 'What you need?'

John took his elbow. 'This way.'

The wiry man stopped them. 'You don't need something? You sure you're not looking for something, boy?'

'No,' said Ted. He added, 'Man.'

'Matilda!' shouted the man, opening his bloodshot eyes wide. He raised his arm as if to strike. Ted ducked, and the man rushed past him, pushing the enormous woman into a wall. She slumped onto the wet sidewalk, her legs stuck out in front of her. She was shaking her head ruminatively. She didn't seem perturbed. Swearing incomprehensibly, the man tottered off down the sidewalk.

Ted and John stepped towards the woman as she laboriously pulled herself up and dusted off snow. 'Fuck's sake,' said Ted.

'On'y making it worse for himself,' muttered the woman, shaking her head and breathing heavily. 'On'y making it worse.'

'She's okay,' said John. 'Come on.'

They stepped into the street and were soaked by a passing bus. They crossed the street, then passed a lumber yard where a dog leaped at them from shadows, snarling and barking. They jumped back, but it was behind a fence, violently pressing its snout into a small hole in the chain link, trying to force its head through. Its feet scrabbled on the asphalt. Ted could see its white teeth in the yellow lamplight.

'Pit bull,' said John, and they moved on, leaving it frantically barking against the fence. They came to Keller Avenue and turned down it, a dark row of squat brick houses and concrete warehouses, then the alleyway with the black Mercedes, and then the glare of a fluorescent lamp outside a steel door with the number they wanted, sprayed in red paint.

There was a rusted intercom panel. John pressed the buzzer.

'What's her real name?' said Ted as they waited.

'Darlene, I think. Darlene Ryan.' John pressed the buzzer

again. 'This probably doesn't work.' He tried the heavy door; it was locked. 'If there's no one here, the only other place Mike knew about was at Jane and Finch.'

'We'll try that next then.'

'Yo,' said a voice above them. They looked up. A black man with long dreadlocks had pushed his head and bare shoulders out of a small window one storey up. A heavy bass throbbed from the upper storey. 'What you lookin foore?'

'Looking for Joey's place,' said John, looking up into the falling snow. 'We're friends of Joey's and, them.'

The man's eyes bugged out; he gripped the windowsill tight. 'HEY!' he shouted, 'LET GO ME FOCKING LEG!' Ted and John recoiled, but the man appeared to be struggling with someone who was pulling him inside. Grimacing, he twisted his body around so he was facing upward. 'LOOK OUT!' he screamed, as something heavy fell from an upper window.

Ted and John jumped out of the way; a black travel bag full of something like crockery crashed to the ground. The dreadlock man had disappeared from the window.

'Hey,' called another voice. An Oriental face looked out. 'What you want.'

'There an apartment of kids,' said Ted, 'white kids? Skin-heads and that?'

'Round the back.' The head withdrew.

The dreadlock man's head popped out of his window. 'Don't know no focking Joey,' he yelled.

'Thank you,' called John, waving idiotically. They trudged down the alleyway until they found another door, ajar. They entered a brightly lit corridor. Electric feedback and the barking of more than one dog seeped from behind a graffiti-scrawled door. Ted knocked as loud as he could for some seconds.

It was opened by a white teenager in shorts and a T-shirt, with dirty hair; he could easily have been one of Mike's courier friends. Around his legs yapped two or three brown-and-white puppies. He looked aggressive and afraid.

'Does Go-Go live here?' asked Ted.

The boy turned. He yelled, 'Petey! PEETEY!' Behind him, Ted could see a big warehouse room with curtains dividing sections. The floor swarmed with barking puppies, guitar amplifiers and beer bottles. Three expensive mountain bikes hung from the ceiling. 'Oh, fuck, he can't hear me,' said the boy, scratching his head. The stereo roared with electric guitar.

John stepped boldly into the room; Ted followed. The boy stepped back, looking at them uncertainly. Suddenly he brightened, seeing something behind them. 'Hey Jimmy, man, hey Jimmy. Roll a hoolie?'

Ted swung around; a mud-splashed cyclist in a wool toque was struggling through the door with a bicycle over his shoulder. Ted stepped out of his way, narrowly missing a small pile of excrement on the floor.

'Jimmy,' said the boy. 'What kind of elastomers you riding?'

'Listen,' said Ted to the cyclist. 'Someone called Go-Go live here?'

The man in the toque frowned, putting down his muddy bike. 'Ask Pete.'

'PEETEY!' screamed the boy.

The cyclist walked his bike to the back of the studio, kicking away puppies and stepping gingerly between piles of dogshit. 'You feed the dogs yet?'

'No dog food,' said the boy.

'You don't feed them fucking dog food, fuckhead. Gives them headaches.'

'Fuck, man,' said the boy. 'PEETEY!'

The dogs' barking intensified. John was trying to shake two off his trouser leg. The dirty-haired boy stood in the middle of the room, immobile.

Ted couldn't help himself; he called to the cyclist, 'How do you know?'

'Know what?'

'How do you know that it gives the dogs headaches?'

'Yeah,' said the boy. 'How do you know?'

The muddy cyclist shuffled back towards them. 'I tried it.'

'You tried it?' said Ted. 'Why?'

'Why?' growled the man. 'Why? Because I expect them to eat it. I should be able to eat it myself.'

'Right,' said Ted.

The dirty-haired boy was nodding. 'That's right. Should be able to eat it yourself.'

John coughed. 'So how do you know?'

'Know WHAT?' shouted the cyclist.

'That it gives them headaches.'

'Because I tried it, right?'

'Right,' said Ted.

'And it *gave* me a *headache*.'

A taller, older skinhead emerged from behind a curtain. He was carrying a beer bottle but looked sober enough.

'Hey, Petey,' said the boy. He pointed at him. 'Ask this guy.'

Ted yelled, 'Someone called Go-Go live here?'

Petey approached the door. 'Yeah, once. She moved out, I think. She's not here now.'

'How long ago?'

'Long time. Years.'

'Ah,' said John, looking at Ted. 'That doesn't help us.'

'You know where she is now?' said Ted.

'Yeah,' said the skinhead. 'I think she's with Angela and them. Three forty-six Wallace. It's at Bloor and Dundas West.'

They walked westward along Bloor, under railway bridges most of the way, beside deserted new housing projects. It was really night now, and Ted's shoes had soaked through. 'My God,' he said, 'why do people live out here?'

John said nothing.

'I had no idea the city was so vast,' said Ted. 'I guess we

only know a tiny part of it. I guess I don't know the real city. This isn't anything like the part we know. I mean we hardly ever leave a few square blocks.'

'I go to Yorkville sometimes,' said John. 'You hungry?'

They stopped at a brightly lit diner that advertised souvlaki and cheeseburgers. It was full of old men drinking draft, and warm. No one looked at them as they came in.

Over a plate of fries and two draft John said, 'This is what Toronto was like before the boom. This is the real Toronto. Full of places like these.'

Ted looked around at the old team jackets, the nylon baseball caps, his mouth full of fries. 'I like it. I could relax here.'

'Jesus,' said John, between deep drinks of beer. 'Remember when, a couple of years ago, when we first came here, how crazy it was?'

'I just came here four months ago.'

'When I came here, after Southern, there was a "help wanted" sign in every retail store, because they couldn't pay people enough to keep them in shitty jobs ... and all those Yorkville cats with cellular phones and everybody working in film or writing ad copy or something. And all those clubs. And there were no apartments for anyone, anywhere. Incredible. You could choose whatever field you wanted to work in. You wanted something, you just plucked it from the trees. You should have seen it at the bank. I drank a lot of fucking champagne.' He took a french fry, then finished his draft. 'A lot of fucking champagne.'

'I've never in my life drunk a lot of champagne,' said Ted.

'Well. You know what? It's no big fucking deal.'

'Yeah yeah,' said Ted, 'Everybody tells me that. After they've done it. It's a cool thing to say. But let me tell you. I'd fucking do it.'

'No. Really. It's no more fun than drinking draft here. No-one really likes champagne that much. It's not worth all the fuss. It's just the idea of it. And because it costs so much. In fact, you could say the same of all that ... luxury. Restaurants, cars, everything. You don't really need it.'

'Well of course you don't really *need* it, John, no one ever has. That's not the point. I mean people have been telling us this since Sunday school and of course it's still true.'

'Yes, I know,' said John, waving a french fry, 'but that's not what I mean. I mean it's actually better without those things. I'm actually happier since that time. There's so much more for us to do now, I mean now we don't have to worry about jobs and, and ... restaurants. Hell, the restaurants aren't even – you remember Manor, and Mr Jourdain's and the Escroquerie, they're not even *there* any more, so we don't have to *worry* about them, you know? And if I'd gone on like that I never would have had all these other ideas, about Mexico, about writing, I mean you wouldn't either. Back then you'd be hauling thirty-five as soon as you got here, writing manuals for IBM or something, and you'd be thinking about buying a car. You never would have got into this play idea, never written it, never met people like Mike and Go-Go –'

'Never be looking for her on a snowy night in fucking no-man's wasteland in Novem –'

'But this is *great*. That warehouse we just saw, and this little restaurant, it gives you –'

'I know all about it,' said Ted glumly. 'When I was a student, in Montreal, I was poor then, and it wasn't deliberate, and I used to have to hang out in places like this. I got all my learning about humble beauty in then. I don't need it any more.'

John shrugged. 'Sure you do. I think ... what I think is that there's going to be a renaissance. Not an economic one. Just that people are going to be more interesting, more productive now, now that all that shit has gone. The world-class bullshit gave us ideas, yes. That we can come up with things, that we could have some kind of culture here. Except that now, the culture I'm thinking won't be New York. It'll be something grittier, something tough. You know?'

'Muscular,' said Ted. 'Berlin before the wall came down.'

'Exactly. Berlin, not New York. Exactly.'

Ted smiled. 'What are you writing, anyway?'

'Novel,' said John, looking away.

'How's it going?'

'I've written a bit. I haven't really got into it yet. I've got some good ideas.'

'Sounds like it. You should write it, dude.'

'So should you. Everyone should write a novel. Especially you. You know all about novels.'

Ted sighed. 'Yes. I know about external focus and zero degree writing, and *fort und da*, and epiphany and deep structure and –'

'No seriously, You could write a great novel. Write one about Janet.'

Ted laughed, and then stopped. He was thinking about it.

'That's what everyone in big cities should do. Back in the boom, everyone quit their jobs and began selling real estate. The whole fucking city, like every Korean grocery store owner, had a hand in real estate. Now there are no jobs and too much real estate, and we could all do the same thing with novels.'

'Every store-owner writing a novel. Sounds great.' Ted laughed and finished his draft, thinking of Go-Go. He felt forgiving and friendly: when he saw her he wouldn't be too apologetic, or worried, just accepting. 'Let's go.'

They found the footbridge the skinhead had told them about, beside a used car lot, a rickety, soot-encrusted, iron structure over a railway shunting-yard, with steep wooden stairs on either side, and elaborate wrought-iron lampposts, none of which supported a working light. As they climbed the stairs the wind grew around them, driving wet snow down into their collars. They paused in the middle of the narrow bridge to look down at the railway tracks.

'They use this bridge all the time to make movies,' shouted John above the wind. 'It looks tough, you know, like Europe, a big old city, you know. It's great for rock videos.'

Ted looked at the snow swirling over the tracks, the green and red signals in the distance, and the dark factories and warehouses on either side, faded advertising painted on their brick walls. A distant siren wailed.

John laughed. 'See. Here's your Berlin culture.'

Ted turned to look over the other side, and a graffito on the weathered wooden surface beneath their feet caught his eye. Something written in faded magic marker. He bent to look at it.

In a childish hand was written:

ThIs waS WHere TYROne and TIfFany knew they Would be haPPy. They lAugh and Cry and said they Love eaCh other. FebruaRy 15, 1991.

He called John, who read it out loud, then said, 'Shit.'

After a moment Ted said, 'That's sad.'

'It's nice, it's happy.'

'No, it's sad. That was years ago. You think they're still together, Tyrone and Tiffany? And it's so pathetic. The sentiment. The naivety.'

'They probably were happy.'

'On this bridge? On this fucking bridge in February?'

'Let's go.'

They walked gingerly down the sleet-covered steps at the other end. Ted said, 'What's most impressive about it is that they tried to write it down. It's proto-poetry. Very good.'

'Lower life-forms struggling towards consciousness, huh? Admirable.'

'Exactly,' said Ted, laughing. 'Admirable.'

But he had almost cried, reading it.

'See, they should be writing their novel,' said John. 'Everyone can write novels.'

They were on a street of houses and factories; the house they wanted, number 346, was dark brick, next to a brightly lit house full of people dancing. The slow bass of reggae boomed from upper windows. A supermarket cart lay overturned on the grass. A Mercedes was parked in the drive.

'Don't walk under the windows,' said John.

They knocked at the dark door of 346 and waited for long minutes. They were about to leave when a white man their age drove a bicycle up the path to the veranda. He wore a yellow rain slicker, short hair; he looked like them.

He got off the bicycle, then hoisted it onto his shoulder and walked up the steps. 'Help you?' He was fumbling for his keys.

'Is Go-Go here? We're friends of Go-Go's.'

'Maybe,' said the man, pushing open the door. 'Come on in.'

'Is she living here?' said Ted, following him into a dark hall.

'When last I checked,' said the man, smiling. 'Go-Go!' he called up the stairs, then disappeared into another room, still carrying his bicycle.

Ted and John stood among the boots and coats of the several inhabitants of the house. Suddenly Ted was apprehensive about seeing Go-Go. What if she were just fine? What if she didn't want to go home? It would be embarrassing.

A door opened upstairs and a heavy woman came down the stairs. She wore a terrycloth nightgown, had short hair. She stopped halfway. 'Yes?' she said dubiously.

'We're looking for Go-Go,' said John.

'I'm Go-Go. Who are you?'

Ted and John apologized and left.

They walked slowly up the steep stairs of the footbridge. 'Only the one at Jane and Finch left,' said Ted.

'Listen,' said John, 'I think we should do that tomorrow, or try to find a phone number or something. You know how long it takes to get up there? And two white guys walking around in the middle of the night ... '

'You don't have to come,' said Ted.

They got home, together, after midnight. The snow was finally gathering on the street. Ted's head spun with the crashing of subway doors, and images of lighted highways, strip malls, bleak apartment blocks. They took off their wet shoes in silence, beside the dark pile of metal lights and poles in the hall.

There had been no answer from the apartment they had found, in a squat concrete block beside a highway. They had had to take a bus from the end of the subway line, then walk a mile or so in snow, and had seen few people. 'It didn't really look scary up there,' said Ted, 'Just empty. Inhuman.'

John sat glumly on the stairs. 'We did our best, right, dude? Don't worry about it. She'll be fine. Besides, it's not your fault, whatever.'

Ted nodded. 'Do we have anything to drink?'

John stood. 'Scotch in my room.'

Ted followed him up the two flights of stairs. He pushed aside a pile of clothes from John's chair; John rummaged in a cupboard. 'Really good Scotch, I think,' came his muffled voice. 'I was saving it.' He pulled out the bottle. 'Got this in London at some AIDS benefit gala. Stole it. There was disgusting excess there. No one noticed. Twenty-four years old.'

'You or the Scotch?'

'Both.' John poured it into two dirty glasses, then collapsed on the unmade bed.

'Steal from the rich,' said Ted, tasting the Scotch. It was instantly warming and nostalgic. He looked at John and settled in his chair, smiling. John looked ridiculous and charming spread eagled on his too-small bed, a blond albatross.

'Well, fuck,' said John in a sigh.

Ted laughed out of affection and took another gulp of Scotch. He sighed deeply. There was a comforting pride in having looked so hard for Go-Go. 'Massive city,' he said. 'So spread out. Miles and miles of ugly places we'll never go, people who never have to come downtown. It's like lots of little small towns joined up. Seriously, we live in a small town. We hardly ever travel outside.'

'I go to Yorkville sometimes,' said John, on his back, balancing his tumbler of Scotch on his chest. Then, 'What is this with Go-Go anyway? Why ... you really crazy about her or what?'

'No. No. I'm attracted to her, yes.' Ted began blushing. 'But I just wanted to sleep with her a couple of times. I wouldn't want to sleep with her again. You know how sometimes you lose interest after ... '

'After one boink. Wham.'

'Well, yes. And besides, she's so crazy, she scares me. I'm embarrassed around her a lot.'

'Guilty, then.'

'Yes. Guilty. And I don't know, I just wanted to do something nice for someone else.' Ted drank more warming Scotch. 'And patronizing. Bloody patronizing.' He shook his head.

'*Mondo* guilt tonight,' said John. 'You're bad, you know that? You are one evil dude. You are wicked, base, venal ... '

'Have you ever been attracted to Go-Go?'

'She's not my type, really,' said John.

'Who is your type?'

'Oh ...' John hesitated. 'Nineteen-year-old chicks at Spleen.'

'You haven't had a girlfriend in the past couple of years, have you?' said Ted.

'I mean the perfect ones, the ones that didn't exist when we were nineteen. In tights and floppy hats and whatnot, diaphanous tops and you know, the ones with their own language and you don't know what they do, they're just beautiful chicks who aren't in the least interested in you and know that you're staring at them. They have completely different lives that we don't understand, and they're totally non-verbal. I want them.'

'Uh huh,' said Ted. 'You wouldn't be able to talk to them at all.'

'No. But I would want to understand them all the same. I would want to be one of them.'

Ted laughed, then became gloomy again and drank more Scotch. After a moment he said, 'I want them too.'

'What did you mean about doing something nice?' said John.

Ted hesitated. 'I guess I wanted to do something that wasn't advancing myself, meeting people that could help me, spending money and so on. I wanted to get outside ...' He stopped, about to say 'outside Miranda's world,' realizing it was John's world too. 'I think your Berlin idea is a good one. I have to stop falling in love with people like Miranda.'

John was silent.

'And Georgina,' said Ted. 'Got a flirtatious postcard from her the other day.'

John grunted.

'Have you ever had anything – I mean has there ever been anything between you and George?'

John said, 'George doesn't think of herself as being flirtatious. She might be shocked to hear you say that.'

Ted considered this and decided to ignore it. 'It must be strange to spend so much time with these women, I mean when you were living with George, and spending so much time with Miranda, it must be ... strange.'

John laughed. 'Yes. I don't find it strange. There's nothing so special about those chicks. This is good.' He held up the Scotch. 'I had a twenty-four-year-old Islay once, at Boss. In fact I had several.'

They talked like this until two or three, when Ted collapsed into bed and slept deeply.

TWENTY

'WHAT DID YOU THINK?' Malcolm asked Ted outside the Parkdale community hall where the dress rehearsal had taken place. 'Just a minute. Jackie.' He turned to embrace an actress in tights and heavy sandals who had just come down the steps. 'Beautiful,' said Malcolm to her ear.

Ted shivered in the cold, waiting for the embrace to end. Light snow was falling; it had been chilly in the rehearsal hall. The actress disengaged, put on her beret and scarf and unlocked her mountain bike. She waved brightly to Malcolm and Ted and rode off.

'She's strong, isn't she?' said Malcolm. 'Very strong.'

'Yes,' said Ted. 'It was good.'

'I knew you'd like it. Brent! Thanks so much. You were so sexy. See you tomorrow night. You kick *major* butt, my friend.'

'It wasn't exactly what I'd imagined, though.'

'No. I had to take some liberties. Open it up a bit. I mean I know it's your script, but I spent a lot of time workshopping it and role-playing parts with the actors, so I feel I really understand it. You know, all the changes I made were just formal. I think they match the spirit of your beautiful, beautiful play.'

'Perhaps you understand it better than I do. I'm not sure I understood why you put the slides in.'

'The slides? You didn't like them? That was Brent's idea. He thought the anti-business subtext really wasn't clear, and we could bring it up a lot more. It was a collective process. That's the way I always work.'

'Anti-business? Malcolm, that was just one character, joking for a moment ... ' Ted looked around at the cold street, the boarded-up shops and lunch counters.

'Gloria baby, I love you *so* much.' Malcolm was hugging the last of the actors.

'So the pictures of factories and sea-birds and so on, that was all anti-business?' said Ted.

'Well, I just thought that whole monologue showed how well the military-industrial complex influences people like that, really shapes them. And I'm not sure the character really is aware of it himself. And I wasn't sure the audience would appreciate it just from his speech.'

'No. They probably wouldn't. I guess that's why you put in the dance segment, then, too.'

'Now, what did you think of that? Billy is just a brilliant choreographer, isn't he?'

'Oh yes. It was very well choreographed. But – '

'He's mister rising young star in Toronto now. We're so lucky to have got him to work for free.'

'Great. And the dance was about, as I understand it, the role of women in office-relationships?'

'Well,' said Malcolm, smiling, 'That's the great strength of your script. It shows so well how all that stuff works, *from the inside.*'

'But I didn't really want to make it ... It's not about that, Malcolm. It's just about this guy and this chick.'

'Oh, I understand that. That's what's so beautiful about it. It's all in there but it's not on the surface of the script. It's not too heavy. You're very good at disguising all that stuff in a story. That's why I thought it would be so perfect in dance, because it's not intellectual, it's physical. Sheer physical theatre. It's so much more expressive this way.'

'But Malcolm, these people, those characters, they're not expressive. That's the whole point. They're not good at communicating, they're uptight and ... ' Ted faltered and sighed. 'Anyway, it doesn't matter. We could hardly change it now, we open tomorrow. You've done a very good job.' He turned towards the street. 'I hope it – '

'Ted, man.'

Ted looked at him curiously. Malcolm's tone had changed.

'All right. Let me explain. You don't understand. I changed all this for your own good. I know this business and you don't.' Malcolm was talking rapidly and sharply. 'You want to get grant money for future plays, right?'

Ted nodded.

'And you want the theatre community to come and see this play so people know who you are.'

'Well ... '

'Trust me, you do. If you want to write plays you need money. And if you want money you're going to have to lick some dick. You're going to have to sell your straight white butt for a change. Now I'm trying to help you. I know this business, and I know what people are going to hate and what they're going to jizz all over. Your play, as you wrote it, isn't going to interest anyone. A straight narrative play about white people? Here? Have you ever *met* one of these Arts Council people? Are you crazy?'

Ted watched his face, suddenly hard and lined.

'It's all politics right now. There's only one kind of play that's going to get any attention at all, and that's what I'm trying to get you.'

'Oh,' said Ted.

'Fuck, man. You are so naive.'

'And they're going to jizz all over this?'

Malcolm shrugged and smiled. His face softened. 'They might. They just might.'

'Phew.' Ted buttoned his overcoat, shaking his head. 'Yes. I am naive. Thanks. Thanks, Malcolm.'

They shook hands. 'Still no sign of Go-Go?'

'No. Her parents called again this morning.'

Malcolm shook his head sadly, then swung onto his

mountain bike. 'See you tomorrow night. Don't worry about anything.'

Ted walked towards King Street, and the streetcar.

As he walked up John's street he passed a couple unloading Tupperware containers and foil-wrapped plates from the back seat of an American car. The man was balding and paunchy, the woman stocky, in a brown corduroy skirt. She patted a sleeping baby strapped to her chest. They both looked tired. The man eyed Ted closely as he passed. Ted looked away, but the man said, 'Ted?'

Ted stopped and stared at him. 'Billy. Billy? Good God.'

'It *is* you,' said Bill McLeod from Sackville, New Brunswick. Then they were shaking hands and Bill was introducing Ted to his wife Carol and the new baby; they were just coming back from a few days at Niagara-on-the-Lake. 'We were in the same graduating class at high school,' Bill told Carol. 'Exactly the same birthday, I remember. Well. You're looking pretty hip, Ted.' He sounded uncertain.

Ted smiled awkwardly, smoothing back his short, gelled hair. He tried not to look at his friend's pallid face, his machined acrylic sweater.

Bill was still holding a plate covered in tinfoil. 'We're visiting Carol's sister,' he said, gesturing to a house. 'We have a place out in Markham. You live around here?'

'Right there,' said Ted, pointing.

'Right there? No way! Right downtown, eh?'

'I don't know how you do it,' said Carol. 'We had so much trouble with the traffic, getting down here.'

Ted smiled. 'I don't drive too much.'

'With kids, you know,' said Bill, looking exhausted, 'it's difficult downtown. You want some space where they can play, and where you feel safe about it. You have any kids?'

'Kids? No. No kids. So what is it you do these days, Bill? You were at Dal, right, MBA?'

'Yes, finished that a few years back, and I got this position with Williams Winwell right away. Analyst. We just got this house, you should come and see it. Just a starter home. We're fixing it up.'

'Wow, Bill,' said Ted. 'Great. That's great for you.'

'You?'

'Me? Well, I don't really do anything. I'm having this play produced.'

'A play? Really? A play.'

'We love the theatre,' said Carol, juggling Tupperware. The baby stirred and moaned. 'We'd better get inside before this all gets cold, honey.'

'And recently I was working on a film set,' said Ted. 'With Julian Claude.'

'The English guy?' said Carol.

'Yes. He's looking a little old now.'

'Really! Julian Claude!'

The baby emitted a piercing wail.

'Wow, Ted,' said Bill weakly. 'I envy you, I really do.'

They promised to keep in touch, and Bill and Carol struggled up the stairs. Ted smiled tensely after them from John's veranda. As they disappeared a taxi pulled up and John got out, wearing his suit and his trenchcoat.

'Ho, dude' said Ted, looking for his keys. John walked up the steps. 'You see that guy going into the house next door?'

'What guy?' John looked tired. He carried a briefcase.

'There was a guy with a woman with a baby, on that porch. They're gone now.'

'Married guy.'

'Yes. That guy's our age. Exactly my age. Exactly.'

'So?' They moved into the dim entrance hall.

'So? That's me, dude. That's us. You know who that was? That's Bill McLeod from Sackville.'

'Billy McLeod? No way. His older brother or something.'

Ted swung his arms, trying to loosen his shoulders. There

seemed to be a band across his temples, too. 'I talked to him, dude. And the wife. We don't know how you do it, she said. Living downtown. The *traffic!*'

'Could have been you, dude,' said John, taking off his trenchcoat.

'And oh, we *love* the theatre! I think I scared the shit out of them. Imagine *living* downtown! I think she wanted to get the baby away from me as soon as she could.'

'Sounds like it's Bill McLeod you should feel sorry for.' John walked into the living room.

'Oh he's doing okay, I'm sure. No one needs to feel sorry for an analyst with Williams Winwell. Wow. What's all this real world intrusion bullshit, all of a sudden?' Ted looked at John, who was standing in the middle of the living room, looking around as if lost, sighing and puffing out his cheeks. 'What's with you? Bob's your uncle?'

'What?'

'Megadrinks with Uncle Bob?'

'Oh. No. More like coffee. He had to tell me he's gone bankrupt.'

'What? Really?' Ted sat on the sofa. 'What does this mean? The Mexico scheme isn't – '

'It's all off.'

'Shit.' John moved into the kitchen and Ted followed.

'Fucking garbage stinks,' said John, sitting down. His tie was loose, as usual.

'I bought some instant coffee yesterday,' said Ted, busying himself. 'What a drag. Where are you going to get money now?'

John exhaled. At length he said, 'Fucking bullshit.'

Ted had no answer to this. 'I need money too,' he said. 'My play opens tomorrow. I owe my share for the rehearsal space. And everything. Rent soon.'

'I know. And I don't know who's going to pay Go-Go's share. Where's this play opening now, again?'

'Little Space. Behind the Bakery.'

'Ah. We'll have to get drunk for it. If we drink a mickey in the parking lot we can run in before it hits us.' John sighed again. 'Actually, my other uncle, Richard, says he can get me a job.'

'Oh my fuck,' said Ted. 'Doing what?'

'Oh, you know. Government bullshit. He's in Ottawa. They're compiling some kind of business guide. I'd have to do research.'

'Wow.' Ted sat down. 'Too funny. Too, too funny.'

'What?'

'Well, actually I kind of panicked recently too. Started reading the classifieds. And there was an opening for a tech writer. Not quite for IBM but close, funnily enough, a software company called Hex or something, Tex-Mex, I don't know. I sent in a resumé. And I actually got an interview. I have to go out to this complex in Scarborough tomorrow.'

John nodded gravely, staring at the floor. 'Had to happen sometime.'

Ted poured the boiling water into mugs. 'There's no milk.'

'You sent out press releases and all that? There going to be critics there?'

'Malcolm handled all that. Shit. I still owe him for the photocopying.'

'You seen it.'

'I saw it today,' said Ted.

'You don't want to talk about it?'

Ted laughed. 'He's changed it completely. It's all about the patriarchy and the military-industrial complex now.'

'Good. Good for him. Were you at the Aquarium last night?'

'Yes,' Ted said vehemently. 'Yes. I was indeed. I have no idea why.'

'Thought you weren't going to go there any more.'

'So did I.'

'They still have Methedrine Mondays there?'

'Yup. The whole thing. Virtual reality room, smart bar, all that. There was a fashion show by Chainsaw Allah and Cathode. And some new group called Roadhead.'

'Miranda there?'

'Oh, Miranda was there. Miranda was indeed there. You ever met her friend Bethany?'

'Beautiful, beautiful girl? Eugenics camp type?'

'Yes. Totally, totally superb babe. Miranda brought her to the Aquarium. Why is another question. They had to talk about something very personal and very important. You know how that happens, when you have to do that in public? So they had to sit on a sofa and talk in earnest tones and smoke and be glamorous in front of everyone.'

'Oh, speaking of being glamorous,' said John, reaching for his briefcase, 'have you seen *Next*? You're in it.'

'Oh no. Oh God.'

John handed him the magazine, open to the page where Ted's full-length photograph dominated. In the photo, Ted's mouth was open and one eye half-closed.

'Oh Christ. Oh my Christ. I look ridiculous.'

'But you were being very funny. I had no idea you were so hilarious when you were drunk.'

'What do you mean?'

'The left hand column is quotations. They're all yours.'

'I don't remember any interview,' said Ted.

'Oh there was an interview all right.'

Ted read, 'The mesh shirt I got from a transvestite duke in San Marino, the smallest sovereign state in Europe.' He looked up at John. 'I said all this?'

'Oh you were in fine form. I remember. Read on.'

Ted read, 'The poor duke had such a crush on me, which I did little to dissuade. The jeans I won from a naive American, who bet me them that I wouldn't run with the bulls in Pamplona. I did. The clogs are *echt Deutsch*; I traded my annotated copy of Horace for them from a tripped-out neo-primitive DJ in a Frankfurt techno bar.'

'Too funny, dude. Too funny.'

'But this is horrific.' He read again, 'And the leather jacket I always wear, because I must always have one slaughtered-animal product close to my skin. I like this one because it still reeks of fear.'

John laughed in a rasping hoot that became a cough.

Ted began to laugh too. 'Come to think of it I do remember that. I wanted to impress the photographer's assistant. She had great purple tights. She asked me, "So how's Julian?", and I said who? and she said "Julian Claude", and I said, oh, Julian, well, he's a little under the weather lately, and she nodded knowingly.'

John hooted painfully, coughing and laughing.

Ted looked at the page again. 'It's a wonder they printed that, in *Next*.'

The phone rang. They looked at one another, as they had begun to do since Go-Go's disappearance. Ted answered it. 'Hello?'

'Ted Owen, please.'

'Speaking.'

'This is Christian at *Next*, I'm in the news department. I was wondering if you'd care to comment on any of the Moonfire group's statements.'

'The what?'

'The Moonfire group, the animal rights group. Have you read their communiqué?'

'I don't know what you're talking about.'

'Oh. You haven't heard.' There was a pause. 'I'll read it to you. There must have been a leak on our side, because we got this communiqué just after the issue hit the stands yesterday morning. They must have seen the page already. Anyway, let me read it. "The Toronto Moonfire Front for Action on Feminist and Ecological Issues, which includes associated organizations Moonfire Women, the Gaia Collective, York Lesbians for Purity, the Soil Foundation, and the entire student government of OISE, is outraged that *Next* would lend credence to the fascism of earth-rape by printing the violent, phallocratic, earth-hating statements of Edward Owen, a right-wing journalist, in its 'My Threads' section, December 7. Owen's supposed humour about 'animal fear' is a chilling reminder that the annual slaughter of billions of animals worldwide for human use, often in conditions of great suffering for the animals, remains a joke to many. The voiceless victims of this genocide cannot protest this degrading humour about their plight. Would *Next* have printed Owen's 'jokes' about the Jewish Holocaust, or about American slavery? Furthermore, Owen's macho boasts about the barbaric practice of running with the bulls – bulls which end up tortured and slowly killed before a large public – proves that this humour originates in his own threatened and insecure masculinity, the imperialist construct which post-modernism has now outdated and linked definitively with the massive environmental catastrophe we now all face. *Next* should know better than to give credibility to such humour and reinforce such destructive stereotypes by publishing Owen's views without comment or context. We demand an apology from Owen and from *Next*. The time has come when violence – verbal and intellectual – must be recognized as such, as no less brutal than physical violence. The two must be equated. If these two apologies are not forthcoming, we promise our own violence in retaliation for such an attack. All the male-dominated media should be warned. Women, rewrite the difference." That's it.'

Ted breathed deeply. 'Oh boy.'

'I don't really get that last line,' said Christian. 'Mean anything to you?'

'Oh boy,' said Ted again.

'It's signed Louise Ellenbock, spokesperson for the Front. Would you like to comment?'

'Well. Could you send me a copy of that first?'

'Certainly. I could fax it to you right now, and you could get me a statement, say, this afternoon?'

'Sure. Except that I don't have a fax. You'll have to send it to me.'

On the other end, Christian sighed. 'Well, that would take days. For now, I'll just have to say you said no comment.'

'All right,' said Ted. 'No comment. Just send me a copy of that, would you, so I can respond to each point?'

'No problem.'

'Christian, what do you think they're threatening, at the end there? Some kind of terrorist attack?'

'It's not clear. That's quite possible. Groups like this have done similar things. We've notified the RCMP, and they were extremely interested. If I were you, I'd watch my ass for a while.'

'For fuck's sake.' Ted kicked his shoe against the kitchen counter. 'Sorry. Christian, are people at *Next* – is the editor worried?'

'He's pretty pissed off, yes. This Moonfire group is planning a conference, on earth-rights, for next month, and we were, the advertising department has been hitting them pretty hard for ads. We were hoping to sell them a special pull-out section, with seminar times and everything. And now that's all in jeopardy. He's not happy, no.'

'Christ,' said Ted as he hung up.

'Get in trouble?' said John.

'Fuck,' said Ted.

'Oh, now don't worry,' said John. 'This kind of thing –'

The front door opened and a small woman's voice said 'Hello,' in such a way as to make Ted and John sit up and stare at the doorway. Then they looked at each other and rushed into the living room.

Go-Go was standing in the hall with a small suitcase. She wore jeans and a bulky brown sweater. 'Hello,' she said, looking at the floor. 'How are you?' Then she picked up the suitcase and walked up the stairs.

Ted and John followed. 'How are you?' said Ted.

'Go-Go, are you all right?' said John.

'We were kind of worried,' said Ted.

'How nice of you,' she said, opening the door to her room. 'I'm fine. I was just away. Visiting some friends.'

'That's it?'

'I was visiting John and Babs. They're old friends. They're doctors. In Caledon. I needed to get away.'

'You were just visiting friends in the country,' said Ted.

'Yes.'

'You look fine,' said John.

'I feel fine. It was very nice, thank you.' She began briskly unpacking her bag.

'Go-Go,' said John, 'You'd better call your parents. They've been pretty freaked out.'

'Oh, for fuck's sake,' said Go-Go. 'They're always fucking freaked out. Of course they're freaked out. Let them chill for a while.'

'So you're okay?'

'Mike's been worried too.'

Go-Go snorted, rummaging in a drawer. 'Mike,' she said. 'Don't worry. I had a long talk with him this morning.' She began pulling out clothes, piling them on the bed.

'He could have fucking told us,' Ted murmured, looking at John.

Go-Go said, 'I hear you've been making a name for yourself, Ted.'

'What? What did you read?'

'In the *Star* this morning. The Moonfire group had a whole article to themselves about your funny animal jokes.'

'In the *Star*? This morning? How the hell did they – '

'What's going on?' said John.

'Ted's been being very amusing about killing animals and

proving his manhood,' said Go-Go, her head in her cupboard.

'Oh Go-Go,' said Ted, 'You don't actually side with – '

'What are you doing, anyway?' said John. 'What are you packing for?'

'I'm moving,' she said. 'Mike and I have decided to move in together. I'm going back to Montreal.'

'Oh.'

'You're moving.'

'Don't worry. I'll pay my rent until you can find someone else.'

'You're moving in with Mike?' said John.

'We've kind of sorted things out,' said Go-Go, a little sheepish. 'And I decided, while I was away, that I don't like Toronto. I've never liked it.'

'The smoking's easier in Montreal,' murmured Ted.

Go-Go spun to face him. Her face was red. 'Yes, that's exactly what I – '

'Okay,' John was saying, 'Okay, whoa, I think it's a great idea.'

She turned back to the closet.

'I was just joking, dudette,' said Ted. 'I think it's great, too.'

'Thanks. You're a great joker. Now if you don't mind – '

'You're not actually going today, are you?' said John.

Go-Go hesitated. She began biting her nails, looking at the floor. 'No. I haven't got a van or anything. But soon. In a few days. I'm just getting ready now.' She stared up at them again, defiant. 'Now I have to change if you don't mind leaving my room.'

Up in John's room John said, 'This means problems. Finding a new room-mate.'

'Good Christ,' said Ted, sinking onto a pile of dirty clothes. 'No tidal waves forecast today, are there? Volcanoes? No *coups d'état* in the works in Ottawa, hey?'

'We should call her parents.'

'I will.'

They sat in silence for a moment. 'Scotch?' said John.

'Any left?'

'A little.'

He poured two small glasses. Ted felt a little better.

'Dude,' said John, 'You planning to go home for Christmas?'

Ted sighed. 'That. Well, I should. I mean I must. But I haven't the money for an air ticket. I've been trying to find someone who was driving.'

'You don't want to drive to New Brunswick in winter, dude.'

'Actually,' said Ted, 'I've just been trying not to think about it. My dad will cough up money for a plane if I really don't have it. But I hate that.'

'Know what you mean.'

They drank in silence until they finished the bottle.

'I should deal with this Moonfire thing,' said Ted. 'Can I write at your desk?'

'If you can clear a space.'

Ted pushed aside the magazines on John's desk and found a clean sheet of paper and a working pen. He began to write,

First, let me make clear my sympathy with the cause of the humane treatment of animals, and with the international feminist struggle. My intention – if intention there was, in a few unguarded jocular moments – in making the comments Next printed, was entirely humorous. Of course some humour is more acceptable than others, and I now realize how insensitive

He sat back, exhausted. How insensitive. The music from Go-Go's beat-box – the same Bile Ducts tune she always hummed, reminiscent of Ted's undergraduate days – reverberated through the floor. He wished there was more Scotch. John was reading a *Playboy*. How insensitive.

'Do you know,' Ted said, 'that when I asked that reporter at *Next* about whether the editor was worried, he said yes, because they might lose some ad revenue. Can you believe that?'

John snorted. 'Of course I believe that.'

Ted looked back at his paper. Louise fucking Ellenbock, whoever the fuck that was. He pictured her in combat boots, on a motorcycle, with a pierced lip. Go-Go upped the volume on her beat box.

'For fuck's SAKE,' shouted John into the heating duct.

Ted thought of Christian at *Next*, and the angry editor, whom he pictured as an old hippy, stamping about and shouting and taking drags on an enormous joint.

Quickly, he tore up the letter he had been writing. He rummaged in John's drawer until he found a clean sheet. Then he wrote,

I was extremely amused to hear of the Moonfire group, and of their surprisingly sophisticated reaction to my social credo, my *ars poetica*, as it were, the central tenets of which are a desire to reassert our dominance over the lower life forms by eating them, and a desire to accelerate, through the use of nuclear power, spray-cans, PCBS, and corrosive cosmetics on soft, pink animal eyes, the disintegration of the hegemony of that tasteless and essentially *déclassé* aesthetic system sentimentally known as Nature – a degenerate invention of unmanly, overeducated Romantics ...

He wrote without stopping for forty-five minutes.

TWENTY-ONE

A WEEK LATER, Ted left his bedroom earlier than normal in the morning because Go-Go had started her beat-box again. He heard the slamming and stamping of her packing from through the wall.

In the kitchen, John was reading the *Star*.

'No *Globe*?' said Ted. 'Or you just want to catch up on the latest murders?'

'No, mister Duke of San Marino, I went out and bought this for a reason you actually might not disdain. Something which might actually interest you.' John held out the paper, folded to the arts section.

Ted scanned the page. 'No way. A review.'

The headline read: 'Young playwright's humane vision.'

'They love you, man,' said John.

'This is incredible,' said Ted, reading. 'Owen's non-linear plot probes gender constructs and deconstructs conventional narrative. I don't believe it. Did you read this? Owen also tackles the environmental problem by subtly relating it to the numbing corporate environment of the characters' worlds.'

'Way to go *Mal*colm.'

'Way to go, Malcolm. Oh, look, there was something he didn't like. However, Owen's characters reinforce negative stereotypes about ourselves, and the rather bleak ending leaves no room for the characters' eventual enlightenment. If Owen accepted his moral responsibility as a playwright, he would do more to show us a way out of our impasse. More positive role models in theatre would go a long way to solving so many pressing social problems.'

'Oh well,' said John. 'That's to be expected. Can't all be Shakespeare.'

'Shakespeare? You think this guy likes Shakespeare? Not too many good role models in Shakespeare. Hamlet. Not a good role model. Not to mention Ophelia. And what about the disgusting appropriation of voice in Othello?'

'Okay. You should be pleased he mostly liked it. I guess there are some communication problems at the *Star*. Your reviewer didn't make the connection between the writer of the play and the character described on page twelve.'

'Page twelve?'

'More enemy of the people stuff. Read on, Mac figgy duff.'

On page twelve was a headline that read, 'Eco-feminists not amused, threaten violence over *Next* controversy.' Beside it was a photograph of the Moonfire group's leader, Louise Ellenbock, a pretty young woman with a spectacular black eye. She looked familiar.

'You know this chick?' said Ted.

'Of course I know her. So do you. It's Louise, Miranda's friend Louise, the editor. You met her at Miranda's.'

Ted sat down. 'Of course. Louise Ellenbock. I knew the name was familiar. Wow. She really took a shine to me. What's with the black eye?'

'Oh, you know,' said John uncomfortably.

'You know what?'

'You know Carlos. He's kind of a crazy guy. I guess sometimes they get into these kind of rough arguments.'

'You mean he beats her up?'

'Well —'

'He beats her up. Great. He beats her up. Terrific.'

Ted scanned the article. Louise's new statement, in response to his letter to *Next*, was similar to the first one, warning of the dire consequences of his levity, condemning *Next* for printing his letter and thereby supporting the industrial-military complex, and threatening 'action'. The reporter naturally described him as a 'right-wing journalist'.

'Yes,' said Ted. 'Right-wing journalist. Enemy of the people. And humane experimentalist playwright. Right on.'

'Exactly,' said John. 'Now you've left Montreal.'

'I guess I have.'

The phone rang; Ted answered.

'Mr Owen? Jack Billman from the *Star* here, wondering if you have any comment on –'

'No. No comment.'

As soon as Ted hung up it rang again.

'Mr Owen? How would you like to have acid dripped into your eyes?' The voice was male, high-pitched, quavering.

'Who is this?'

'If you were a rabbit you wouldn't know either. Just some big hand dripping acid into your eyes. You think that's funny?'

Ted hung up. 'They've got our home number,' he said to John.

'Oh,' said John uncertainly.

'How the fuck?'

'Well, you've started to meet quite a few people here. And they had your number at *Next*, right? They had to have your number for the photo. And they said there was a leak. Someone inside *Next*.'

'For Christ's sake.'

The phone rang again.

'Leave it.'

John turned on the answering machine and turned down the sound. The ringing stopped. The tape seemed to continue rolling for an unusual time. Ted felt a huge urge to listen to the message. He moved to the machine.

'Don't,' said John. 'You don't want to hear. We'll listen to them all later.'

Ted put down the paper and found his hands were shaking. 'Fuck,' he said in a tone of surprise.

'It's a little worrying,' said John. 'But don't let it scare you.

They'll get bored with it.'

'Fuck, man. I'm not into this. I'm really not into this. I'm going to move to New Brunswick. I'm going to go to library school.'

'Or nursing. Or rehab. Speaking of moving, you know Go-Go's really leaving today. She's got a van and everything.'

'Does that mean we help her?'

'I asked. She doesn't want help.'

Ted took the newspaper and went upstairs to Go-Go's room. Her room was dismantled; the posters were down, the futon was rolled up, and boxes full of clothes and books filled the hall. Go-Go was bending over a trunk full of clothes in the middle of the room. 'You seen this?' said Ted.

'The article on Moonfire?'

'No, the review.'

'Oh, yes. Congratulations.'

'Funny, huh?'

'It's great for you. Excuse me.' She pushed past him with another box, dumping it in the hall.

'You need any help? You have people helping you load the van?'

'Yeah. I'm fine.' She was stretching to reach a top shelf.

'Here,' said Ted, moving into her room. He reached up to help her, tripped on something and swayed into the bookshelf. A pile of paperbacks came tumbling down. 'Shit,' he said. 'Sorry.' He bent to pick them up.

'Ted, I don't need any help. Thanks.'

'Okay.' He stood up. 'Well, it's kind of weird you moving .out like this. I mean it's not the room-mate problem. It's just kind of sad.'

She said nothing, picking up the books.

'I'm happy for you,' said Ted. 'I really hope it works out in Montreal. I hope you're happy there.'

'Thanks. By the way, Ted, you haven't forgotten the money, hey?'

'No no.' Ted put his hands in his pockets. 'A hundred bucks. I haven't forgotten. You really helped me out there. I haven't thanked you enough.'

'Because I really need it now, with the move and all. I need it now.'

'Okay,' said Ted. 'Sorry. I'll get it to you.'

'Before I leave this afternoon would be best.'

'Right.'

The phone rang again.

'Ted-DY!' came John's voice from downstairs. 'I think you might want to hear this one.'

'Excuse me.' Ted rushed down the stairs.

John was standing beside the answering machine, engrossed in a letter he had just opened. He had turned up the volume on the machine. 'So,' a calm man's voice was saying, 'if you're interested, we'll need to see you on Monday the fifth, that's next week, on the eighteenth floor. Come to my office first and I'll show you around.'

'Who is it?' said Ted. He found he was whispering, as if the speaker could hear him through the machine.

'Huh?' said John, looking up. 'Oh. IBM, I think, or something.'

'So give me a call,' the man continued, 'today or tomorrow and let me know your decision. Take care.'

Ted grabbed the phone just as the machine bleeped. The caller was gone. He rewound the message, careful to stop before hitting the first message, which he didn't feel up to hearing, and listened again.

'Shit,' he said at the end.

'Fuck,' said John, folding up his letter.

'I've got the job,' said Ted.

'So have I,' said John. His face looked fallen and grey.

'What?'

'Uncle Richard's come through. They want me in Ottawa.'

'Oh. They want me at Hex Software.'

'Hex what? Doing what?'

'Writing manuals. Remember I had an interview, in Scarborough?'

'Oh yeah.' John looked around at the living room, confused. 'So you'd have to work in Scarborough?'

'Yeah. It wouldn't be so bad. There's a subway.'

'Right.' John was staring at his letter again. 'Lot of money,' he said.

'But you'd be living in Ottawa.'

John blew out a great stream of air. 'I don't know.'

The phone rang again. Ted turned down the volume on the machine. There was a loud rapping at the door; Ted saw two bike couriers with headbands and goatees peering through the glass. One was talking into a walkie-talkie. They waved to John and Ted.

'Go-Go's help has arrived.' Ted went to open the door. They came in noisily calling for Go-Go. They had parked their van on the front lawn.

A crash from upstairs signalled that she had begun to move her furniture in the hall. The two couriers clattered up the stairs to help her, leaving a whiff of sweat.

'Let's get out of here,' said Ted. 'Let's go out for lunch.'

'I don't have any money,' said John.

'Neither do I,' said Ted. Another crash, followed by happy hoots, came from upstairs.

Ted remembered the money he was to find for Go-Go. He pictured the grey-carpeted Hex Software offices, the quiet doodle-deedle-doodle of the new telephones, the simple, nondescript clothing he would wear. He thought of the noise and smoke of Penumbra, and Aquarium, and the chiselled heads of the boys who looked like Max there, and he automatically felt hung-over, although he wasn't. He thought of the foreign voice on the phone when he had tried to call Max. He thought of the cold balcony where he had tried to kiss Miranda. He decided to accept the job.

TWENTY-TWO

December 15
Dear John,

More wild snowflurries, cowardly, niggling Peter Lorre weather without any real manly snow. It's pitch black at five these days. I'm up in your empty room because I'm sick of writing on Georgina's futon. I have a steaming pot of tea and I can't see out the window. Might as well be in a farmhouse in New Brunswick.

Good talking to you last night, you seem to be doing very well. Very sober. A little odd, actually. You seemed so serious about work you reminded me of you three years ago. And what were those hints about a woman? Tell all.

Even that didn't really seem possible when you were here.

Speaking of years ago, I ran into Dick Forsdyke – remember Forsdyke and Phibbs on the Students' Council School Spirit Committee, tried to kill the Gazette, Forsdyke iS a pRick all over the place? Remember? Anyway. Too funny. Let him be a warning to you.

I can't face the thought of my own work tomorrow, getting up in darkness, that bloody subway, then the shuttle bus to the big mirror building beside the highway, and that bloody hearty small talk in the fluorescent cafeteria. All my coworkers can talk about is highways and cars and the best route in to work and how long it took them today because of what accidents. They never ever go downtown because it's so difficult to find parking there, can't understand why anyone would want to go, especially when they have everything they need in Brampton or

Bramalea or Christ knows. They seem both a little afraid and a little domineering with me, as if I'm to be respected yet need to be taught a lesson, like sergeants training an officer recruit.

The work is predictably easy, and not totally dull, although it soon will be. Of course I'm restrained at every possible turn in my writing by square-headed editors whose arseholes must be by now quite distended with the Cadillac gas-tanks they all have rammed up them. I'm trying to slip the word cunt into a little promo piece I'm doing, though, in some combination of letters or an anagram or something, something like calling Tex-Mex's 'dedicated search for quality' its 'careful hunt.' Rather adolescent, but keeps the time passing.

I have a cubicle with a computer and my very own notice-board. Sometimes I have to stay late and work on something urgent, and all the secretaries and accountants and almost everyone else leave bang on the dot of five, which can get rather depressing when it's as black as this outside at four-thirty I exaggerate five. At least my debts are paid off.

I've actually been buying food, too, real food like eggs and canned soup, sometimes even before I need to eat it. There is often orange juice and occasionally even coffee in the fridge. I haven't graduated to fruit and vegetables yet, although I admit I have begun to wonder about where to get them.

The house is worst on Sunday. People are starting to respond to the ads in Next and they're coming to look at the rooms. Just an endless stream of losers and weirdos. Half of them seem to think it's crucial to tell me about their food allergies right away. I'm the one who has to show them around because Malcolm and the Mole are always out. The hallways echo a lot without those rugs of your parents' – hey, did they turn out to be valuable? I wish we'd thought of them before.

Thanks for paying rent until the end of this month; Go-Go has too. So if we haven't found replacements by then we're fucked and I'll have to move.

Can't wait to organize a move in January, mondo fun.

Also can't wait for Christmas in Sackville, whoo boy, big time. The deserted streets, everybody drunk the whole time, fighting with Anna and her con-man asshole husband – of course Mom is furious that I missed the wedding, as if I could just take the three hundred bucks for the air ticket out of savings or something, cash a goddam RRSP or something as Anna's friends would – and the Richardson's annual egg-nog party with all those fun Christmas carols. Dad ended up paying for my ticket, of course. I fly to Halifax, then take the train, because it's cheapest. Mondo fun. Nothing like Halifax airport in December.

Actually, it will be nice to see them all, but I think five days will be just enough.

I guess I'm depressed. This Christmas thing has always struck me as idiotic. All these streamers and electric lights over these grey streets where no one can walk for long anyway without wanting to duck into the nearest bar and get sodden. Toronto under Christmas lights is almost indistinguishable from Sidney or Moncton.

I wonder where all my fall enthusiasm has gone. When I think of my first impression of Max, and of Miranda, I remember being utterly optimistic. I've given up hoping for Max's phone call now. I wonder what's happened to him. Everyone has rumours.

And Miranda I saw last week at Penumbra and she was with Bethany again and silly and distant, exchanging knowing looks with her and giggling all the time. I said we should get together (why? why? because she looked so incredibly powerfully confidently silky beautiful, that's why) and she said sure, we should have coffee, that I should call her, and I called her the next day and left a message on her machine and she hasn't called me back. Yesterday I ran into Petunia and it took her a few seconds to remember me, incredible, and then she got all friendly and asked me if I was going to Miranda's party, which I hadn't even heard about, so she got embarrassed and tried to cover it up. She gave me an invitation to a rave called Dark Apostle Tuesday.

Georgina hasn't replied to my last letter either, and it's been a month. I still have no idea what she thinks of me.

Trouble is, dude, you *did* remind me of Forsdyke last night.

Listen, I feel guilty about breaking up the household. If it wasn't for me, Go-Go would never have left. Everything seemed to change after we went on that god-awful trip through the snow. Real World Intrusion Syndrome.

She called yesterday from Montreal, all sweetness. She's *so* much happier, she says, God help us all. No, she was really very sweet. And I'm happy – no, relieved for her.

She was even almost apologetic. So confident – and rather condescending, come to think of it. As if I was the fucked up one. She said something rather cutting about answering machines. She doesn't have one, of course, because she thinks that if you need to be 'tuned in' all the time you're insecure. Hint hint. For Christ's sake. As if *not* having an answering machine wasn't in itself a pretentious gesture these days. But of course she doesn't think like that. And who knows, Montreal may be different.

Anyway, she's *so* happy because – aside from not having an answering machine – for fuck's SAKE why does that irritate me so? – she's taking some courses in photography and working in some craft collective making earrings, which she sells at some market. And people are *so* relaxed there – hint hint, again – that she doesn't even have an answering machine; nobody does. (I don't even believe that part.)

Actually, I really am relieved that she's happier. But I can't help still seeing Montreal as one simple thing: failure.

But what successes do I face here? Tomorrow, the darkness, the subway and the cafeteria, and my cubicle. I can see already that there's really no potential for advancement. I could, I suppose, if I stayed for years, start making some decisions about publications, like the font size and colours of the graphics, and I could, I suppose, begin to help with decisions about marketing strategies and so forth. Terrific. My salary would continue to rise.

On nights like this I start to remember what it was like to work on my MA thesis in the library, on my own, at my own speed. If I didn't feel like going in tomorrow I wouldn't. I actually wrote to Lozere last week, asking about the chances of getting into the program for January. I don't know if I'm serious or not. I haven't heard back yet, but I know Lozere will do everything he can to get me in and get me funding and everything if I decide to. They've always been incredibly supportive of me. Actually I feel guilty about it. I just rejected it all. And I feel guilty because I tried to reread Barthes's *Lover's Discourse* the other day, and found I couldn't concentrate at all. I used to love that text. Now I can hardly understand it. It's depressing to think that I've let that little muscle atrophy.

Okay. I suppose you'd rather hear something positive. What successes? Read in the paper yesterday about Andreas's film. He suddenly got some money and shot a short in two weeks. It's out and he's a success. Big success. Called 'Pictures of Gunnar'. His Icelandic family immigrant thing, cut with scenes of the alienated modern end of the family, the cynical young protagonist in the big city. The critic loved one scene in which the 'wickedly funny' protagonist says that he can't abide a street in which there's no pixelboard time display.

Oh well. He went out and made the film and I didn't, so he has a right to use whatever he can find. So. I still can't bring myself to go see it.

My own wild success continues apace. I actually did go ahead and write that architecture piece, and fired it off all round, but no one seems to want it. It's too long and not journalism and too poetic and cerebral. You have to be already famous to get stuff like that printed. I have to go on with interviews with chefs for a few years first. Actually, even that has subsided. *Cities* is suffering terribly, cutting back all pages but their monthly guides (to restaurants, antique markets, bicycle shops, pool builders ...), so I'm not even getting the profile pieces.

Which isn't too big a loss.

Malcolm is asking me for another play. He assures me that the last one did very well, even though we only broke even and no one has asked us to put it on anywhere else. He says not *losing* money is a great success in this town. He should know. He seems to know everyone and be regarded as quite a success.

Apparently after putting on three plays as a company we can apply for grants. But he wants a native-issues play so we can get some native actors, or he says we won't get anything, and he wants me to do it, as long as I change my name. I tried my hand at an environment-and-the-patriarchy thing, intentionally this time, but just couldn't take it seriously. I used to have an idea that theatre was something different. I'm not sure what, now.

No women, even on the distant horizon. I find myself, sadly and sinfully, fantasizing about Janet. I actually wrote her a flirtatious letter recently. Prick. I hope she has the sense not to reply.

Phew. Sorry about this length.

Hang in there.

Ted

December 16
Dear Mom and Dad,

Yes, I have indeed decided to go back to school. You didn't sound too surprised on the phone last night. I guess you guys were right after all. It's a much more appropriate milieu for me. I contacted Lozere this morning, and he's being sweet and accommodating, as usual. The prodigal son returns. The funding is unclear, but he thinks he'll be able to get me at least a TA-ship next term, and then I'll be eligible for departmental and SSHRCC funding in the summer term. Thanks for your offer to help out. All I'd need would be money for this first term, until I can get back into the grant swing.

I fly home on the 23rd, so I'll be in time for the Richardsons' egg-nog party, as usual.

Congratulations on the wedding. It sounds like a great success. Sorry I missed it. I wrote to Anna explaining and apologizing and congratulating her though. I don't imagine she missed me much.

See you soon.

Love

Ted.

December 16

Dear Janet,

Thanks for the *beautiful* card. I was wildly happy to hear from you. I'm so glad you sound so happy. Yes, what you heard is true. I'll be there in early January. Please thank Jenny for her offer to house me; I'd love to take her up on it for a week or two while I look for a place. Please send her phone number. And send yours! I'm dying to see you. I'll give you a call as soon as I arrive. Coffee in the Santropol, perhaps?

Love,

Ted.

TWENTY-THREE

IN A FURY OF RUSTLING Ted pulled out the balls of newspaper that stuffed his new nylon bag and scattered them over the mound of clothing that spilled from Georgina's tiny closet and over the futon. The bag was bright fuchsia, amorphously large and corseted with useless straps, but an excellent deal; only twenty bucks at Toronto's Largest Discount Bag Store. Standing up on the futon, he waded through clothing and crackling newspaper to the closet.

Lucky he didn't have much to pack; his trunks were still in storage, waiting for the permanent Toronto address that would never come. He had never had to unpack them, even. But his original backpack wasn't big enough for the new clothes he had amassed. Georgina's closet wasn't big enough for them. Japanese silk ties and linen trousers (when, when had he thought he could wear these?) and the thick leather jacket and even a pair of thong-back underwear from Yorkville – red, *red* no less – patterned the futon like a terrible beach towel. He surveyed the lifeless mess. He didn't really have to pack right then, as his flight wasn't until the following evening, but he had nothing else to do.

The window was open, and it was strange to hear street noises – the odd car, a distant jackhammer – after so many weeks of muffled nascent winter. There had been a freak thaw, a strange pre-Christmas lull in the cold, coupled with bright sunshine, that brought a few dazed birds out to chirp.

Ted wondered briefly why they hadn't migrated. Perhaps birds didn't migrate any more, had devolved beyond it. Perhaps seasonally migrating birds was another myth he had always accepted from his antiquated children's readers, like milk delivery and the word 'fishmonger'.

A sweet cool draught – it must have been close to ten degrees outside – filled the room with the outdoors. It was pleasant, but disorienting. Ted felt torn by conflicting nostalgias.

He began stuffing underwear into the new bag. A ball of newspaper on the futon caught his eye: the word 'Queal'. Carefully, he unfurled the crumpled scrap. It was a long obituary. Augustus Tumiston Plexor Queal, dead at twenty-nine.

It was last week's newspaper. Ted hadn't been bothering to read the newspapers since his decision to leave; not much point really. And he had grown tired of reading the massively popular outrage directed daily, in every daily's Letters section, at the insensitivity of right-wing journalist Ted Owen.

He began to read. Gus Queal, the beloved driving force behind the City Core Development Program's successful Reading Series, dead at twenty-nine. (Twenty-nine? He had looked forty-five.) Well-known for his work with both internationally successful writers and local unknowns, tireless and disinterested supporter of local arts scene. Risk-taker but warm and friendly man, often in spotlight – most recently because of much-publicized lawsuit against Zack Rudnicki, a little-known Toronto writer, for illegal use of the CCDP Reading Series name. Suffering from mysterious heart ailments for last two years. Condition aggravated recently by stress of legal battle. Suffered heart attack in office while on telephone – apparently talking to Rudnicki. Memorial service tomorrow.

Ted giggled despite himself, and was about to crumple the paper up again when another word caught his eye: Bentley, in the social announcements near the obituary. Mr and Mrs Frederick Bentley pleased to announce the engagement of their daughter Miranda Clara to Arthur Harris Crispin, son of Mr and Mrs Edward Crispin.

Miranda and Arthur, to be married in the spring. Of course.

No one had told Ted. But he hadn't seen any of them for a couple of weeks. And it had probably taken everyone by surprise. Then again, it probably shouldn't. Ted realized, slowly, that he really wasn't surprised at all, and then felt dispirited and cynical. He crumpled the paper into a tiny ball, working on it for some seconds, then threw it through the open door into the corridor. At least that was that. He resumed packing.

From far away, downstairs, he heard the phone tinnily echoing through the naked rooms. He went on packing; he was sick of taking calls about the rooms for rent, and sick of showing spindly vegetarians the deserted house. It wasn't his affair any more.

But the phone kept ringing, and its distant whine began to irritate him. He slowly rose from the bed, and stepped down the stairs whistling, hoping it would stop before he found the phone. By the time he reached the sunny kitchen the ringing was loud and frantic.

'Hey-ellow,' he said as frighteningly as he could.

'Hello,' said a gentle voice, a young man's. 'Could I speak to Ted Owen please?' The voice was smooth, confident, yet impeccably polite. And familiar.

'Speaking,' said Ted cautiously.

'Hello Ted. It's Max here. You'll remember me; we met on a train.'

Ted felt a hot wave of sadness rush over him like a blush. He wanted to sit down. 'Max!' He laughed, loud and short. 'Yes,' he said. 'Yes. Of course I remember you. Hello Max. How are you?' There was a knot in his throat. 'Thank you for calling me.'

'I've tried to contact you before. I take it you live at a whirlwind pace, which is admirable. I'm sure you must. And, first, I want to congratulate you on doing so well. I see your name everywhere. You seem to have fairly taken Toronto by storm.'

'Not exactly,' said Ted, sitting down on the floor. 'Not

exactly. I've just quit an extremely mind-killing job. And now I have no money and no work here.'

'Well, I can hardly believe that. I mean, no money is one thing, and as I'm sure you've reminded enough smug stock-brokers' daughters, it's irrelevant. You're the enlightened one. I'm surprised at you. As for no work, what are you talking about no work? Your name is everywhere, the cry goes up, the city clamours for more Ted Owen, fame and receptions are dangling from every lamppost, yours for the effortless and arbitrary taking. You can do anything you want now. You're valuable.'

Ted laughed, wiping away a tear, remembering the spell of Max's relaxed voice. He wanted to ask him what he was wearing. 'Well, it's too late to think about that now, because I'm leaving. I've decided that I'm going back to school.'

'Congratulations,' said Max. 'I'm sure your department is extremely pleased. That's bad news for me though. Actually, it's quite a disappointment for me. I had something I was so sure would interest you. What made you change your mind about the city? I suppose anyone with real intellectual training would find it hard to ...'

'No, no, it's not so much that. Well, it's partly that. But there are a lot of things that went into it. I don't really want to talk about it right now, it's too long and.'

'Of course. And painful.'

Ted laughed again. 'Well, I'm afraid of you trying to convince me to stay. Don't start. I don't even want to hear what you're doing.'

'Well, if your mind is really made up, I won't attempt it, no. Have you got good funding for the next term?'

'Of course not.'

'Won't take long, though, to get back in the swing of it, will it?'

'No.'

'Congratulations again,' said Max.

'Thanks,' said Ted. He twitched, hearing a shout nearby. It was only children in the street outside, of course: it was warm, the window was open. He watched a slow-moving fly float through the open window, in from the December day. The world was turned upside down. 'What's your new project?' he asked.

'A magazine,' said Max.

'Oh,' said Ted weakly.

'In fact it's more than a "project", at this point. It's definitely happening now. The mock-up is ready and we've sold enough advertising for a first issue. We even have an office. I'm speaking to you from there now. King and Peter. You should drop in before you go. Ogden's been showing me how to play wargames on the new Mac design system which you'd find amusing. Do you know Ogden?'

'Ogden Starelsky? The designer?'

'Yes. He's art directing. You do know him.'

'No, no. Miranda and ... Petunia used to talk about him. Reverentially. He's supposed to be quite a star.'

'Oh, he's very good, yes.'

'What's it to be called?'

'*Apache Surgery*.'

Ted drew in his breath. 'That's good. That's very good.'

Max laughed. 'You think? Thank you. We were also considering *Digmeister*.'

They laughed together.

'But we thought,' Max went on, 'it was limiting, too clearly meaningful, and that people might not catch the irony.'

'You're right. But *Digmeister* is good.' Ted laughed again, and looked at the open window. Talking to Max was like drinking fresh water. He gulped at it. 'What's going to be in it?'

And then Max told him all about it, matter-of-factly. Art, culture and fashion, with an emphasis on the 'alternative'. Monthly, tabloid size but glossy paper. Only black-and-white art and photographs. Art direction by Starelsky, photographs promised by Andy Nottingham and Spirella, an essay promised for the first issue by Godfrey Williamson, who was now at Trent, as Ted probably knew – and Ted did know, and he had heard all these names mentioned with awe by John and Go-Go and Miranda – and with a literary section in every issue. That's where Max had thought of Ted. Perhaps Ted knew of someone literary who would be interested in editing the section?

'Editing the section?' said Ted, miserably. 'Shit. No. Maybe. I'll think about it. Let me take your number there, I'll call you if I ... '

Max gave him a number. Writing it on the doodle-scrawled cover of the phone book, Ted felt a twinge of superiority. He wasn't going to get too excited about this phone number this time. He had taken Max's number before. This time he had his own life to lead. 'The first issue must be swallowing an enormous bite of money, surely? Who's funding it?'

'Oh I've got money.'

'Oh.' Ted watched another tremulous fly negotiate the window. He thought of getting back to his packing, but couldn't let Max go. 'Perhaps I'll submit something to you from Montreal.'

'Oh please do. And, listen, I don't want to sway you in any way, but I do want you to consider this position. Judging from what I know of you and what I've read by you and of you, I'm convinced we would work extremely well together. And I know you would love the others. It's quite an interesting concept.'

'Oh, I'm sure of that,' sighed Ted.

'So if you ever reconsider your decision, I'll be here. We don't need to find someone for another week or so anyway. Give me a call. I hope to hear from you soon anyway.'

'Certainly. Max, what kind of money would you be thinking of paying?'

'Well, for the first couple of issues the money will be rather dicey.'

'Of course.'

'We'll have to see how the advertising evens out, and what we can all expect. After the first issue I could make you a definite offer. I'll need everyone to work the first couple of months for free. But I could assure you that I would make it up to you once we were on even ground.'

'Of course,' said Ted, feeling superior again. They chatted about Montreal for a few more minutes and said goodbye with the understanding that Ted would call Max very soon.

As Ted hung up he tried to resist the sadness that now invaded him. The money thing was too risky, and he had decided that pursuing Max's elusive glamour was all behind him now. Still, it all did sound very bona fide this time. And Max *had* edited *Haze* ...

He went upstairs and sat on the pile of clothes. He took out his wallet and stared at a picture of Janet, recently reinserted. She was sitting at an outdoor café table on Prince Arthur, squinting in the sun. It was shortly after she had cut off most of her hair. He remembered her not wanting him to take it. He couldn't help noticing her sandals again; they appeared to be made of some kind of wood.

He put the picture down and tried to think of Lozere's welcome, or of teaching. The first seminar he had to give could be exciting. There would be departmental committee meetings. They used to be in a lounge next to the cafeteria; he remembered the committee-meeting smell of wet winter boots. And socks.

There was a slam as the front door opened and closed, then a thumping as heavy objects were dropped. Ted sat up, listening. It was unusual for Malcolm or the Mole to be home in the day. He called, 'Hello?'

'Hello?' came a woman's voice. A young woman.

Ted went to the top of the stairs and looked down.

A twenties black hat and a long shimmering raincoat with many pleats and folds, and a pile of suitcases around her. The woman looked up and Ted saw the straight copper hair framing the face, the bright blue eyes; she was smiling energetically, and her whole face seemed to shine.

'Georgina!'

'Hi! Hello! Hello!'

Ted stumbled down the stairs as she stumbled up them. They embraced in the middle. She seemed to hold onto him for a long time.

'What's going on? Why are you here?'

'I'm back. Sorry I didn't warn you. You don't have to get out of your room or anything.'

'Well, that's ... You're back! For how long? For good?'

'Yes. For good.'

They were still standing on the stairs. She turned and swooped down on her suitcases, lugging them into the living room. Ted helped speechlessly. Her satiny raincoat rustled. Her black cloche fell off and revealed her hair, a slightly different colour, gold rather than the pale straw he remembered, with a faint wave.

'I'm sweating,' she said. 'Weird weather.'

'You changed your hair.'

'Did I? The colour? What colour was it when I left?' She was shedding the rustling raincoat, revealing a long black knit dress with buttons down the front. It was clingy and soft. She threw the new hair out of her eyes.

'There's a bit more red in it now. Looks great. Looks terrific. I love it.'

She blushed, and sank into the sofa. 'So tell me everything. Where is everyone? Where's John?'

'Long story. You want tea?'

So Ted made tea and they sat in the sunny kitchen with the window open. Ted told her about Go-Go, her disappearance and her change, and about John in Ottawa, and Miranda and Arthur and Queal's death, and his play and Malcolm, and his decision to go back to Montreal and school. He didn't tell her about his picture in *Next* and the Moonfire controversy.

Georgina laughed and frowned at all the appropriate moments, drawing her feet up onto her chair and resting her chin on her knees, sipping her tea from a chipped cup. She wore little black ankle boots like cut-off cowboy boots, which she soon kicked off. Ted said, 'So you stayed much longer than anticipated, in Japan.'

'Not really.'

'I thought you were only going for two months?'

'Oh.'

'And why are you back now? How was it? Tell me all about it.'

'Well, it's always the same there, you know. It's very ugly and a lot of work. I made some money. Are you hungry?'

'Yes,' said Ted with surprise, because he was suddenly starving.

'Want to go out for some food? The Bakery? I just have to take a shower and stuff. Can I use your room?'

'Let me clean it up a bit first,' said Ted, rising.

'Shut-*up!*' she sang, and ran out of the room in her stockings, and up the stairs.

The whole afternoon passed in the Bakery, over coffee and muffins and chocolate croissants. Georgina talked elliptically and desultorily about shoots and stylists and the other girls and hostess bars and free air tickets, and laughed frequently. Ted still couldn't picture anything she described. He felt reckless, leaving the next day, and asked bold questions about boyfriends, admirers.

'Yes,' she said, 'there were a couple of guys.'

He was surprised at her ease. 'Anything serious?' But then she hung her head again and looked sad, so he said, 'I haven't, there hasn't been anyone here. For me.'

'I find that hard to believe.'

'No, seriously.'

'Do you think you'll start to see Janet again, when you go back?'

Ted hesitated, then smiled. 'No. Certainly not.'

'Oh Ted.' She was smiling warmly at him now. 'It's *so* good to see you again.'

'You too.'

'Do you want to go out to dinner tonight?'

At eleven that night they returned to the dark house, swaying and giggling in the cold entrance hall. As soon as the sun had disappeared, at five that afternoon, the air and ground had suddenly frozen again, and they hadn't been dressed warmly enough.

'I think it's an excellent decision,' Georgina was saying, rubbing her hands. 'It doesn't sound as if she's good for you.'

'I agree,' said Ted, leaning against the wall. 'It's just that it *seems* good for you, to have a supportive partner, someone who will always listen to you and indulge you. But it's not. It's really not. It weakens you somehow.'

'Well I'm not sure about that. Jesus it got cold all of a sudden.' She was struggling with the shoes, trying to kick them off her feet.

'I think I'm a little drunk, actually,' said Ted. 'God, that was wonderful, George. I can't even imagine how much you must have spent. On wine alone!'

'Shutup. I'm rich for now.'

'I've never had food like that before in my life.'

'He was quite the talk of the town when he was at Bandit. I'm surprised he has this new place at all. He must owe everyone in town money.'

'Who's this now?'

'Ritchie. The chef. At Theft, where we just were.'

'Yes yes. Of course.'

'You know he's only twenty years old. Never been to cooking schools. Makes it all up.'

'What was that dish I liked? Borneo Filet of Chèvre?'

'Rind. Borneo Filet of Chèvre Rind. I liked the Detroit

Bamboo Shoots. And the Calypso Duck, which I don't think really had any duck in it at all.'

'Ah, you are so unlucky to be a vegetarian. Because you missed the great carnal delight of the Grilled Provimi Veal Liver with Suburban Mango Sesame Sauce. It was bliss and heaven. Where does he get the names?'

'Oh, he's really into symbolism. He'll tell you all about the names. They symbolize spice trade routes and patterns of oppression. He's big into oppression, the Third World. He thinks eating his food is socially progressive.'

'Christ,' said Ted.

'He can be charming, though, really. He's just a little crazy. He pisses people off because every time the restaurant he's at goes bankrupt or he fights with the owner he steals all the CD's when he leaves. Even tonight we heard the same music you used to hear at Bandit and Anarchy and Dog Goes Bong. He took them all. He's crazy. He does a lot of coke, still, like everybody.'

'Everybody?'

'In restaurants. All the artiste chefs are on coke the whole time.'

'Wow. I didn't know ... How do you know so much about the restaurant scene?'

'Oh,' said Georgina. 'I used to spend a lot of time with someone who was a ... who was involved with it. Brrr.' She had her shoes off, and was rubbing her hands over her arms. Then she turned and leaned into Ted backwards, with her arms folded in front of her, just leaned into him as he leaned against the wall.

Gently, he rubbed his hands up and down her folded arms. 'Freezing, isn't it,' he said, a little too loudly. He could smell a faint but unmistakably musky perfume on her neck. Her hair was almost in his mouth. Her arms were soft in the black woollen dress.

Then she pulled away and moved toward the kitchen.

'I have some brandy in my room,' he said, following her. 'Cognac actually. I could use a little warming drink. Like some?'

'Sure,' she said, stopping. She turned and faced him.

'Oh. Okay.' He froze for a moment. 'Shall I bring it down here?'

'No no. Let's go up.'

'Yes. It's warmer,' said Ted, and moved towards the stairs.

In his room he kicked at the pile of clothing and the fuchsia bag, ploughing it off the futon. He turned on the one low lamp and turned the overhead light off.

'I think I left some candles in here somewhere,' said Georgina, sinking onto the futon with her legs folded gracefully under her. 'In the bottom drawer of the chest.'

Ted rummaged, found silky underwear and then candles strewn among it. He pulled them out carefully so as not to drop anything embarrassing on the floor. 'Found them.'

Georgina giggled. 'It's okay. It's just underwear.'

'The cognac is in the closet somewhere.'

Georgina lit the candles and melted them onto an ashtray found among the debris while Ted fumbled, cursing, in the closet.

'Here it is.' He brought out the half-empty bottle as she turned the lamp off. Only one corner of the room glowed, faintly orange in the candlelight; the rest was dark. Ted pulled two cloudy glasses off the dresser and sat with her on the futon, his legs stuck out in front of him.

'Come and lean your back against the wall,' she said, patting the pillow beside her. 'It's comfortabler.'

Ted settled in beside her and poured the cognac. Her thigh was touching his knee. 'So,' he said, 'Tell me about these guys in Japan.'

'Which guys?'

'Guys who were in love with you. Tell me about your men.'

Georgina turned her head to face him and put her hand behind his neck. Her fingertips felt light and hot. She pulled his head towards hers and he kissed her once, tentatively, and pulled back. She smiled and kissed him again firmly, her hand still behind his neck, turning her whole body against him.

Her mouth was soft and loose. Ted felt the hair move all over his body. Then they were kissing and touching for real, tongues and hair and mouth. She smelled so much more astoundingly of honey and sea and incense than Ted had imagined; it was unbelievable. Ted was stiff and incredulous, refusing to let himself become excited.

He pulled back again, brushing hair from her face. He put his arm around her and sat back against the wall. He said, 'Did you get my postcard?'

'Yes. I guess. Which one?'

'About ... I don't know, six weeks ago.'

'Oh yes. The Rothko. Beautiful. I love that whole early abstract thing.'

'You didn't reply.'

'No.' She was playing with his hair, one hand on his thigh. 'I was with someone.'

'Ah. Who?'

She shrugged and rolled her eyes.

'No, really. Who?'

She giggled. 'An architect.'

'A Japanese architect?'

'No, no. American.'

'An American architect. Bastard. Bastard.'

She laughed.

'And?'

'And what?'

'Is it over, finished, or ...'

'Oh. Well it was never really ... I don't know.'

Ted sighed. He began to kiss her again, but she turned her head. He stroked her thigh through the soft wool dress.

'There was someone here, before,' she said suddenly.

'I know,' he said.

'You do? Oh – John told you.'

'Yes. And, well, that's his photographic equipment in the hall, isn't it? The man leaves traces.'

'What? The photographic – oh *that*. *Him*. No no, that belongs to Lucas, I haven't seen him for ... is that what John told you? That I was going out with him?'

'I think so. He called him your prick boyfriend. But you're not?'

She rolled her eyes. 'Not for ages. I hardly ever was. I don't even think about him.'

'Oh.' Ted sipped his brandy. 'So there was someone else?'

'Well, I think it's over now. I'm surprised John didn't tell you about it.'

'John knew? No, he would have told me.'

'Oh, John knew all right.'

'Uh-huh.' Ted leaned back against the wall. 'Do I know him?'

'I think you met him. Anthony.'

'Anthony. No. Anthony. Not the sculptor? The one at that shitty art show, the first day I met you?'

She nodded.

'Wow. I *knew* I hated that guy. Wow. You liked that guy? Sorry. Of course you did. He had black jeans and long hair and didn't shave, and he's a sculptor, and everyone knows sculptors have the biggest egos and are invariably assholes. The way of the world. The world is a totally excellent place for a very good-looking asshole.'

She was smiling, laughing a little, fingering a worn patch in his jeans. 'He's not always an asshole.'

'Oh I'm sure. And he's very, very talented. I know. I've talked to women about sculptors before. He doesn't ride a motorcycle, does he?'

'You're the asshole.'

'Good. Kiss me.'

They kissed gently for some minutes. Ted put his hand on her small breast, felt the roughness of a lace bra under the dress. She shivered a little and laid her head on his shoulder.

Ted said, 'I guess that's why you were sad when I first met you.'

'What?'

'The sculptor being an asshole.'

'Oh ... maybe.'

'And that's where you stayed when you came into Toronto. With him?'

'Oh Ted, stop it. Not always, no.'

'Sorry. It's just that I had a mad crush on you all that time.'

'You did not.'

'What! How could you not have seen?'

'Stop. Asshole.'

'I can't believe you didn't ...' He stopped. 'I guess your life is complicated.'

'Not really.' She was kissing his neck. 'Just before I left. It was a little crazy.' She sighed. 'He was being a bit of an asshole. But so was John. And Anthony got really upset.'

'John?'

'I hadn't heard from Anthony for weeks, so I thought it was all over. But the thing with John started it all up again. He just went insane.'

'Thing? With John? My John? I mean, this John?'

Georgina stared at him. 'I thought you knew. I thought everybody knew.'

'You had a thing with John?'

'Oh. I'm sorry. I didn't need to tell you. It was just a short thing. I was sure he would have told you ...'

Ted was rigid, staring straight ahead of him. His body felt numb. He was thinking fast. 'No, John never told me.'

'Well Anthony got really crazy about it. And that was the end with Anthony. The thing with John was just a little thing, it wasn't serious. He was an asshole too, you know.'

Ted was silent, trying to regain the excitement he had felt in his body a moment before. His limbs felt full of sand. 'Wow. I mentioned Anthony to him, once, too. He didn't say a word. No wonder. I can't believe it.'

'Oh, Ted, don't worry about it. Your friend doesn't have to tell you everything. It wasn't – '

'I told him, too,' said Ted with a rush of pain. 'I told him I was – I had a crush on you. How embarrassing. So he dumped you?'

'Ted.'

'Wow. He must have been ... I wonder what he was thinking. When I confessed to him. He must have found it funny. No wonder he never wanted to talk about you.'

'I'm not surprised,' she said drily.

'How long did it last? Was it going on while I was living here?'

'Once, when I was back from Japan, but that was ... It was really over just before you got here. He was much more deeply involved with Miranda, really, all that time.'

'With who? With Miranda? Oh my – '

'He didn't tell you that either?'

Ted exhaled forcefully. 'No. No he didn't.'

'*That* caused even more problems. She was pretty broken up about it. And Arthur was too. But they all seem to be friends again now.'

Ted was silent for a moment. He began a loud laugh, but it sounded forced, so he stopped. He exhaled again. 'Holy shit. I never get it. I never fucking get anything.'

They sat in silence for a moment.

'Ted,' she said. She moved suddenly onto his legs, straddling him. Her long skirt rode up on her thighs. He felt her bare thighs gripping his, her breasts and hair in his face. She was holding his face in her hands and kissing it. Ted kissed back, cupping the small breasts in his hands. She began to unbutton his shirt, and he unbuttoned the dress. He forgot about Anthony, and, eventually, about John.

TWENTY-FOUR

WHEN TED WOKE UP he knew the freak weather had continued. The pink light on his face through the blind felt warm. Georgina had drawn away from him and was lying curled on one edge of the futon. Peeking from under the heavy duvet were her thin shoulders, her thin red hair.

Ted pushed back the duvet and stood. He stepped over Georgina and pulled up the blind. A bright square of light fell over the bed, and Georgina stirred and groaned. He bent to kiss her shoulder, feeling very naked in the sunlight, and she shrank under the duvet.

He pulled on his jeans, a shirt and shoes without socks, and left the room, closing the door as quietly as he could.

In the sunny kitchen he opened the window, then the sliding doors onto the snowy garden. He could hear the trickling of water, the dripping of melting snow, and another one of those inexplicable birds. He laughed aloud, then breathed deeply, feeling healthy and silly. For the first time in months, he wanted breakfast, a ridiculous vulgar American breakfast with bacon and eggs and cereal.

He looked in the fridge, but of course found nothing. In the front hall he pulled on his coat and went out to buy supplies.

On the veranda he was dazzled. It had been weeks since he had been out of doors in sunlight. On the street, he walked gingerly between patches of melting snow, feeling fragile, just recovered from fever in some tropical memoir. 'I must have been tended to,' he said aloud in his Colonel-of-the-Raj accent, 'by Bapur or faithful Bombadall, for there were several empty insect-saliva gourds on the hut's earthen floor. How many days had passed? I crawled to the grass door, and surveyed the disastrous scene without. Not one of my company remained alive, but a tattered Union Jack —'

He silenced himself as he drew up to the grocery. A family burst out of the glass door in a flurry of Cantonese. He let them pass and entered.

The shop was filled with the lusty shouting of the tightly wrapped black bundles that were Portuguese women, and the scent of garlic sausages and votive candles. At the butcher counter two shrunken Mao-era grandmothers in grey pyjamas shrieked at one another.

As Ted wandered around the store, he strained his ears to make out individual words in the angular tongues. The Portuguese seemed more than usually filled with *zh-sh-ch*, like a language designed to hush squalling babies. The shrunken women sounded furious with one another, but they were smiling. It could have been about murder or incest or Nietzsche versus Kierkegaard or recipes, the best way to make dim sum, or the way the warm spell had made puddles in the basement. He wished he could make it out. There were stories all around him.

He picked up bacon, eggs, still-warm bread, coffee, milk, frozen tubes of juice, trying to resist making *bubbabubba* noises like a helicopter, or some kind of *grunkle-grunkle-grunkle*, like a large backhoe revving up. When he got outside the store, he was confident, he would find the appropriate noise for his present energy. Perhaps just a full-throttle scream, or a sort of *yaawooo yaawooo*. There would be time to experiment.

At the counter one black widow smiled at him and punched his purchases into the cash, still yelling at another one, waving a finger. Ted smiled back, wondering how many years they were allowed to live before they had to don the mourning. This one could have been thirty-five or fifty.

Outside, he skipped among the slush piles, swinging his shopping bags. He would have to find a name for the black widow's husband, who died so young. Hernando. Armando.

Armando headed a small construction company, or worked in a bar, one of those fluorescent-lit cafés with a grainy satellite feed, stayed there late every night with the other red-faced men with moustaches, watching their team getting pasted again by Juventus, by Bayern Munich . . .

Ahead of him a teenage girl struggled with a pram. Ted slowed as he came up behind her, his eyes drawn to her spectacular high-top basketball shoes. They were hugely puffy, fluorescent orange, striated with purple zigzags and logos, the laces undone. He followed closely behind her, his eyes fixed on the sneakers, trying to see if they were the kind with the little flashing lights on the soles – LED's, probably, although LED had an anachronistic ring to it now: he couldn't remember what the letters stood for, or indeed the last time he had heard them. LED. It was all LCD now. Liquid crystal something. And VGA. He should ask the Mole.

His steps in time with hers, he glanced up at the rest of her ensemble – tight black jeans, an orange bomber jacket – and she looked around suspiciously. It was only then that he noticed that she was black, her hair straightened and recurled.

He stopped short, because he had thought suddenly and vividly of the railway tracks, the night of his trek with John. Tyrone and Tiffany. He tried to remember the inscription.

They laugh and cry and said they love one another.
February 15, 1991.

The teenage girl drifted away, repeatedly looking over her shoulder at him, her orange shoes flashing. Ted looked down at a puddle. Tyrone and Tiffany. Now that was life. That was living. He wondered why he had never written anything like that on a bridge.

Here Ted and Janet Had a Boring and Emotionally Loaded
Argument about the Elitism of the Academy.

Here Ted Apologized to Janet for Not Being
Supportive Enough.

He chose an alleyway at random and walked among the garages. He tried to imagine Tyrone and Tiffany meeting Janet, and giggled at the impossibility of it.

And the other thing was, she wouldn't really be interested.

He remembered the sooty bridge, his wet feet, his stomach knotted over Go-Go. The distant siren, the brutal pounding of bass. A wave of sadness, or something like it, something pure or releasing like tears washed over him. Fatigue.

There was something there that Janet would not understand and he was glad he had seen. And she possibly wouldn't have reacted at all. Janet would never meet Tyrone and Tiffany.

How could she? Perhaps in some kind of formalized multi-culturalist food bank way. Perhaps at some kind of social service office, he supposed. Community Outreach. He pictured Janet volunteering at the Community Outreach Office, spending the rainy and uneventful morning indignantly agreeing with her sister volunteers about the harmful yet concealed side-effects of antibiotics, spectacles, inoculations, Band-Aids – when in would roar drunken, tearful Tiffany in puffy high-top basketball sneakers with flashing red lights and a pram and Janet would be, quite simply, appalled.

Ted snorted, finding it funny. He realized he could write it down, make something out of it. He would make Janet wrinkle her nose as if she smelled something bad, he would have her remark to one of her sister workers about the running shoes, or something more naively suburban, a red spandex top – he would have snottiness oozing out of her like ... like whatever snottiness was, like mucus, and this would enrage Tiffany and then ...

He began to walk quickly. He had to get home and write it down. His head was filling with details. He could see Janet's volunteer boss – not Janet, though, he would have to name her something similar, something plain, Karen, Jennifer maybe – he could see the head of volunteers at the Community Outreach Office, New Day Community Outreach, fat Ilsa – no, Ilsa was too obvious, something Scandinavian, Baltic: Alfreda, Jasminka, fat Jasminka with her hysterical letters to *Next* magazine. She would have a bit of body odour, poor old Jasminka.

He broke into a run, the shopping bags smashing against his legs, possibly breaking the eggs, but he couldn't stop. Jasminka! Jasminka was too good. He could see the New Day office and the AIDS prevention notices in several alphabets pinned to the cubicle dividers and the separate baskets for various recyclable materials – white paper only this bin, coffee cups here, discarded pen caps here, this bin *blue* plastic only – and Jennifer at her desk, in her rainy window, just after she had had her hair cut, again, smoking and looking out the rainy window and about to cry. Just before Tiffany's arrival. He felt sorry for Jennifer. Just as he felt sorry for Tyrone and Tiffany and – another wave of guilt or whatever it was, like nausea – for Go-Go.

He slowed, breathing heavily. The garage doors glittered. There would be someone, someone beautiful and – sad, perhaps? Or unnoticed? No. Unpredictable, or simply dangerous – here he began to run again, feeling the tension rise – but with the emotion of the alcoholic Consul's devoted wife, what was her name? – anyway, someone, a guy, possibly a guy not unlike Ted, would feel very strongly about someone, a woman, he would be irrationally, emotionally – and he was thinking of Georgina now, her thin limbs and hair, her nervous lovemaking – someone would be glazed-eyes, stomach-knotted in love.

He ran all the way home.

He crashed into the house panting. He put the bags down on the kitchen table and stood still, slowing his breathing and listening. Georgina still wasn't up.

He found a clean frying pan, buried deep in a cupboard, and

put bacon in it. He opened his mouth wide and yelled, 'Ya ya ya ya ya.' This wasn't quite right. Then he clenched his teeth, drew his lips apart and grunted as he imagined a wild boar would grunt, although he had never seen one except in *Asterix*.

He began to clean the mouldy coffeemaker, thinking more calmly now. It would have to be in Montreal, and all the volunteers would be Concordia students, and they wouldn't speak a word of French, although most of their clients were Haitians – or worse, it was *Ottawa*, they were Carleton students, God help us, they were *Carleton film students* ...

The wild boar grunted with delight. He would have to write it all down fast. Then again, he probably wouldn't. It was sitting in him like memory. The bacon smelled exquisite.

Then he remembered his flight that night, New Brunswick in December. Montreal in January.

He put down the coffee pot and stared straight ahead. With leaden clarity, he was remembering a windowless cinder-block room three stories underground, under the Arts building, where he had led a tutorial in his last term. He even remembered the name of the class: *The Disappearing Subject: Sex, Ego and the Self in Japanese Animated Science Fiction*. His most regular audience had been three boys in team jackets and sweatpants who spent the three hours absorbedly drawing rocket ships. One of them used to frown deeply and display a moist centimetre of tongue when working on a particularly tumultuous section of exhaust fumes.

He thought of the reserve-room librarian, the one they used to call Orca, and her peculiar smell of potatoes and vinegar, how he had described this to Janet once and how indignant she had been. 'They can't *all* prance around in high heels and frills,' she had said.

He stayed motionless for several minutes.

Then he turned off the element under the bacon, and walked into the empty living room. There was a scrap of paper on the floor, beside the phone, covered with phone numbers.

He examined it till he found the number marked 'Concord. reg.,' and dialled.

'Registrar's office,' came a harried voice.

'Hello,' said Ted. 'I'd like to cancel my registration.'

It took some minutes and explaining. The woman didn't want to refund him his tuition, and Ted couldn't explain to her that since he hadn't yet paid anything it wouldn't be at all difficult. She finally agreed, and Ted hung up, feeling weightless.

He was frying eggs when he heard Georgina's bare feet on the stairs. She came in wearing the same black dress. 'No, no,' he said, 'You're not supposed to get up. I'm making breakfast in bed. Go back to bed.'

'That's okay,' she said quietly. She sat at the table.

Ted glanced at her. She was pale, her hair flat. She wasn't smiling. 'You okay?'

'Yes. What are you doing?'

'Bacon, eggs, coffee, fresh bread, cereal. I don't suppose you got this a lot in Tokyo. Some dismal miso soup or something, right? Incredible how it occurred to someone to eat *fermented bean curd*, I mean who –'

'I don't eat breakfast at all.' Something hard in her voice made Ted look at her again. She was staring out the back door, frowning.

'You should try this though,' said Ted. 'It's a great day for breakfast. There'll be coffee in a minute. We'll have it in bed.'

'I'm not hungry,' she said. 'I have to go in a minute.'

'Oh.' He stared at his eggs, then scooped them onto a plate. He turned off the element. 'Where do you have to go?'

She turned her head and looked at him blankly, then stood, smoothing her dress.

'Don't you even want coffee?'

'No.'

'When are you coming back?'

'Probably this evening. You'll probably be gone.'

'I'm not going. I cancelled my registration. I have to stay a few more ... maybe for a while. I have to stay.'

'Oh.' She was frowning again. 'Where ... what are you going to do?'

'I'm going to take Max's offer. Work on the magazine. And something's happened, I don't know – I've had an idea. I can't go now. It's very clear. And fuck it, there are all kinds of things to do, you know, I always had this feeling I had to get paid and get a *car*, you know, and John had this excellent – John was really smart about this one thing – '

He paused for breath. Georgina was staring at him.

'It sounds silly, but I have this ... I want to write a story. I have an idea and I want to write a story and it sounds like just a little thing but I'm really excited about it. I have to stay and do it.'

'Where are you going to live?'

'I ... ' Ted faltered, looking at her. 'I thought I'd live here. There are two extra rooms now. We wouldn't have to find two more roommates.'

Georgina moved towards the door. 'I have to go. You know ... that would mean we would be living together.'

Ted felt something in him tighten and hurt. 'Well, living together, not *living* together ... I see why it frightens you, but it shouldn't. I think ... well, we can talk about it. It's not a problem either way.'

She hesitated for a moment in the doorway. 'See you,' she said, and she was gone. He heard her moving quickly up the stairs.

Ted sat at the kitchen table with his plate of glassy eggs. He had lost his hunger. He looked out the doors at the garden. The sky was even bluer. He got up and shut the sliding doors. He sat at the table until he heard Georgina come down the stairs and out the front door.

Once the door had closed, he got up and went to the living room. He found Max's number on the piece of paper and dialled. After many rings, a sleepy man's voice answered. Ted asked for Max.

'Max? No Max here. Wrong number.'

Ted repeated the number.

'That's the number here. But there's no Max. I've been living here for three years, dude. I don't even know a Max. You must have got the number wrong.'

Ted paused, swallowed, then hung up. He looked at the number again. He dialled directory assistance and asked for a number for *Apache Surgery* on King West.

There was no listing for *Apache Surgery* or anything like it on King or Queen or anywhere. He hung up again, and his hands began to shake. 'You fucking idiot,' he said. His voice echoed. 'You big dummy.'

Rapidly, he began to calculate his finances. He had withdrawn his remaining hundred and fifty dollars the day before and spent almost fifteen of it on breakfast.

'Max,' he said, 'I'll kill you. I'll fucking kill you.' But he knew he didn't mean it. 'You big dummy.'

Swinging his arms, he began to wander the house. There was always *Cities*; he could call Derek again, ask him about profiles or something. Maybe he could do the TV listings. But Derek hadn't returned his last three calls. Maybe Andreas was making a new movie, needed someone to lift lights. For Christ's sake.

He looked into Malcolm's immaculate room, with its posters and Chinese parasol on the ceiling. He stepped into Go-Go's empty room and said, 'Cockshit piss.' He looked out her window onto the leafless, muddy street and said 'Bumfart poop.' He began to pound his fist into his palm; he was avoiding looking in Georgina's room, with its rumpled futon.

Forcefully and inescapably, like a collapsing ceiling, the image came to him of Georgina's neck, a curl of copper hair, her narrow shoulders, the shallow breasts with their brown nipples.

He shook his head and shouted, 'Bum bum B U M!'

He scanned the street below, as if she were about to reappear. Perhaps she would reconsider at the bottom of the street, come running back to him.

He turned and shuffled up the stairs to John's room. Dustballs littered the wood floor. He sat heavily among them and waited for a sound, in case Georgina was on the front steps. His head buzzed, as if someone had clubbed him with a dictionary. The odour of bacon fat was beginning to turn his stomach.

He supposed he should call Concordia back, explain it was all a mistake, re-register. It wouldn't be hard if he did it right away. The thought of this made him immensely tired, so he lay down on the floor.

Definitely, Georgina was not at the door or on the steps or about to be. He thought of the cool flesh of her shoulder under the pink window, and then, with dizzying fatigue, about what he would try to say to her, when he saw her next – 'Hey, listen, don't apologize, we all go through – ' and realized he wasn't expecting to see her much, at all. Before he could leap out of its oncoming path, he was hit by an unfortunate image of Georgina and John, and shuddered.

Her quickness, when naked, her lightness – it was all rather unleisured, really: excited, yes, but ... with John, big heavy John ... He shook his head to clear it.

Sighing dramatically, he rose and wandered out. He peeked in at the Mole's hole, recoiling at the smell of stale clothing. He stared at the tangles of wiring, the towers of grey plastic components. There was a plastic Mr Spock doll on top of the monitor. Ted smiled.

He wandered back into the empty living room and sat on the floor. It was ridiculous, really, the thing with John. He said indignantly, 'What John? *My* John?'

He was laughing aloud when he heard a timid knock at the front door. He froze, remembering the ad in *Next*. He tried to keep totally still, but in a few moments the knock came again. He rose, dusted himself and went to the door.

There stood a young woman with a hat, wide-brimmed and black, and an astounding face. Dark brown eyes, bright cheeks and swollen red lips. As far as Ted could tell she wore no makeup. Thick black hair framed her face. She wore a large man's raincoat.

Ted was embarrassed for his appearance. He had only seen women like this in films. 'Hi,' he said briskly.

She smiled. 'Hi. I've come about the room for rent. I called yesterday.' There was a faint French accent.

'Oh, that's ... well, I guess there is still a room for rent, though I'm not sure which one.' He stepped back. 'Come in, I'll show you all of them.'

'It's so warm,' she said as she followed him in.

'Yup,' said Ted. 'Goddam Russians.'

'What?'

'The Russians are changing the weather. To f–screw us up. Communist plot.'

'Except the Russians aren't Communist. Let's call it a CIA plot. Or why not a new republic? A Kazakhstan plot.'

'Done,' said Ted, looking at her in surprise. 'This is the kitchen.'

He went on to tell her the story of the house, whose rooms would be sublet and whose would be rented for good, the lease and the heating problems, the Mole and Malcolm and Georgina.

Her name was Maïcke, pronounced Mike – her real name was Dominique. She was a Ph.D. student in English, studying Woolf. Ted got enthusiastic about Woolf and told her that he preferred *Mrs Dalloway* to *To the Lighthouse*, despite official opinion, and she said she disagreed, had he read *The Waves*?

He almost said yes, because he wanted intensely at that moment to have read it, but he hadn't. He noticed a fine bright purple bra strap hiding under the loose neck of her dress. The dress was long and gauzy. Muddy little drill boots.

She asked him what he did, and he said he didn't know, but he thought he would be starting soon on this new magazine. He showed her the empty rooms, and, rapidly, Georgina's, with its rumpled bed and his clothing spread around. Aside from some lipstick on the pillow, which he was sure she didn't notice, there was no trace of Georgina; her bags were still in the front hall and she had taken all her clothes.

They went back into the kitchen. 'It's lovely,' said Maïcke, 'Charming. I can't wait to meet the others. They sound so – ' She sat on the one remaining chair and crossed her legs; they were bare under the long dress. Ted leaned against the counter, aware of a heavy perfume he had not smelled at the Bay before. She was rummaging in her bag, pulling out a slim cigar box; the writing on it was Spanish. 'I have a sense of – ' She paused to light a dark cigarillo. Ted watched wide-eyed as she puffed. She raised her eyebrows. 'Would you like one?'

'No. I mean, I don't think so. But go ahead.' The smell of the smoke was intensely foul.

'Tell me about this delicious Mole. He sounds – oh, I meant to ask you, do you like risotto?'

'Do I like what?'

'It's expensive. To make, and time consuming, the shopping part. But therapeutic. I *love* to make it. You need a lot of wine.' She smiled at him. 'Does he wear an astronaut suit? Or a Star Trek costume?'

Ted laughed. 'Oh he's quite sane. He's hardly ever here, though. You may find Malcolm's friends a bit – ' He paused, distracted; she was delving into her bag again, frowning briefly as she accidentally extracted a postcard. She held it up to reread it; Ted glanced at the picture, a port with white hotels, something like Nice or Marseille. She frowned again, shoved it back into the bag, and pulled out a silver flask. Then she smiled, unscrewing the top. 'Would you find it completely disgusting if I offered you a drink?'

Ted felt himself grinning. 'Not at all. Not at *all*.'

He filled two mismatched glasses with her Scotch. The fug of cigar-air was making him dizzy. 'I'll show you the garden,' he said. 'It's lovely in the fall.'

They went into the muddy garden. The sky was clouding over, but it was still warm. The snow had almost all disappeared, leaving sparse patches of brown grass. There was a smell of earth. 'Lovely,' she said, with true warmth. 'It's beautiful.'

Ted pulled up the rusting garden chairs and they sat together, shivering. She was staring away from him, at the next garden's fence. 'So pretty,' she said softly.

He glimpsed the purple bra strap again, and looked away. He could smell thawing dogshit from the alleyway between the houses. It smelled like fields. There was the distant buzzing of an airplane; for a second he thought it was a lawnmower, and smiled.

He sipped the Scotch: smoky and dark, definitely single malt, probably Islay. He said, 'So you've only got the thesis left, is that right?'

She nodded quickly, staring at the fence.

'How many years do you figure ...' He stopped. Something in the stiffness of her head, the way she kept her face from him told him something else was happening. He watched her cheek quiver slightly, and sat back in the rusty chair with a sudden and intense feeling of relief, of relaxation, of arriving home. She was crying.

ACKNOWLEDGEMENTS

The idea for this book came from Alex Pugsley, the money from the Explorations Program of the Canada Council; I am very grateful to both. Many thanks also to Richard Bingham, Malcolm Brown, Katherine Bruce, David Donnell, Linda Frum, Kim Jenkinson, Ceri Marsh, Jeremy McCormack, Darlene Rigo, Kate Sykes, Pippa White, Nicole Woolsey, the Taro Grill, Biagio Ristorante and my tireless and generous editor, John Metcalf.

JEREMY MCCORMACK

ABOUT THE AUTHOR

Russell Smith was born in Johannesburg, South Africa in 1963 and grew up in Halifax, Canada. He studied French literature at the universities of Poitiers, Paris (III) and Queen's. His master's thesis was on the surrealist poetry of Paul Eluard. He works as a freelance journalist in Toronto.

How Insensitive is his first book.